Tuesday Means Trouble

A Story Smith Mystery

Maggie FitzRoy

ISBN print: 978-1-7330262-6-0

ISBN ebook: 978-1-7330262-7-7

❀ Created with Vellum

To my husband, Jim, for his quiet, unending support.

ONE

Philadelphia, Pennsylvania
Tuesday, July 21, 1955

Shirley Bianco was supposed to be working. But, nope, she sure wasn't. She was being naughty.

I lifted my binoculars for another peek.

Shirley was *at* work, but she wasn't sifting flour, baking cookies, or making muffins.

She was making out, passionately, with some guy in the front seat of her Chevy, parked behind Thelma's Bakery, where she'd told her husband, Lenny, she started work at six a.m.

Only now it was six-thirty, and from my hiding spot behind a big bush I could see she'd been lying to him, which he'd suspected, which was why he'd hired me, Story Smith, Philadelphia's newest private eye.

I was also a woman going it alone in a man's business, and needed the work, so when Lenny Bianco showed up in my office, I'd quoted him a bargain rate he gladly accepted.

"Shirley's not worth a dime more," he'd growled as he scribbled me a check and slapped it on my desk. He told me the address of the bakery and the kind of car Shirley drove, then declared, "I just need proof that she's a lying floosy so I can get out of paying alimony. Can you do that?"

I'd assured him I could.

And now I had proof. Except it was too dark to take pictures. Not that I was close enough to get any decent shots anyway with my little Brownie camera.

When I could save up enough money, I'd buy myself a good camera and a long lens. And a gun. I knew I shouldn't be in the P.I. business without a gun. Because it was dangerous. And I didn't want Steve Evans to keep worrying about me.

Steve was my competition, an experienced P.I., and too handsome for my comfort. He'd helped me solve my first case, but even so, I didn't want my safety to be his concern.

I shifted my position behind the bush to relieve the cramping in my legs. The grass under my bottom was wet with dew and I tried to ignore the gooey chill creeping up my back.

How long should I sit here watching two middle-aged lovers paw each other like a couple of teenagers in heat?

"Hey, lady, what're you doing?"

Startled, I turned and looked up. A young man dressed in a white coat and white pants was staring at me with a bemused smile, like he knew exactly what I was doing. He was on a bicycle, the reason I hadn't heard him coming.

I put a finger to my lips. "Shhhh."

"You're spying on Shirley, aren't you?" He was whispering and grinning like he was enjoying this.

I whispered back, "I'm a private detective, working for her husband. Do you know her?"

"Sure." He ran a hand over his white coat. "I'm head baker here. She works for me."

"You call that work?" I hitched my head at the car, where soft kissing and moaning sounds were coming from the rolled down windows.

He chuckled. "We start work at seven. She tells her husband she starts at six. Which means she and Billy Boy get to spend an hour together every morning. Sometimes in her car. Sometimes in his. Sometimes, I suspect, in a nearby motel. Although motels cost money."

I peeled myself off the ground and backed away from the bush, motioning for Shirley's boss to follow me a short distance down the sidewalk. The sun was coming up and I didn't want Shirley or Billy Boy to see me.

"Do you know Billy's real name?" I asked. "Who is he?"

"I think his name's Bill Shuster. He works in a store down the street. Probably tells his wife the same lie that Shirley tells her hubby."

"How do you feel about what Shirley's doing?"

My source shrugged and gave me a sly smile. "What do I care? It's her business. But I do get annoyed when she wanders into work a half hour, or more, late. That bothers me. Especially when her husband calls and asks to speak to her and I gotta tell him she's out getting flour or sugar. Everybody who works here knows they gotta lie for her."

Shazam. I had her. I didn't need pictures. I just needed one or more of her co-workers to snitch on her and be willing to testify in court if it came to that. I asked Shirley's boss if he'd be willing.

"Sure," he said. "Whatever you need. She's not that great of a worker anyway. Thelma, who owns the place, should have fired her a long time ago."

———

The big wet patch on the back of my pants felt dry enough to not be embarrassing by the time I got to my office.

My friend Wendy, a receptionist down the hall, greeted me with her customary smile as I walked past her open door.

She jumped up from behind her desk. "Hi, Story. Exciting day so far?" Wendy envied my life, as if it was out of a movie. She wasn't completely wrong.

"Not as exciting as my first case, but it went well. Got what I needed for my client who came in yesterday." I bent my elbow and flexed my bicep like Superwoman. "Another success on the books at least."

"I don't know if you'll ever get another case as exciting as your first one." Wendy's smile widened. "You got lucky there."

"This morning did go pretty easily in comparison." I shrugged. "Nobody shot at me at least."

And nobody died.

But I hoped Wendy was wrong.

I hoped more exciting cases would come my way. Thrilling, challenging cases that would help me grow as a P.I. and succeed in my new business.

I told Wendy goodbye, continued down the hall, unlocked my

door, and let myself into my tiny office. Settling down behind my desk, I started to type a report on Shirley Bianco.

And then she walked in.

Not Shirley, a young woman.

Right away, I sensed she was trouble. An answer to my wish for a thrilling case? Already? What was it they said about being careful about what you wished for?

I don't know why I sensed she was trouble. Except that watching her slowly and hesitantly approach my desk gave me a tickly, spider-crawling-on-my-neck feeling. Which I ignored because she looked like money. And I needed money.

I couldn't afford to be choosy about clients. I'd only had two cases so far. Shirley Bianco and my first case, which had recently ended successfully. If you didn't count the unfortunate deaths of some of the people involved, which were not my fault.

Eager for my next challenge, I ignored the flashing lights and wailing sirens going off in my head and gave the young woman before me a welcoming smile.

It wasn't like she looked dangerous. Dressed in a jade green figure-fitting dress and beige high heels, she wobbled up to me and stopped. Biting down on her lower lip, uncertainty flickered in her eyes as she met my gaze.

If anything, she looked harmless and fragile. And nervous. Maybe I was feeling nervous because she looked nervous.

I pushed my chair back and stood up to greet her. "Can I help you?"

"Story Smith? Are you Story Smith?"

"I am."

She was perspiring, too, her face covered with a sheen of sweat.

Then again, so was I. The day heating up to be a steamy one, so I'd left my office door open to allow air to flow between the window behind my desk and the hallway.

"How can I help you?" I asked.

"I'd like to hire you." She smoothed her perfectly coiffed shoulder-length auburn hair. "If you're available, that is."

Was I ever, but I played it cool. "I do happen to be taking new cases. Could you give me an idea what this is about?"

She pressed her rosy-red lips together, inhaled deeply, and fixed troubled eyes on mine. A striking shade of light brown, they were starting to water. She opened the large purse on her arm, took out a tissue, and dabbed her tears.

"Please ..." I gestured to the chair next to my desk. "Have a seat."

Nodding, she sniffed and sat.

My uneasy feelings about her had now morphed into concern. Sensing that she needed a moment to compose herself, I sat back down, faced her, folded my hands, and waited.

"It's about my father," she said, finally, her voice strained and shaky. "I'm afraid he's about to be arrested for murder."

"Oh..." I said, widening my eyes. "The murder of who?"

"My mother."

"Oh," I said again. Wow. No wonder she looked so emotionally distraught. "I'm sorry ... about your mother, I mean. And your father. How awful."

She fished another tissue out of her purse, dabbed her cheeks, then nodded. "Yes. You have no idea. My life has been hell. Which is why I'm here. I need you to find out who really murdered my mother. And clear my father's name."

I had many questions, but where to begin?

"How was your mother killed?" I asked, grabbing a pen and pencil out of my top drawer.

"Someone shot her in the back of the head." She dabbed away another tear. "When she was grooming her horse in the stables."

"Stables?"

"The stable on our estate. Grand Gables."

Suddenly, I knew who she was. Gripping my pencil, I swallowed hard and stared at her. I'd heard about her mother's death. Just like everyone else in Philadelphia who'd been reading the papers or watching the television news. Wealthy socialite gunned down with a single bullet. No murder weapon found. No apparent motive. Grieving husband and daughter, claiming to have no idea who would murder their loved one, or why.

Grand Gables was a large estate in nearby rural Chester County, in Brandywine Valley. Wealthy area. My instincts about money had been correct.

"I've heard of you," I said. "This happened to your mother, when? About a week ago?"

She nodded. "Last Tuesday."

"It's been in the news," I said. "But I can't remember your name."

"Celeste. Celeste Cranston. My father is Philip Cranston. My mother was Lorna Cranston."

"So, you're saying that the police suspect your father?" Of course, they did. They always look at the spouse first.

"Yes, they suspect my father." She spit the words out. "Problem is —they're not looking for the real murderer because they're convinced it's him." Her tone was icy and bitter. "That's why I've come to you, Miss Smith. I need you to find the monster who did kill my mother. I know it wasn't my father."

"How can you be so sure? What makes you sure he's innocent?"

Her expression turned fiery. She leaned toward me. "Because I know him. He loved her. He had no reason to kill her. He's a good person. He doesn't deserve this."

"Doesn't deserve what?"

"Being persecuted by the police. They're at our house every day. Questioning, questioning, questioning him. Badgering him. They won't leave him alone. Give him time to grieve."

I didn't want to lose her business, but I felt compelled to be honest. "They always suspect the spouse first, Miss Cranston," I said softly. "And it's only been a week. Perhaps they *are* investigating other suspects."

She shook her head. "I hope they are. In the meantime, I want them to leave my father alone. He doesn't deserve this."

Something about what she was saying bothered me. She seemed more upset about her father's plight than her mother's murder. From the little I knew of Lorna Cranston, she had been well-liked, a nice person.

"Do you have any idea who killed your mother?" I asked. "Did she have any enemies?"

"No. She had no enemies. That's why I'm hiring you. I need a professional investigator. I need to give my father some peace. Give him some hope. He's suffering terribly. I can't bear watching him go through this."

Now I was really intrigued and wanted to know more. About Lorna Cranston and her seemingly perfect life, and about Philip Cranston, poor, suffering widower.

I didn't just need this case—I really wanted this case. But I was curious. Why me? I was trying to figure a way to delicately ask that question when Celeste seemed to read my mind.

"You're wondering why I've come to you, Miss Smith."

I nodded. "Yes, as a matter of fact."

"You've heard about me. Well, I've heard about you. Right before my mother was killed *you* were in the news. Attractive blonde female private eye finds missing doctor's wife. With tragic, dramatic consequences, that were…"

"Not my fault."

"No, of course not." Celeste shrugged. "The point is that you were hired to find her—and you did—when it looked impossible. You impressed a lot of people. You impressed me. With your tenacity. With your courage."

"I had help." For some reason I'd felt it necessary to mention that, although I wasn't going to say his name. Steve Evans. I didn't want to give her any ideas about hiring that highly experienced gumshoe instead of me.

A wry smile came over her face. "You're being too modest. Go ahead, take the credit."

I shrugged. "Okay, thanks, I will. And thank you for having faith in me. I'm sure I can help you."

But I didn't promise to clear her father's name. For all I knew, the police were on the right track with him. My job was to find out.

"What do you charge?" She reached into her purse and pulled out a black leather wallet.

"I charge by the day," I said, naming my fee.

She didn't flinch. She pulled out a wad of hundred-dollar bills and spread them out on my desk. "Here's a thousand dollars. Which should do for now. Hopefully you'll find the real murderer before this runs out. In which case, keep the change."

I tried to keep my expression nonchalant. I don't think I succeeded. "Thank you," I murmured.

"I can tell you're wondering about the money." She pursed her lips. "I received a very generous trust fund from my grandfather when I turned twenty-one last year. I'm an only child, and it's nobody's business what I do with my money. Please don't let me down. I'm counting on you, Miss Smith."

"Story," I said. "Please call me Story."

She shrugged. "Okay. And please call me Celeste."

I scooped the money off my desk, stuffed the bills into an envelope in the side drawer and closed it tight. "I'll need to ask you a few more questions. Then, I'll need to meet with your father."

"Of course." She looked relieved. As if a burden she could no longer bear had been taken off her slim shoulders.

Gadzooks. I was glad to take it. This was my lucky day. The challenging case I'd wished for.

Too challenging? After all, as Steve would tell me when he heard about this, I was still very much a rooky in the P.I. business.

But was I going to let that stop me? No way.

So ... why couldn't I shake the niggling feeling that this case was going to be trouble?

Big trouble.

Two

The next day, I headed to Grand Gables, with an appointment to meet Philip Cranston at noon.

Celeste had assured me he would be there, and that he would be happy to answer any questions, no matter how long it took.

"Does he know you were planning to hire me?" I'd asked.

"He will by the time you get there," she'd told me with a thin smile. "I wanted to be sure you would take the case first."

"Will he be upset that you hired me?"

"No. Why should he be? He can use all the help he can get."

Unless he's not the innocent man his daughter believes he is, I mused to myself as I drove my T-Bird convertible through bucolic Chester County. As usual, I had the top down, allowing the warm breeze to wrestle my hair as I relished the freedom of the open air.

My white 1955 Thunderbird is my baby, a precious gift I never take for granted, even if Steve says it's too conspicuous for a private eye.

I think Steve's jealous, and anyway, I like driving it with the top down whenever possible. Especially on a day like today. Sunny and not too hot.

I motored through the small, quaint town of Chad's Ford and then I was back on a two-lane country road with few cars and the welcoming earthy scent of freshly plowed soil.

Passing horses grazing in open fields, and wealthy estates framed by miles of white fencing, I wondered which mansion off in the distance, if any, belonged to Steve's parents. He'd grown up in the area, which made me think about him. And the more I tried to *not* to think about him, the more I thought about him. Blast it all.

Steve had helped me solve my first case, even though I'd really wanted to find my client's missing wife on my own. Grateful in the end, I had invited him to help me celebrate at a country inn.

But our evening out had proved more romantic than I'd wanted it to be. Steve is handsome, and I'm attracted to him, but he has a reputation as a love 'em and leave 'em kind of guy and I had to keep reminding myself to keep my head to spare my heart.

Not that anything *truly* romantic happened, in any kind of physical, Shirley Bianco-Billy Boy making-out kind of way.

No. Our date was romantic because while we had dinner and talked and laughed, dreamy love songs like "Some Enchanted Evening" played in the background, and the candle on our table gave Steve's chiseled cheekbones a golden glow, and the people around us kept giving us cute little smiles, like were getting engaged or something.

And then Steve said he wanted to see me again.

I'd told him I'd need to think about it, but that I was sure we'd be seeing each other around. "You know," I'd stammered, "as competitors in the P.I. biz."

Now, here I was, driving through his old neighborhood where he'd told me he'd grown up. Which was clearly upper class to my middle class—and why was I thinking about this anyway?

I needed to think about Philip Cranston, and what I was going to ask him. Because if the police were questioning him every day there had to be a reason.

What if he was guilty? What if everything I discovered led to him? What then?

I ran a hand through my breeze-tangled locks and told myself I'd deal with it if, and when, it happened. Right now, my job was to find his estate.

I pulled over to the side of the road and unfolded the handwritten map Celeste had given me. Five miles after leaving Chad's Ford I was to turn right onto Bluebird Lane, and then three miles after that I needed to look for the entrance to Grand Gables.

"Okay," I muttered to myself. "Almost there. I can do this. Whatever happens, I'm ready."

———

I wasn't ready for Philip Cranston.

I wasn't sure what I'd been expecting. But I wasn't expecting him.

Waiting for me on the front steps of his magnificent white brick mansion, he was leaning against one of the massive Roman pillars framing his front door. His warm, welcoming smile made me feel like there was no one in the world he'd rather see.

His three-story home reminded me of Tara in the movie *Gone with the Wind*, only grander.

And Clark Gable didn't hold a candle to him in the looks department.

Probably in his mid-forties, he was one of those men who'd still be handsome and distinguished at ninety-nine. Tall, around six-foot. Lean, fit, dressed in white pants and a white button-down shirt. Brown hair streaked with white, which somehow complemented his outfit.

Was he aware of that? I was betting yes. Even as I pulled up and parked, I could see the man oozed charisma. And knew it.

He bounded down the steps and came over to me as I got out of my car. Reaching for my hands, he clasped them in his big, strong, warm ones. "Welcome to Grand Gables, Miss Story Smith," he said with the gleeful air of a host welcoming a dear friend to his home. "I'm so glad you've come."

Feeling for a moment like I'd been invited for tea or tennis, I was momentarily shaken and withdrew my hands, which he'd held just a tad too long for my comfort. I like to pride myself on being able to quickly size someone up, but this man had me rattled.

He was quite possibly a murderer. But I couldn't imagine it. Even on my guard, I found myself liking him.

"Philip Cranston, I presume?" I said, matching his smile.

But why was he smiling? His wife had been shot and killed only a few days before.

And why was I smiling? I was there because his wife had been shot and killed a few days before.

"Yes, I am Philip Cranston. Please, please, come in," he said, gesturing for me to follow him up the steps. He held the front door open and waved me inside, his manners so confident, so smooth, so courtly, so old-fashionably chivalrous, that I half expected a manservant to come and take my cloak.

Only there was no manservant, and I wasn't wearing a cloak. This was 1955, after all, and summertime, and I was wearing a plain blue dress and white pumps, which I was starting to regret because I suddenly felt underdressed in Philip Cranston's world.

From his marbled foyer, he ushered me into his cavernous living room with high ceilings, Victorian furniture, walls dotted with paintings, and a dark wood floor covered with exotic carpets from the Orient.

He walked up to the large, wide fireplace that took up most of one wall, and turned to face me, watching—arms folded across his chest, a slight grin on his face—as I admired his home.

"You don't look like a detective," he remarked. "But I like that. I like that very much." His voice was deep, with a touch of amusement. "Celeste told me to answer all your questions, and to not hold anything back, and of course I will do that. So please..." he gestured, palm up, to a velvet sofa facing the fireplace. "Have a seat."

Two large leather armchairs flanked the sofa and he folded himself into one of them. Facing me, he leaned forward and met my gaze. "I confess I was taken aback when Celeste told me she'd hired you, but not completely surprised. My daughter loves me, and the girl does have a mind of her own."

What he had not said piqued my curiosity. That his daughter loved her mother and wanted her murderer arrested and brought to justice.

"I'm sorry about you wife, Mr. Cranston," I said. "It must have been quite a shock. Such a tragedy."

"Yes." A hint of pain erased the polite, admiring smile he'd been giving me since I sat down. His gaze lingered on my legs, then lifted to my face. "Lorna was a wonderful wife and mother. No enemies in the world. I can't imagine who would have wanted her dead. And I have no idea why the police think I might have wanted to murder her. It's outrageous."

I smoothed my dress over my knees. "Do you have any suspects in mind at all, Mr. Cranston?"

"Please call me Philip, and no, I don't. The only thing I can think of is that maybe someone envied her life, her wealth, her beauty, her family. Resented her for all she had, you know?"

He sighed, then looked away. "Then again, maybe it was just a crazy person roaming the neighborhood with a gun, who just happened to find Lorna in the stables and for jollies shot her dead." He narrowed his eyes at me. "That could have happened."

"That is a possibility," I said. "Though not likely."

He pressed a hand to his forehead. "I know. That's what the police say. Which means they're not looking for such a person. They're focusing on me. And I don't even own a gun."

"Do you have any enemies? Any at all?"

"None that I can think of."

"Were you faithful to your wife, Mr. Cranston—Philip?"

"Of course." He didn't look the slightest bit upset by the question. Or defensive. And he hadn't hesitated to answer.

"Where were you when Lorna was shot?"

"I'd assumed you heard all about it on the news."

"I've heard a lot about your wife's murder on the news." I nodded. "But I want to hear your version of events. Where were you when she was killed and what was your reaction when you heard about it and what did you do next?"

He cocked his head. "You're good. I'm glad Celeste hired you. I know you're going to clear me with the police."

The questions I had asked were common sense questions, nothing genius. And the gleam in his eye was uncomfortably flirty.

"I'll clear your name if you're innocent," I said sweetly.

He laughed. "I can assure you I am completely innocent." Then he turned serious. "I was at the racetrack when Lorna was shot. Many people have vouched for that, and I have many witnesses about where I was that day. Still, the police keep badgering me. I don't know why." He smiled. "Thank God for you. I have faith you will come up with alternative suspects who they can focus on and leave me alone."

"Why were you at the racetrack?"

"It's my hobby and my profession. Grand Gables is an equestrian estate, Miss Smith. We race and breed a few of our horses. The others Lorna considered her pets, although she did compete in jumping events."

"I understand she was grooming one of her horses when she was shot."

"Yes. Thunderbolt. Her favorite."

"Was the horse harmed?"

"No. Just horribly spooked, from what I heard."

"Who found Lorna?"

"Our neighbor and Lorna's best friend, Francine Montague. They were supposed to go riding together. When Francine went to meet Lorna at the stables, she found her, then hurried home, and called the police."

"Tell me everything you know about the crime."

He took a deep breath, let it out long and slow. "Lorna was brushing Thunderbolt. Someone snuck up behind her. Shot her in the back of her head. Once. She fell face forward into a pile of straw at Thunderbolt's feet. Then the shooter fled, taking the murder weapon with them. That's all I know."

His tone was flat, no emotion, just a recitation of facts, a quick, short version of a story that he'd likely repeated many times to the police and others.

"What time did it happen?"

"Around eight a.m., I believe. After breakfast, which Lorna and I had enjoyed together. Right after that I headed to the racetrack."

"Did Lorna keep a regular schedule?" I asked. "Did she usually brush Thunderbolt at the same time every day?"

"Pretty much. After grooming her horses, she usually went riding. Sometimes alone and often with Francine. Celeste and I don't like to ride. That was Lorna's passion."

"So, Celeste doesn't take after her mother? Is there a reason she doesn't like to ride?"

He smiled wryly. "I think you better ask her that. She and her mother were not particularly close. Celeste loved her mother, don't get me wrong, but she and Lorna were very different."

"What about you and Celeste?"

He smiled. "She's a Daddy's girl."

"An only child?"

"Yes. And spoiled, I must admit. Lorna and I had hopes that she'd get married, like all her friends were doing. Unfortunately, Celeste has her mind on one young man, who she dated a few times, who threw her over."

"Threw her over?"

"He wasn't interested in continuing the relationship. Celeste is hardheaded. I don't think she's given up on him." He raked his fingers through his thick salt and pepper hair. "Such a shame—and now Lorna will never see her daughter walk down the aisle."

"What about your marriage. Was it a good one?"

"It was wonderful. Lorna had her interests and I had mine, but we had much in common. Our horses, for one. Although for me, it's all about breeding them and racing them. Lorna, though, just enjoyed riding them, and loving them, like I said, as her pets."

"Who told you that your wife had been shot?" I asked softly.

He squeezed his eyes closed, as if revisiting the painful memory.

I waited.

Finally, he opened them and looked at me. "The police found me at the racetrack. I insisted that they take me to Lorna immediately. I watched them put her in an ambulance and drive away. Slowly. There was no point in rushing her to the hospital, an officer told me. But he didn't have to. I could see she was gone. So much blood."

I winced. "What did you do next?"

"What do you mean?"

"Did you break down?"

"I was in shock. Celeste ran up to me. We held each other and cried. Then the police took me to the station for questioning. I can't remember much. Only that I was at the station for a long time. I don't know why. I couldn't tell them anything that would help."

Tears formed in his eyes. He wiped one off his cheek, looking like a lost little boy. I wanted to get up and put my arms around him and tell him it would be okay.

But that was ridiculous, and it would have been unprofessional. I got a grip on myself and stayed on the sofa.

He sniffed, then brightened as his gaze slid to someone coming up behind me. "Annie," he said, standing. "We have a visitor and I'm afraid I've been terribly rude. Could you please bring us some iced tea? Unless…" he looked back at me, "you'd like something stronger?"

"Oh, no thank you." I turned to Annie, who I assumed must be the housekeeper. "I mean nothing stronger, iced tea would be …"

My eyes widened. Annie was no typical housekeeper.

A cross between Audrey Hepburn and Marilyn Monroe, she was somehow both impish and sexy. Hair pulled high in a ponytail, with curly tendrils framing her cheeks, she looked to be about twenty, and wore a uniform that flattered her slim, leggy, busty figure. Above-the-knees-short, the slate gray dress was fitted at the waist and had a low neckline that teased a glimpse of her cleavage.

Cleavage? Why had Lorna Cranston been okay with that? *Had* she been okay with that?

Annie's smile faded as she looked me over. "You didn't tell me you had company, Mr. Philip," she said in a girlishly alluring voice.

I was amazed at her ability to pull off being simultaneously innocent and mysterious. While looking great in gray.

"This is Story Smith, a private eye hired by Celeste to clear my name," Philip said. "Story, meet Annie Leeds, my housekeeper."

Annie slid me a frosty smile. "Very good, Mr. Cranston. I shall go get your iced tea now. Miss Smith, would you like ice in your glass?"

"Sure," I said, "thank you."

Philip waved a hand, like he'd just thought of something. "Wait a minute, hold on."

Beaming at Annie, then at me, his charm in full bloom, he said, "If you don't mind, please hold off for now, Annie. I want to take Story on a tour of Grand Gables, take her to the stables. I think she needs to see where dear Lorna died."

THREE

I had many more questions, but taking a break to visit the murder scene wasn't a bad idea. Maybe it would spark more questions.

"Where's Celeste?" I asked Philip, hoping she would join us.

"Upstairs in her room. She wanted to give you a chance to interview me alone. She won't want to come with us to the stables because it upsets her too much."

"I understand."

Annie twirled the large pink feather duster in her hands. Feathers dancing just inches from her dainty chin, it was the cleanest feather duster I'd ever seen, more stage prop than cleaning tool. "Will that be all, Mr. Cranston?" she asked demurely.

"Yes, thank you." He smiled. "I'll summon you when we return."

"Very good, sir." Shooting me a quick cool glance, she curtsied and scurried away.

I had the distinct feeling she didn't like me. When I was certain she was out of earshot, I murmured, "Annie surprises me."

Philip raised his eyebrows. "Oh, how so?"

"Her uniform, for one. It's rather revealing, don't you think?"

"Oh, that." He chuckled. "She's young and she just likes to look pretty." He whispered, "She's good at her job, so we let that go. Lorna was fond of the girl, thought of her as almost a second daughter."

Huh. I needed to ask Celeste about that.

"Where was Annie when Lorna was shot?" I asked. "From what I heard on the news reports, nobody was home at the time. You were at the tracks. Celeste was staying with a friend. What about Annie?"

"She had the day off." Philip shrugged. "Anyway, enough about my maid. Are you ready to head to the stables now?"

"Okay."

"Then follow me."

He led me into a chandeliered dining room, its walls adorned with photos of distinguished ancestors, then through a spacious, well-equipped kitchen to a wide back porch. From there, steps led down to a patio and large swimming pool, which we walked around before taking a ten-minute stroll across pristine green pasture to the stables.

The stables were impressive. Resembling a small castle, they were built of stone with high windows and three turrets, like something out of the Middle Ages. Whimsical and imposing and large enough to house at least twenty horses.

Why would someone with murder on their mind choose such an exposed location to do the deed? It wasn't as if the stables were surrounded by trees. Only pasture and wide-open fields, dotted with grazing horses.

They would be seen coming from any direction. So maybe Lorna's murder had not been planned. Maybe someone had paid her a visit and they got into an argument and, unfortunately for Lorna, that someone had a gun.

Or ... did that someone know she was home alone? Meaning no witnesses? Meaning her murder was premediated?

But what about workers?

"Do you have a crew of stable hands?" I asked Philip. Eyeing a pile of horse manure just inside the entrance to the stables, I hopped over it to spare my pretty white pumps.

Philip grabbed my arm to steady me. "I'm sorry. Clive should have seen to that."

Releasing me with an embarrassed grin, he said, "It's hard to get good help right now. Clive is all we have at present. He's probably off riding one of the horses. They need daily exercise you see, and now that Lorna's gone..." He heaved a heavy sigh. "Well ... we're managing without her, but not well."

My ears perked. "Was Clive on duty when Lorna was shot?"

He shook his head. "No. Like Annie, he had the day off. That was one of the first questions the police asked."

"Which means Lorna was out here alone?"

He nodded. "As she often was." Lightly touching my elbow, he directed me past several empty stalls.

Suddenly, out of nowhere, a gigantic black spider dropped down from the ceiling, inches from my face.

"Eeeeah!" My piercing scream made Philip jump about a foot in the air.

"What's wrong?" He reached for my arm as I backed up, breathing hard, mouth agape as I stared at the monstrous furry arachnid.

"I'm scared of spiders," I hissed.

He laughed. "Oh ... is that all? What a relief. I thought— I didn't know what to think."

"Arachnophobia," I whispered. "I have arachnophobia. I'm sorry, I didn't mean to scare you."

He laughed again. "Come on, I'll guide you around that big bad boy." With a firm grip on my elbow, he zig-zagged me around the creepy thing and we continued our stroll through the stables as if nothing had happened.

Or, at least he was able to act as if nothing had happened. I had to will my legs to hold me up, they were shaking so badly.

We continued past more empty stalls, then halted at one occupied by a dark brown stallion with a black mane. A sign above the stall read: "Thunderbolt."

My chest tightened. "Is this where it happened?"

"Yes." Philp reached his hand over the stall's gate toward Thunderbolt.

The stallion snorted loudly and shied away. Stamping a hoof, the horse glared at Philip, as if saying, "Don't touch me."

A chill trickled down my spine. Lorna's favorite horse didn't like her husband—maybe feared him.

"Poor Thunderbolt has yet to get over what he witnessed." Philip pressed his lips together. "Clive said it might take some time. That's why he's not out in the field with the other horses right now. He needs time to heal."

That sounded plausible. But I knew next to nothing about horses. Which put me at a disadvantage. I needed to talk to Clive.

"Was Lorna in the stall with Thunderbolt?" I peered inside. It didn't look roomy enough to me.

"No, she had led him out and was grooming him here." Philip pointed to where I stood.

I jumped back and looked down. No blood. No trace of the horror that had happened here. Just hardpacked earth and a smattering of hay.

A creepy feeling raised goosebumps on my arms.

"Here?" I bent down and scrutinized the area, not sure what I was looking for.

"It's been cleaned up," Philip said. For a fraction of a second, I thought I detected a hint of irritation in his voice. But when I glanced up at him, his handsome face was the picture of patience.

"I thought she fell in a pile of hay," I mused out loud. "Why was a pile here, outside the stall?" I went to stand up. He reached for my hand and helped me to my feet.

"Clive must have raked the hay over some manure that he planned to come back and dispose of later." Philip wiped the dirt from my hand off on his trousers. "Can't think of any other reason. Maybe you can ask the police if they found anything under the hay. If they did, they're not telling me."

"I'd like to speak to Clive, and I plan to visit the police station soon," I said. "Ask for a report and hope they'll give it to me."

"Good luck." Philp put his hands on his hips and looked around. "Are you finished here? Think you've seen enough?"

"For now."

"Okay. Let's go back to the mansion. I'll give you a tour of my house, show you the master suite, and Lorna's room."

I nodded. "Good idea. But first..." I stepped toward Thunderbolt's stall. The horse was eyeing us warily.

"We should go," Philip said. "Let's not upset him further."

I hadn't upset Thunderbolt. Philip had. How would the horse react to me?

I leaned over the gate to the animal's stall and extended my hand. Thunderbolt snorted softly.

"Don't—" Philip's voice was sharp.

"Here boy," I whispered. Was that how you talked to a horse? I had no idea. But it worked. Thunderbolt stepped toward me. Close enough for me to touch him. I ran my hand over his nose. He let me. He didn't move. He seemed to like it. I did it again, then whispered, "Good boy."

"Let's go," Philip said, "before he nips you."

"I think he likes me." I turned around. For a fraction of a second, I thought I saw fear on Philip's face. Or maybe anger. Or maybe it was just my imagination.

Because he started laughing, then waved me to follow him out of the stables. "I think you must have a way with animals. I think that's why Thunderbolt likes you and not me."

"Maybe," I said lightly. But I wasn't so sure.

———

Celeste greeted us when we returned. "I hope Father is cooperating with you, Story, answering all your questions." She went over and gave him a hug. "Annie said you'd gone to the stables."

"Story and I are getting along fabulously." Philip grinned at Celeste and then at me. "I'm grateful that you hired her, and now I'm going to show her around upstairs."

"Great idea," Celeste said, "Let's all go."

She bounded up the spiral staircase, with me on her heels and

Philip following. Calling over her shoulder, she asked me, "What did you see at the stables? Anything that struck you as significant?"

"Not really. But I met Thunderbolt."

"Ahh. That poor horse."

"He let me pet him on the nose."

"Lucky you."

We reached the second floor and a long hallway that branched off into three wings.

"Why lucky me?"

"Thunderbolt's not crazy about everyone. Me included," Celeste said, "but that's not surprising because I don't really like horses. I'm afraid of them and they know it."

Philip said, "Tell Story why you don't like horses."

She grimaced. "I fell off one when I was four."

"One that her mother made her get on to ride," Philip said. "She wasn't hurt, but she's never been on one since."

"Right." Celeste wrinkled her nose at her father, looking annoyed. "But that's enough about me. Let's go see Mother's room. Maybe it will give you an idea of the kind of woman she was, Story. Which hopefully might lead to some clues."

We headed straight, toward what I assumed was the master wing of the mansion.

I asked, "Where do the other wings lead?"

"To guest rooms," Celeste said. "This house is as big as a hotel. We could house a small army."

"Rita gets her own suite when she's here," Philip said. "And she's here a lot."

I turned around to look at him. "Who's Rita?"

"Lorna's sister. I'll introduce you to her at the funeral tomorrow."

I stopped, almost tripping on a small lump in the carpet. "Funeral? You haven't held it yet?"

"Not yet." Celeste sighed. "We had to schedule it so that people could get here from out of town. Mother had many friends, and we expect it to be packed."

"We want to give her the send-off she deserves," Philip said softly.

At the end of the hall, Celeste pushed open a door to our right. "Mother's room," she announced, then pointed to a door across the way. "And that's Father's room. Their rooms are adjoined, but having a room of her own gave Mother her own space."

Indeed.

Walking into Lorna's room, her interests were plain as day. Paintings of horses on the walls. A horse motif on the bed quilt.

Pictures of Celeste and Philip sat upon a large bureau, alongside photos of horses, one of which I was certain was Thunderbolt. I picked it up and examined it. "Is this Lorna?" I pointed to the woman next to the horse.

Peering over my shoulder, Celeste murmured, "That's Mother."

It was the first picture I'd seen of Lorna. She was short— slim, petite, dark-haired, with a perky smile. She looked as youthful as Philip, although she had to be in her forties.

I put the picture back and walked over to her closet. Sadly, it was filled with riding clothes she'd never wear again. Black boots lined the floor. English riding helmets sat side by side on the top shelf.

"Excuse me ... Mr. Philip ..."

I turned around to see Annie standing in the center of the room, without a feather duster. "Excuse me, sir," she said, "but there's a man downstairs who says he wants to speak to you."

Philip frowned. "Who is he?"

"Says he's from the insurance company."

"We're busy," Philip said. "Get his card and tell him I'll call him to set up an appointment later. The nerve of him just showing up."

"No, wait." Celeste touched her father's arm. "I'll go speak to him. You stay here with Story."

"Insurance?" I looked back and forth between Celeste and Philip.

"Life insurance." Philip ran a hand through his hair. "Yes, please, go deal with him, Celeste. I'm sure his call is just a formality. Nothing you can't handle."

Annie followed Celeste out of the room, leaving Philip and I staring at each other in strained silence.

"I've been meaning to ask you about life insurance," I said. "That's one of the questions on my list."

Philip went over and closed the closet door. "Of course, Lorna was insured." His voice was tight. "Although I can't recall for how much." Turning to me, he gave a pained sigh. "Lorna and I insured ourselves after Celeste was born. In case something happened to one of us and the other had to raise her alone." He shook his head. "I don't know why I have to deal with this *now*."

I didn't see the problem, and I wanted to talk to the insurance agent, even if he didn't. "Look, let's go downstairs, and you can talk to this man yourself. Get it over with."

He hesitated, eyes uncertain, his face oddly flushed.

"Come on." I headed for the door before he could stop me. "This probably won't take long, and if nothing else, I'll get my insurance questions answered."

"No, Story. Wait ..."

I pretended like I hadn't heard him and hurried down the stairs.

"Stop!" Philip shouted. "Wait for me."

I stopped when I reached the first floor. Then together we walked into the living room.

I stopped. Suppressed a gasp.

It couldn't be. No.

I blinked. Blinked again.

Celeste was sitting on the velvet sofa. And in the armchair next to her sat Steve.

My Steve.

Steve Evans.

Four

"Story?" Steve bounded to his feet. "What are you doing here?"

"What are *you* doing here?" I moved toward him, feeling confused, as if in a dream, my heart racing, my cheeks suddenly on fire.

"You!" Philip rushed up to Steve. "You're the insurance agent?"

"Not an agent, I'm a private investigator representing Philadelphia Fidelity." Steve faced Philip square on and narrowed his eyes. "They've hired me to investigate your claim."

Then, looking as rattled as I felt, Steve shifted his gaze to me. "But I don't understand why you're here, Story. What's going on?"

"That's what I want to know," Philip snapped. His eyes flashed fury. "You're the jerk who stole my daughter's heart and then ditched her and left her crying her eyes out for weeks—and now you show up *here*? Claiming to be from my insurance company?" He turned to me, then to Steve, then back to me. "And you two know each other?"

"We do." My legs shaky, I made my way to the sofa and collapsed onto it next to Celeste. I looked at her, hurt. I'd been so proud to have landed this case. Now my confidence was shattered. Now I knew why she'd hired me, a rooky female private eye.

She'd known, from the news, about my connection to Steve. And she'd seen me as a possible way to get back with him. Only she hadn't needed to hire me after all. Because here Steve was, hired by her father's insurance company, no doubt to find evidence that her father could be guilty, so it would not have to pay his claim.

"Celeste hired me, Steve." I met his gaze, enjoying the surprise I saw in his dreamboat dark brown eyes. "She hired me to clear her father's name, to find out who murdered her mother because she's convinced her father didn't. But now I think she also hired me to get back with you." I turned toward Celeste. "Am I wrong?"

"No," she murmured. "Not completely."

I glanced back at Steve. He looked at me with that lopsided grin of his, the grin that made my heart pound, that set my blood on fire. No, no, no. This was no time for that.

"You sure have a way with women, Steve," I said, hoping no one noticed how red my face must have been. "And congratulations on your new case. Hired by Philadelphia Fidelity? Wow, I'm impressed. Bet they're paying you well. Too bad we're on opposite sides of this case, though. We made a good team."

I bit down on my lip. Had I gone too far? Had I said too much?

"Yes, we did make a good team." Steve's voice was strangled. He raked a hand through his dark brown hair and turned to Celeste. "I can't believe you did this."

"Did what?" She glanced sheepishly at her father. "Hired the best P.I. in the business? Story was the one who found that doctor's wife. You only helped her from what I understand."

"Story is an excellent private eye and I congratulate you for hiring her, Celeste." Steve's tone was warm and genuine. I wanted to hug him. And I wanted to strangle him. Here he was again, entangled in one of my cases.

Was this some kind of joke? Was fate having fun at my expense?

"Get out!" Philip shouted, pointing to the front door. "Get out of my house, whatever your name is, and don't come back."

"Name's Steve Evans." Steve folded his arms across his chest and spread his legs wide, clearly not going anywhere. "I'm here at the request of your insurance company and I need to ask you some questions."

Philip scowled. "Tell them to send somebody else. I'm not dealing with you, you cad. You broke my daughter's heart."

Celeste jumped up. "Father, stop."

"I didn't mean to hurt you, Celeste," Steve said. "We dated a couple of times and that was all. I never took advantage of you. You can't claim otherwise."

"You kissed me."

"Once."

"I thought you loved me."

"I'm sorry you thought that. I never meant to lead you on."

"You're the only one I ever loved." A tear slid down Celeste's cheek. I felt sorry for her. I could relate. I had the same feelings for Steve, although he could never know.

I would not let that happen to me. Besides, I had my business to think about. Starting now.

"Get out!" Philip shouted again, jabbing his finger in the direction of the front door.

"No." Steve shook his head. "Not until you answer some questions. If you have any hope of processing your claim, that is."

Philip glared at him. Angry silence filled the room.

"I don't understand, Steve," I blurted. "What do you need from Philip now? He hasn't even buried his wife yet."

Steve stared at me. "He didn't tell you?"

"Tell me what?"

"That he filed a claim to cash his wife's policy the day after she was murdered."

"What ...?" I went numb. Philip had lied to me. He'd told me he couldn't even remember how much the policy was worth.

"How much was Lorna Cranston insured for?" I asked in a choked whisper, then held my breath, dreading the answer.

"He didn't tell you that either?" Steve looked at me with pity. "One million dollars."

———

"Father!" Celeste ran over and grabbed him by the shoulders. "Tell me that's not true."

Philip didn't say anything, didn't move a muscle, just stood there meeting her anguished gaze.

She shook him, her long nails digging into his shirt. "Tell me it's not true!"

"He can't," Steve muttered. "Because it is true."

Celeste pulled away, all color draining from her face. She met my eyes and shook her head. "He didn't tell me, Story ... he didn't tell me."

Nodding, I whispered, "This looks bad."

Bad for Philip, but also for me. I'd been paid one thousand dollars to prove this man did not murder his wife, and now it looked like he'd had the classic, age- old motive. Money.

I needed this case. I wanted to believe he was innocent, not only so I could keep my fee, but also for the challenge, and to seek justice for Lorna. But now, how could I believe anything Philip Cranston ever told me again?

"I can explain," Philip said.

We all looked over at him. Celeste, tears streaming down her face. Me, pressing my lips together so I didn't say anything I'd regret. Steve, hands on his hips, a slight smirk on his face.

"Make this good," Steve said, tapping his foot. "We're waiting."

"I panicked." Philip said, shooting me a please-believe-me look. "Lorna was dead, and I didn't know what to do, so after the police let me go home, I searched for her life insurance policy. I found it in the top drawer of her bureau. Was surprised at how much money she was insured for. Surprised and relieved because I knew I'd need that money."

"Why?" Celeste stood up. Her eyes red and puffy, she shook a fist. "Why did you need the money, Father? We're not poor!"

"Because I knew Grandpa would discontinue my allowance." Philip ran a hand down over his face. "I knew as soon as Grandpa learned your mother was dead, that he would cut me off. I panicked, I panicked."

My list of questions for Philip was growing as fast as my respect and admiration for him was going bye-bye. "Wait," I said, furrowing my brow. "Who's Grandpa?"

"Arthur McKay," Steve said. "Right, Celeste? Your mother's father?"

She nodded.

My eyes met Steve's. I didn't deserve the sympathetic smile he was shooting me.

I mentally kicked myself. Hard. Steve had done his homework before coming over here. I had not, expecting to get everything I needed to know from my client, not even considering that he might be a liar.

Boy, I still had a lot to learn about being a crackerjack detective.

Meantime, I'd have to soldier on. "Enlighten me, please, Philip," I said, turning to him with an expression of forced patience. "Are you saying that your father-in-law has been giving you an allowance to live on? For how long?"

He lifted his chin, his eyes flashing defiance, as if daring me to judge him. "For as long as I've been married to his daughter. He could afford it. He gave Lorna and me separate allowances every month. In addition to letting us live at Grand Gables for free." He looked at Steve, then back at me. "You might as well know that."

"Already did," Steve murmured.

Philip shrugged.

I couldn't believe this. I struggled to think. Maybe this was good news. Why would Philip murder his wife—when his lifestyle depended on being married to her? That would be stupid.

With her head buried in her hands, Celeste sobbed softly.

Steve went over and patted her gently on the shoulder. "I'm sorry," he said. "I think I should come back another time. Unless your father wants to hold off on trying to process his claim."

"No!" Philip shouted. "Why should I? My wife was insured for a million dollars and now she's dead, so I'm entitled to that money."

"No, you are not. Not while you remain a prime suspect in her murder." Steve looked at Celeste. "There's no point in discussing this further right now. I'll come back another time." He turned to me. "Story, could I have a word with you, please?"

I gave him a grim smile, nodded, and followed him out the door.

Outside, he reached for my hands. As if magnetized, they went to him.

My breath caught in my throat as we stood there, his warm hands squeezing my cold ones. My memory flashed back to the last time we'd held hands, on a plane ride home, after we had solved my first case.

It had taken everything I had not to surrender to him then.

And it took everything I had not to surrender to him now.

I pulled away. Steve and I were not going to solve *this* case together. Either he would win, or I would win.

The truth was what mattered. Justice for Lorna.

"Be careful, Story." Steve reached over and ran a finger down my cheek. "Philip Cranston could be a dangerous man. I don't want you to get hurt."

I smiled. "Thanks, Steve. But I can take care of myself. I'll be okay." I widened my smile. "And I'm sure I'll be seeing you around."

His eyes glinted. "Yes, you will. Starting tomorrow at Lorna's funeral. You're planning to attend, right? Many people will be there who I'm sure you'll want to talk to."

The funeral. I'd forgotten about the funeral. "Of course." I raised my chin. "Of course, I'll be there."

"Good." He grinned. "As will I. See you then."

FIVE

Lorna's funeral was a somber, crowded affair.

Hundreds of mourners dressed in black had packed the pews of St. Paul's Lutheran Church by the time I arrived. Flower arrangements flanked Lorna's satiny white, rose-draped casket at the front by the altar. The mournful sounds of a hymn I couldn't identify filled the sanctuary as I found a seat in a back row.

Celeste and Philip had not asked me to sit with them, which was fine with me because I preferred to attend as a family acquaintance, not a sleuth out to catch an evil killer.

St. Paul's, on the outskirts of Brandywine Valley, was not a large church. I suspected some of the mourners who'd come to the noon service were curiosity seekers, given that Lorna's unsolved slaying was still a hot news item. The reporters and photographers standing around out front made it clear that the wealthy woman's funeral would make the papers and television news tomorrow.

As I looked around, trying to catch a glimpse of Steve, a shiver of excitement, mixed with apprehension, ran through me. The world wanted to know who murdered Lorna Cranston and I was going to find out.

Nothing and no one would stop me.

Craning my neck, I finally saw Steve in a middle pew, next to a stained-glass window depicting Jesus carrying a lamb. The sun shining through the colorful glass bounced bright yellow and orange rays onto Steve's dark brown hair, making it look as if he was wearing a halo.

I bit back a smile. A halo? Ha. Steve was no saint, that was for sure.

I moved my gaze to the front row, where Celeste and Philp sat side by side. A woman wearing a wide-rimmed black hat sat on Philip's right and an elderly man sat next to Celeste on her left.

The woman was likely Lorna's sister, Rita, and the man was probably Lorna's father, Arthur McKay. I needed to speak to both, and I planned to introduce myself after the service.

My eyes moved back to Steve. He must have felt me looking at him because he turned around, met my gaze, and winked.

I waved back.

Then the music stopped, and the chapel fell silent as the pastor moved to the pulpit and began the service with a prayer. Then the choir sang *Amazing Grace*, which was followed by more prayers, and a homily by Philip that told me nothing about Lorna that I didn't already know.

Dry-eyed, he spoke about how wonderful she was as many people sobbed softly and wiped their eyes.

I shifted uneasily, wishing he would at least shed a tear so he would look less guilty. After all, he was speaking about his beloved wife. Could he have murdered her? He claimed to have many witnesses who vouched for his alibi. But what if he'd shot her right after breakfast, before going to the racetrack? Or hired someone?

There were many people I needed to talk to, including the police and those so-called witnesses.

The service ended. Determined to speak to Arthur McKay and Aunt Rita, I made my way toward the front of the church as people streamed past me on their way out. Lorna was to be buried in the graveyard next to the church, another opportunity for the news cameras to capture, for reporters to describe.

Looking at each face heading down the aisle, I told myself that any one of them could be the murderer.

The police apparently thought so, because several police officers stood by the door, watching people leave.

"Story." I stopped. Steve was hurrying toward me and darn, did he look good in black. Then again, when didn't he look good? "Glad you could make it," he said, his eyes taking in my black dress, black stockings, and black heels.

"Wouldn't miss it." My cheeks went hot. "I'm on my way to meet Celeste's aunt and grandfather."

He took my arm. "Come, I'll introduce you."

"You?" I blinked. "You know them? Oh, wait, of course you do. You dated Celeste. Aunt Rita was probably planning your wedding."

He squinted at me. "Do I detect a hint of sarcasm in your voice? Not nice, Story. But yes, I do know the family. Although it would be fairer to say that I know of them. I grew up in the area, but I'm much older than Celeste."

"Not that much older."

"Eleven years. She's twenty-two, I'm thirty-three. My cousin told me Celeste had a crush on me, and to make my cousin happy, I asked her out on a date. She was cute and fun, and we went out a couple more times. Nothing came of it, except in Celeste's imagination. I had no idea she was so bonkers for me."

He nodded at the casket. "I met Lorna. She was a nice woman."

"Philip remembered you," I said. "What did you think of him?"

"Not so nice to me. Overly protective of his daughter. Kind of haughty. Polite. But a phony. Watch out for him is all I can say."

Celeste hurried over to us. Even with the black hat and veil covering half her face, I could see her bristle at the sight of Steve's hand on my arm.

"I was hoping you could introduce me to your family," I said, pulling away from Steve. "Your aunt, your grandfather?"

She nodded. "Oh, sure." She turned to the woman with the big hat. "Aunt Rita, this is Story Smith, a private investigator I hired two days ago to find Mother's killer."

Aunt Rita's eyes went big. She looked like her sister—short, slender, wiry—although there was a fragility about her that I'd not detected in the photograph of Lorna. "Private investigator? Celeste, whatever for? The police are investigating, aren't they?"

Celeste sniffed. "As far as I can tell they're not looking at anyone but Father."

"Oh..." Rita gave me a weak smile and reached over to shake my hand. "In that case I'm glad to meet you, Miss Smith. We all know Philip is innocent, so I can't wait for you to prove it."

Rita introduced me to the older man with her, who, as I'd suspected, was her father, Arthur McKay.

He leaned toward me and whispered in my ear, "I'm not so convinced that my son-in-law is innocent, dear, so good luck."

Shocked at what he'd said, and his sarcastic tone, I could only nod. I needed to ask him what he meant, but now was not the time.

My gaze fell on Annie Leeds. Standing at the end of the pew, she was giving Philip an awkward, wistful smile, like she longed to be part of the family, but knew her place.

Not surprisingly, her black dress was low cut, and molded to her body, and her pointy-toed heels, which added at least five inches to her height, had to be killing her feet.

I felt sorry for her. Until she turned and graced me with the same cold stare she'd given me at Grand Gables.

What had I done? I headed over to speak to her.

But Steve was quicker. He hustled over to her side and made a remark that made her laugh, and then the next thing I knew, they were heading down the aisle together, chatting like old friends.

I couldn't believe it. He was interviewing her and using his masculine charm to set her at ease.

I followed them, and the rest of the family, out of the church to the graveyard.

Miffed that Steve had beat me to the housekeeper, I wondered what she was telling him.

No doubt she was privy to more dirt about the Cranston family than anyone knew.

———

The grave had been dug. Throngs of mourners circled the yawning hole in the ground that awaited Lorna's casket.

I went to the front and watched as the crowd gave way for the pall-bearers.

Filled with the scent of freshly disturbed earth, and the lilies in people's hands, the air felt heavy.

Someone handed me a lily. The pallbearers moved closer. Lorna's casket was slowly lowered into the hole.

A dove in the distance cooed mournfully. Around me, people cried and then stepped forward and one by one tossed their lilies onto the casket. I hadn't known Lorna, but my eyes welled with tears as I threw my flower onto the growing pile.

A hand touched my shoulder. "Life's short, isn't it?"

I turned and looked at Steve, nodded, and wiped a tear from my cheek.

"We can never know when our time's up," he said. "Which means we need to embrace the good things in life before it's too late."

I blinked at him. "The good things?"

"Like love."

I smiled. "Great pickup line, Steve. Especially effective at a funeral."

"I'm not being cute." He looked hurt.

"You're talking about me and you, aren't you?"

"Yes ..."

I whispered, "Well, this is not the time or place."

"Let's go to dinner again. On a real date."

"We can't." I shook my head. "That would be a conflict of interest. Don't you think?"

"Would you go out with me if we didn't have a conflict of interest?"

"Uh ... maybe ... but right now, I can't ignore that we're competitors. I was heading to talk to Annie Leeds when you skirted around me and got to her first."

"Right." He gave me a sheepish grin. "Sorry about that. She looked particularly vulnerable at that moment—so I decided to take advantage."

"So ... what did she tell you? Anything juicy?"

He stared at me. "We're competitors ..."

I gave him a look.

He nodded. "Okay, okay." He cleared his throat. "Well, for one, she's a Piney. That's what people from the New Jersey Pine Barrens call themselves. She didn't tell me much, but I sense she comes from a poor but proud family that she couldn't wait to escape from."

"Interesting ... and so?"

"And so that's why she took a job as housekeeper to the Cranston family. It was her way to make a life for herself in a place of wealth and luxury. Even as a bystander."

I nodded. "Okay. And so?"

"And so, what?" He arched a brow.

"There's something you're not telling me. Something big. Spill."

A corner of his mouth twitched up. "You're perceptive, Story. For a rookie."

"Spill, Steve."

He sighed and leaned closer and whispered, "Annie is in love with Philip."

"What? Did she *tell* you that?"

"Of course not."

"Then ...?"

"It's the way she looks at him and the way she talks about him. Her employer is old enough to be her father. But that maid is in love."

Six

Steve's juicy theory about Annie sent me back to Grand Gables early the next morning. I was going to talk to that woman, whether she liked me or not.

Only Cranston family drama waylaid my plans.

When I pulled up, Annie was hauling a suitcase out of the trunk of a big, shiny, black car. Looking peeved, she shouted something at Celeste, then wrangled it up the steps and into the house.

Shaking her head, Celeste grabbed a large cardboard box out of the trunk and stamped after her.

Philip came out the front door, followed by Rita, who was waving her arms and yelling, "I'm staying, and that's that."

What was happening?

"Rita's moving in." Philip announced as he opened my car door, then helped me out. "Insists we need her, but we don't."

"Oh." I watched Rita snatch a small suitcase out of the back seat. Setting it on the ground, she pulled another larger one out of the trunk, set it down, then turned and give Philip an aren't-you-going-to-help-me look.

He held up a finger to say he'd be right there.

I asked him, "How long is she staying?"

"Who knows?" He blew out a breath. "Probably for the rest of her life."

"What about her husband?"

"Doesn't have one. Never did. She's an old maid."

I pressed my lips together. I hated hearing a woman called an old maid. It was insulting. What was wrong with never marrying?

That was my plan. I had been secretly engaged once and what should have been our fairytale story ended in tragedy when I broke it off. Dean killed himself and I blamed myself. I learned that love could be dangerous. And that I should protect my heart if I didn't want to get hurt—or hurt anyone else—ever again.

Rita came over to us, limping. As she came closer, I noticed that her right leg seemed to be slightly shorter than her left. And thinner below the hemline of her skirt, which I hadn't noticed at the funeral.

"Hello, Miss Lady Detective," she said with a strained smile. "Here to help?"

"To tell you the truth, I was hoping to speak to Annie, but I can see she's busy."

"Oh, she'll be busy for a while." Rita pointed to an upstairs window. "That's my room. I need all the help I can get moving in because it's hard for me to carry anything heavy." She glanced at Philip. "I don't know if my brother-in-law told you, but I had polio when I was three."

"No, he didn't tell me that. But he did tell me you're moving in. For how long?"

"Indefinitely." She batted her eyes at Philip and the way she was grinning at him erased years off her face. She suddenly looked like a teenage girl with a not-so-secret crush, nibbling her lower lip. Really? Was I really seeing that? Was she really looking at her dead sister's husband like that?

Annie could wait. I needed to talk to Rita.

"Tell you what," I said, lightly touching her arm. "Let me grab a couple of things from your car and I'll take them up to your room and then you and I can talk? Okay?"

She and Philip exchanged glances but I'm not sure what they were communicating to each other. She raised her eyebrows, like she was waiting for him to give her the go-ahead, which he finally did with a brusque nod.

Their relationship struck me as more than a little strange. She was moving herself into Philip's home, which apparently didn't thrill him, but he wasn't stopping her. She either didn't notice or didn't care about that, but she did want his approval to speak to me.

With a shrug, I went over to her trunk, grabbed the last two small suitcases in it, and headed inside. Trudging upstairs, I met Annie coming down. She looked tired and gave me a wan smile. Better than the chilled stares I'd gotten before. Maybe there was hope for us.

Celeste met me in the hall and directed me to her aunt's room. Or, rather, rooms. She had an entire wing, with a spacious bedroom that connected to a sitting room and bathroom, with an outdoor balcony overlooking the front of the estate.

I set the suitcases on the bed and went to fetch Rita.

She was in the kitchen, downing a glass of lemonade. She offered me one and I accepted, and we carried our beverages out onto the back porch to talk.

"I don't know what I can tell you, except I know Philip didn't murder my sister." Rita waved for me to sit in a white wicker rocking chair facing the patio and pool, then lowered herself down in the one next to me.

We had a lovely view. Sunflowers around the porch, swaying in a light summer breeze. Horses grazing in the distance. Puffy white clouds moving across a stunningly blue sky.

Quiet. Serene. Hard to believe a brutal slaying had happened here.

I turned to Rita. "I'm curious. How you can be so sure about Philip?"

She took a minute to answer, rocking back and forth as she sipped her lemonade. "I've known Philip most of my life," she said at last. "Longer than Lorna, actually." She glanced at me, then away. "I know his heart and that he loved my sister. He would never have done anything to hurt her."

"What do you mean, longer than Lorna?"

She ran her tongue over her lips. "Philip and I dated briefly in college. Swarthmore. I majored in English, he in Economics. We met at a dance, where a friend had dragged me against my wishes. I felt shy and awkward there, insecure, like I didn't belong. Who would ask a cripple to dance? But he did. Then, he asked me out, and I couldn't believe my luck."

"You dated?"

She sighed. "Briefly. Until I brought him home to meet my parents. And my younger sister, Lorna."

"And he ...?"

"Fell in love with her. And she with him."

"She stole your boyfriend?"

Rita sighed again. "Yes ..."

"Were you angry?"

"I was hurt."

"What did your parents think?"

"They hated Philip. From the beginning. Not because he ditched me for Lorna. But because of where he came from. Camden, New Jersey. Working class family, his father a car mechanic. 'Not our kind, dear,' my mother warned Lorna. But she didn't listen. She and Philip eloped."

I was amazed at the lack of bitterness in Rita's voice. "I never stopped loving Philip," she said softly. "I love him still."

I gripped my glass, cold against my fingers, and felt a chill run through me. Could she have murdered her sister in revenge? Had she harbored a rage that grew and grew until one day she'd snapped? Swallowing hard, I glanced over at her, wondering if I was sitting next to a monster.

She gave a cool laugh. "I know what you're thinking. And, no, I didn't shoot my sister. I loved her, and I love my niece, almost like a daughter. And now that Lorna is gone, Celeste is going to need me more than ever. Which is why I'm moving in. And staying."

She was taking her sister's place. And proud of it. That, in a way, was revenge.

"But Celeste is twenty-two," I said. "A grown woman. What if she tells you she doesn't need you?"

Rita gave a satisfied smile. "It wouldn't matter. Because Philip does, whether he knows it or not. I've been waiting for him to come back to me all these years. For him to realize that he chose the wrong McKay sister. Now is my time to prove it."

———

After basically declaring that she had designs on becoming the next Mrs. Philip Cranston, Rita was done with me.

She stood up, drained the rest of her lemonade, and wished me luck, saying she needed to go direct the unpacking of her belongings.

Which meant interviewing Annie right now was not an option, although I was more eager than ever to speak to her. Steve believed Annie was in love with Philip. I *knew* Rita was.

Had Lorna known how her sister had felt about her husband? Did she care? I remembered Philip mentioning that their neighbor, a woman named Francine, was Lorna's best friend. If Lorna had concerns about Rita, maybe she'd confided in Francine.

Now I needed to meet Francine.

I found Philip in his study, obviously trying to stay clear of the activity in Rita's room, where I could hear Celeste arguing with her aunt about which clothes should go in which closet and why did she bring so much stuff ... and how long did she plan to stay, anyway?

Forever, most likely. I was sure glad I wasn't a Cranston. They had money but money was a major cause of their problems. If not a motive for murder.

"Come in," Philip called when I knocked on his door. Gripping a golf club, he was practicing his putting skills—sending golf balls across the room and into a glass laid on its side. This time his usual charming smile hinted at embarrassment. "I'm sorry you had to witness all this," he said, scooping a ball out of a small bucket by his feet.

I waved my hand. "No, no, it's been most enlightening. Rita told me how you and she met."

He squeezed the ball and moaned. "I knew she would. It makes me look like a cad."

"She's still in love with you."

"I know. I don't deserve it, the way I treated her."

"Did Lorna know how she felt about you?"

He bounced the ball up and down in his hand. "Rita never kept it a secret. She was always telling Lorna how lucky she was to have me. Lorna usually brushed it off. What else was she going to do?"

"What about you?"

He slipped me a sly smile. "I can't help it if women find me attractive. I was flattered. Never did anything about it, though, if that's what you are insinuating. We never had an affair."

"Why are you letting her move in here? Celeste doesn't seem happy about it."

He placed the ball on the floor and tapped it. It missed the glass. "My father-in-law owns the deed to this estate." He went over and picked up the ball. "If Rita wants to move in here, I'm sure it's fine by him." He shrugged. "It gets her out of his house. She moved in with him after my mother-in-law died a few years ago, declaring that he needed her. I'm sure he's delighted to have her be my problem now."

I felt sorry for Rita. How awful to be considered a burden. Then again, it could have led her to commit murder. I'd table my pity for now.

"I'd like to talk to Francine, your neighbor," I said. "Could you give me directions to her place?"

He put the ball back on the floor, tapped it lightly, missed the glass again, then frowned. "Why do you want to talk to her?"

"Didn't you say she was Lorna's best friend?"

He went over and snatched up the ball. "Yes, so?"

"So maybe she knew some things about Lorna's life that you didn't."

"Secrets?" He narrowed his eyes at me. "We didn't keep secrets from each other."

"How do you know? Secrets are secret."

He laughed. "Wow. Very good, Story. I'm so glad Celeste hired you."

I smiled. "So am I."

He winked. "It's a plus that you're so pretty."

My smile froze. I stared at him. What did my looks have to do with anything?

He laughed again, this time nervously. "Relax. I didn't mean anything by that. Although you are ... pretty, I mean. That Steve Evans is sure besotted with you—which you don't seem to mind. I saw the two of you chatting at the funeral."

"We worked together on my last case."

Philip shrugged. "Good for you. Please tell him to back off me. What was he doing at the funeral, anyway?"

"Just doing his job."

Philip grabbed another ball from a bucket, placed it between his feet, gave it a light tap. It sailed across the floor and into the glass. With a satisfied smile, he looked back at me. "Anyway ... Francine. Her estate is just west of here, adjacent to ours. No fences between here and there, so why don't you go over to the stables and ask Clive to saddle you up a horse? It would be quicker than driving."

I shook my head. "No thanks, I'll take my car."

"But Francine would love it if you came calling on horseback. You'd instantly become her new best friend."

That didn't gladden my heart. Given what had happened to her last best friend. "I have no idea how to ride a horse," I said. "I prefer to drive."

"Come on ... I'll have Clive give you a quick lesson, then guide you over there. It'll be fun."

I met his gaze. Was he serious?

"I'm serious," he said. "And I mean it when I say Francine will be impressed. You'll connect with her instantly once she sees you're a horse person."

"But I'm not."

"But you could be ..." For some reason he was appealing to my sense of adventure. The trait that had led me to become a private detective in the first place. The part of me that had caused me to quit a safe, respectable, financially secure job as a newspaper reporter. And now I was digging up dirt about people. Finding out things they didn't want me to know. Risking danger at every turn.

So ... how dangerous could it be to ride a horse?

"Okay." I glanced down at my pedal pushers and sneakers, then frowned. "Do you think I'm dressed okay?"

"Sure."

I gave a half-hearted shrug. "Okay ... I'll do it. I've been wanting to talk to Clive anyway."

"Good girl." Philip's eyes danced with admiration, making me feel as if I'd just won an Olympic gold medal or something. "Come on, let's head to the stables."

SEVEN

Clive was outside, brushing down a dapple-gray horse, when we strolled up.

The stable hand was short and wiry, with a tanned leathery face. I guessed his age to be around forty. Wearing a cowboy hat, short-sleeved shirt, jeans, and scuffed brown boots, he greeted us with a questioning smile. "Mister Philip, Miss ...?"

Philip introduced me and filled him in on our plan. "Story's never ridden before," he explained, "so we need to get her an easy rider. Maybe Spotlight?"

"Yep, Spotlight be good." Clive looked me up and down. "Suppose what you're wearing will do alright. You just wanting to ride to Miss Francine's and back? That all?"

I nodded.

"Miss Francine at home?" he asked Philip.

"Probably. Why don't you two just ride over and see?" Philip winked at me. "Story doesn't mind taking a chance that Francine might be out. Anyway, a ride over there will give my lady detective a lay of the land."

It wouldn't hurt to explore Lorna's world on horseback, I assured myself.

Still ... I bit down on my lip. "Spotlight will go slow, right?" I looked at Clive, then at Philip, who seemed mildly amused by my sudden case of nerves.

"Slow enough, I reckon." Clive ran a hand over the dapple-gray. "This is her. I'll go get you a saddle."

This was Spotlight? I reached over and patted her neck. She twitched an ear. Otherwise, she didn't move. She looked placid enough. Not too big. Kind of old, which had to be good. I didn't need young, skittish, or fast.

Clive returned with a saddle and threw it onto her back.

"I've got to be going," Philip said. "I'm leaving you in good hands, Story. I hope Francine can help you. She knew Lorna better than most anyone."

"Okay, thanks."

I turned back to Clive. He adjusted the straps on the saddle, then told me to put my foot in the stirrup to hoist myself up.

"These here are the reins," he said, placing them in my hands. "Two things to remember. Pull back on them to make her stop. And when you want her to go, or go a little faster, nudge her with your heels. Just a little. Not hard. Harder you nudge, faster she's going to think you want her to go. You don't want her to just take off."

That I did not want.

"Uhm ..." I remembered all those riding hats in Lorna's closet. Hard helmets, with chin straps. "Shouldn't I be wearing a helmet or a hat or something?"

"Nah." He spat on the ground. "We're not going to be doing that kind of riding. Not going to cantor or gallop, no jumping. You'll be fine."

He took hold of Spotlight and led me around in a couple of wide circles as I squeezed my legs into her flanks, using every muscle in my body to hold on for dear life. "Good, good," he said. "You're ready. We're going to go real … slow … which is what Spotlight likes anyway. Let me go get Jet."

He dashed into the stables and came back with a magnificent black horse much bigger than Spotlight.

"How many horses live here?" I asked as Spotlight shook her mane to scare off flies. Just that bit of movement made me tense and I gripped the reins harder.

"Jet's mine, so counting him, eleven."

"Philip owns all the others?"

"Technically, they was owned by Miss Lorna. But Mr. Philip breeds three and races two." He tossed a saddle onto Jet's back, mounted the horse, then came over next to me. "We'll ride together," he said. "Just try to relax, nothing bad going to happen if you do what I say."

"Sure." I nodded vigorously. "Sure, sure."

We rode in silence across a grassy field then came to a trail that skirted the edge of a woods and took it. To my left I noticed areas that seemed to be arranged for jumping. Pieces of fence, bushes, barrels.

"I understand that Miss Lorna was a show jumper," I said, willing myself to relax as I swayed back and forth in the saddle. True to his promise, Clive was taking us slow.

"Yep." He grinned over at me. "She used to compete—and she was dang good."

"I don't remember seeing any trophies or ribbons in her room."

"Oh, they's in the library." Clive widened his grin. "Mr. Philip probably be glad to show you if you want."

I made a mental note to check out the library. Maybe I could interview Annie there.

After another fifteen minutes—and what felt like many acres—we came within sight of a huge barn. The largest, cleanest, most pristine barn I'd ever seen. Nothing compared to the stables at Grand Gables, but impressive all the same.

We went around it and came to a red brick mansion. Three-story. Colonial. Lots of windows, lots of chimneys.

I heard a horse galloping up from behind us and craned my neck around.

A woman rode up on a snow-white horse and met my eye as she halted, pulling back on her reins with a dramatic flourish. "Hello. May I help you?"

Her deep voice had a questioning tone, but she relaxed once she saw who I was with.

"Clive. What brings you here?" she asked as her horse pirouetted in a tight circle, controlled and graceful, as if performing some kind of horse ballet.

I got the impression I was supposed to be impressed, and I was. Even more so by her riding outfit—bright white jodhpurs, short sleeved quartz-pink and white shirt, black leather gloves, and shiny black riding boots.

My sneakers and pedal pushers had never felt so inadequate.

"This here's Miss Smith," Clive said. "She's a private detective hired by Miss Celeste to find out who killed her mama. Miss Smith, this is—"

"Francine Montague, right?" I suddenly wished I had just driven over because the woman on the horse in front of me did not look the slightest bit impressed that I had come calling on horseback.

My T-Bird convertible, on the other hand, probably would have at least elicited a smile.

"Yes, I'm Francine." Her voice was cool, but her expression confused. "I don't understand. Why exactly have you come?" She led her horse through a few more ballet circle-moves, then closed the gap between us. "I've already spoken to the police."

"I'd just like to talk to you." I gave her my best I'm-harmless grin. "Philip Cranston tells me that you were his wife's best friend."

"True." She cracked a tiny, tenuous smile.

"So ... I was hoping you could give me some insights about Lorna's life. That could perhaps give me some leads to go on. You know, as to who might have wanted her dead."

"Right." She cleared her throat. "Yes, yes, of course, I'll talk to you." She slipped off her horse and secured it to a nearby post.

Turning back to me, she waited for me to dismount as well.

Only I had no idea how to do that without killing myself.

Clive got off his horse, hurried over, and instructed me to swing my right leg over Spotlight's back as he held the reins.

I ended up on my butt.

Jumping to my feet, I dusted myself off. "Sorry, I'll get the hang of this. First time."

"Really? Who could have guessed?" Francine pointed to her house as Clive secured Spotlight next to her horse. "Come on, let's go inside to talk."

She glanced back at Clive. "Are you going to wait for her?"

He shook his head. "Rather not. I got work to do, Miss Francine."

"Don't worry about it then," she said. "I'll take Miss Smith back myself."

We entered her mansion through a back door and went into the kitchen, as clean and pristine as the barn. White tiled floors. White wooden cabinets. White and blue curtains on the windows.

We sat down at a massive, oval-shaped kitchen table, next to a window with a view of the barn. I watched Clive ride off, fast, kicking up swirls of dust, then turned to Francine sitting across from me.

She removed her gloves and then her riding helmet, revealing a head of thick, wavy dark brown hair. Her eyes were an unusual shade of avocado green, with fine lines around them indicating she was approaching middle age, though still youthfully attractive.

"What inspired you to pay me a visit on horseback?" she asked. "Don't you have a car?"

"I do, but Philip thought you'd be impressed if I came by horse." I ran a hand through my tangled locks. "I told him I'd never ridden before, but he dared me to try."

She sighed. "Dear Philip. That man can be quite persuasive."

"He appealed to my sense of adventure."

"He's good at that."

I wanted to ask what she meant, but I'd come to talk about Lorna, not Philip.

"About Lorna ..." I took a deep breath. "I was hoping you could give me an idea of what kind of woman she was. Was she well liked? Did she have any enemies?"

"Everyone loved her. No enemies, that I know of, anyway." Her eyes misted up. "I still can't believe she's gone."

"You were the one who found her," I said softly.

She nodded. "It was awful. Awful, awful, awful."

"Can you tell me—"

"No. Please, I don't want to talk about that. I don't want to think about that. I wouldn't have agreed to speak to you if I thought you were going to ask me about that. I've already told the police ..." She covered her face with her hands.

I waited a few seconds, then softly whispered, "I understand. I won't ask you to relive it. But were you at Lorna's funeral? I don't recall seeing you there."

She raised her chin and wiped a tear from her cheek. "No, I couldn't bear to go."

She pushed her chair back and stood up. "Excuse me, but I need to go get a tissue. Would you like a glass of water?"

"Yes, please."

She disappeared for a moment, then returned with drier eyes. She took two glasses from a cabinet, filled them with water from the sink, then added ice cubes from the freezer above her refrigerator.

I took a sip, then slowly set my glass down. "Why couldn't you bear to go to the funeral?"

She was gripping her glass with both hands. "I would have sobbed through the whole thing. Didn't want to cause a scene."

"But many people were crying. That's expected at funerals."

"I know, I know. Still, I couldn't deal with seeing Lorna lowered into the ground." Her eyes started tearing up again. "I just couldn't."

I hadn't wanted to upset her, so I quickly switched gears. "Tell me about Lorna. Tell me the good things you remember about her."

Francine's eyes brightened. "She was easy going. Fun. Adored horses. She and I went riding all the time."

"She competed in shows?"

"Yes, she competed in show jumping. So did I, but she usually beat me." No bitterness in her voice. She sounded genuinely proud of her friend.

I smiled.

Francine met my gaze, and her mood took a sudden turn for the better. She took a sip of water, then leaned toward me with a gleam in her eye. "Lorna was lucky, too," she said. "Really lucky."

I blinked. "Lucky? How?"

"She got to be married to Philip."

I blinked again. "And ...?"

"And what? You don't think he's good-looking?"

I shrugged, surprised by the question, uncertain how to answer it. Good-looking or not, he was a murder suspect. "Sure, I guess. He's above average in looks for a man his age, but—"

I was about to say that looks weren't everything when it occurred to me that this was the perfect time to bring up Rita.

"Did Lorna seem concerned that other women found her husband attractive?" I asked. "Did she talk about it? Act worried?"

"Oh, no. She'd just laugh. Thought it was cute."

Cute? I raised my eyebrows.

Francine ran a finger around the outside of her glass. "Her sister Rita flirted with him, but Lorna never took it seriously. She told me she didn't care. That Rita didn't mean anything by it."

"Did you believe her?"

"Of course."

"Did Lorna have any hobbies?"

"What do you mean?"

"Any other interests beside horses?"

"Oh, yes." Francine's eyes grew big. "I'm glad you brought that up. Because I've been thinking about it, and I think it might have had something to do with her death."

My eyes went big. "What do you mean?"

"Lorna had a psychic medium," she whispered. "A man she went to see all the time. At least once a week."

I drew my brows together. "Psychic medium? You mean, somebody who talks to the dead?"

She nodded, then whisper-hissed, "They also predict the future. Or so they claim."

"But why? Why would Lorna go see such a person?"

"She believed he could put her in touch with her mother, who died a few years ago. She didn't talk about it much with me since I'm not a believer. But she sure believed. I think it gave her comfort."

I wondered why no one had mentioned this to me. "Did Philip know? Celeste?"

"Yes, oh yes." Francine waved a hand. "But I think they were embarrassed by her strange preoccupation with the occult. I know Philip was."

Thoughts chased each other in my mind. What kind of person was this psychic medium? Could he have had anything to do with Lorna's death? And if he claimed to predict the future, had he warned her that she was in danger?

Fascinating questions, which I kept to myself because there was something about Francine that gave me pause. What if she had murdered Lorna because she had designs on her good-looking husband?

My list of possible female suspects was growing. This was getting ridiculous.

"Are you married?" I asked.

"No. I'm a widow. My Monty's been gone four years, God rest his soul. He was many years older than me."

"I'm sorry," I said.

"Don't be." She sniffed. "We had a wonderful life together. And he left me very well off."

Hmmm. I took a sip of water from my glass, then asked, "Do you happen to know the name of Lorna's psychic?"

She cocked her head. "I sure do. It's Victor Bravo. How could you forget a name like that? Sounds fake if you ask me. He lives in West Chester, I think."

"You think?"

"Pretty sure. He's not far from here, though I don't know the address." She made a face. "Lorna asked me to go with her several times, but I wasn't interested. Although I think you should be. I bet he's quite a shady character. Anybody who makes his living the way he does ..."

At least it was a lead. I had absolutely nothing else to go on at this point. "I appreciate you sharing this with me," I said. "It could be important."

"I forgot to tell the police when they interviewed me. I told them I had no idea who would want to kill Lorna." She stood up, signaling the end of our chat. "I hope I've helped you."

"You have." I stood, too. "And now, can you take me back to Grand Gables? I don't dare try going it alone."

She settled her riding helmet back on her head and tightened the chin strap. "I told Clive I would."

"Slowly," I said. "We need to go slow. Real slow."

She smiled. "Of course. Philip would never forgive me if I let you get hurt."

I was glad she felt that way. And that she was as patient and under-standing as Clive had been, even more so. She helped me mount. Stayed next to me as we made our way back. Cheerfully brattling on about Lorna and the competitions she'd entered, and the prizes she'd won, giving me a chance to relax.

I was getting the hang of horseback riding. Feeling good. Proud of myself for taking the risk. It was fun.

Then we came within sight of the stables. And Spotlight took off like a racehorse, galloping at breakneck speed, obviously anxious to return to her cozy stall.

Heart pounding, gripping the reins, I dug my knees into her side and by some miracle, held on. Tensing every muscle to the breaking point, bouncing wildly out of control in the saddle, I didn't know what to do next.

I panicked, tried to think.

Then I remembered. To slow down—pull back on the reins.

I pulled back. She sped up. I pulled harder. She went faster.

To hell with the reins. I threw my entire body over her neck, dug my fingers into her mane, and pressed my knees even harder into her side.

Gallump ... gallump ... gallump ...

Everything blurred. My heart pounded to the beat of her hooves. I wanted to scream but couldn't.

I started praying.

And by some miracle, continued to hang on.

Until we reached the stables.

And Spotlight came to a sudden halt.

I flew into the air.

And landed in the outstretched arms of Steve Evans.

"Story," he said, the corners of his mouth curving up into a grin. "Fancy meeting you here."

———

I gulped in air, my heart beating so fast I thought it would burst.

Gazing up at Steve's face, inches from mine, I told myself I was dreaming. Had to be.

Only I wasn't.

"Steve," I gasped. "What are you doing here?"

He widened his grin. "Funny how you keep asking me that question."

"Set me down," I pleaded.

Bad idea. My legs were shaking so much I couldn't stand. I stumbled backward. Steve grabbed my arms and pulled me upright. "Steady, steady. You could have got yourself killed."

"I know."

"Good thing I was here. Can I at least get a thank you for saving your life?"

"Thank you," I squeaked.

He let go of my arms. I wobbled over to Spotlight and grabbed her reins. Not that she was going anywhere. She was home.

Francine galloped up, dismounted, and took the reins from me. Without saying a word, she led Spotlight into the stables and returned a few minutes later.

"What happened?" she demanded. She was breathing hard and clearly furious. "You were supposed to stay with me."

"I tried," I cried. "But she just took off. Where's Spotlight?"

"In her stall." Francine slipped off her horse, looped the reins over her arm, and took off her gloves. She went over to Steve and shook his hand. "Francine Montague, next door neighbor. Thank God for you, sir. If you hadn't been here, I shudder to think what would have happened."

I suddenly remembered my manners. "Francine, this is Steve Evans, private investigator hired by Philip's life insurance company."

She narrowed her eyes. "Life insurance?"

"I'm here about Lorna's policy," Steve said, then turned to me. "Philip refuses to speak to me and I was hoping you could talk some sense into him. Celeste said you'd gone to see Lorna's friend on horseback. I didn't know you knew how to ride, so I headed to the stables. Something told me I might be needed."

"Something told you right." I frowned. "But I'm disappointed in Philip. He is only making things more difficult for himself by refusing to cooperate with you. What do you need from him?"

"Bank records. I shouldn't reveal any more than that because I want to respect his privacy."

I glanced over at Francine, who was obviously listening, with keen interest, to everything we said. I lowered my voice to Steve, "Why do you want Philip's records? Maybe I can convince him to let you see them."

"The insurance company would like to know why someone who was living the life of a well-to-do gentleman would have taken out a million-dollar life insurance policy on his wife," Steve said, his voice low and tense. "Maybe crushing debt? Which would be a motive for you know what."

"Philip told me he bought that policy over twenty years ago and basically forgot about it," I whispered. "Does knowing that make a difference?"

Steve rolled his eyes. "Not really. If Philip had forgotten all about that policy, why did he rush to cash it in before his wife's body was cold?"

"What are you insinuating, sir?" Francine called over to Steve.

"Nothing. I'm merely investigating a claim," Steve said, his tone smooth, his expression guarded. "Why?"

"Philip did not kill Lorna. I know that for a fact," she snapped.

Steve faced her square on, hands on his hips. "How do you know that for a fact? You found her body. Does that mean you saw the murder take place? Are you covering for someone?"

"Of course not!" Francine turned and quickly mounted her horse. She pulled her gloves back on and glared at me, anger flashing in her eyes. "I'm done here, Miss Private Eye. I will not stay and listen to the nonsense coming out of this man's mouth. I hope you find out who killed my friend because her husband did not."

She galloped away.

"Thanks for your help," I called.

She held up a hand and waved it without looking back.

"Interesting," Steve remarked.

"She likes Philip. A lot."

"I can tell." His voice was dry. "What do you think?"

"About what?"

"Do you think she knows more than she's letting on? Because I do."

"Hard to say." I was tempted to tell him about the psychic medium but decided to keep that tip to myself for now.

"I know one thing." Steve reached over and patted my shoulder. "You have yourself another complicated and dangerous case, Miss Rookie Detective."

I shrugged. "Complicated? Yes. Dangerous? Why do you say that?"

He squinted at me. "Just a feeling."

"You're jealous. Jealous of my case."

"Not true." He leveled a curious gaze at me. "But I am wondering ... what possessed you to ride a horse over to the Montague farm rather than drive there?"

My lips attempted a smile. "Philip suggested it. He basically dared me."

"Ah-ha. So, he appealed to your sense of adventure. Your willingness to try something new that you've never done before."

I gave up on the smile. "I guess you could say that."

"He's a clever man and he's playing with you, Story."

I shook my head. "No, he's not."

"He's using his charm to manipulate you."

"No, he is not." Steve's insinuations were making me uncomfortable. Because he seemed to be inferring that as a female, I was susceptible to Philip's charm—and I suspected he might be right. Philip had a way of charming women and I needed to be on my guard.

"I'm worried about you," Steve said softly. "Have you got yourself a gun yet?"

I swallowed hard. "No. I haven't had time." Which wasn't exactly true. I was afraid of guns, but if I was going to succeed in this business, I needed to get over that.

"Well, we're going to make time, then." Steve said. "I'm going to help you buy one and I'm going to teach you how to use it."

EIGHT

"What are you doing?" I shouted at Philip when, after leaving Steve, I found him on the porch with Celeste and Rita. All three were sitting in rocking chairs with drinks in their hands, looking oddly relaxed under the circumstances.

Confusion creased Philip's brow as he languidly looked over at me. "What are you talking about? Did you enjoy your ride over to Francine's? You look rather flustered. Did she say something to upset you?"

"It wasn't anything Francine said." I glanced at Celeste, then at Rita. "But we do need to talk, Philip. Now. Preferably in private."

Philip took a sip of his drink. It looked like Scotch on the Rocks. He rattled the ice cubes. "Anything you have to say to me can be said right here. I'm not hiding any secrets from my daughter or my sister-in-law." He pointed to the rocker beside him. "Have a seat, doll."

I stared at him, then sat. His flippant attitude was making me mad. I just came out with it. "Why are you withholding your bank records from the insurance company, Philip?"

He hesitated. Hovering his drink in front of his lips, he shot me an innocent-naughty-little-boy look over the rim of the glass. "Who says I'm doing that?"

"Steve Evans. I just saw him at the stables."

"Oooh." Celeste was slurping something orangey-pink and fizzy. "Steve's here? Where? I need to talk to him."

"Your father wouldn't see him, so he just left," I said.

She made a pouty face. "Darn."

I sighed. I was getting nowhere and wondered how long they had been imbibing. Rita, too, looked a great deal more relaxed than she had earlier. Wearing a silly, satisfied grin on her face,

she was drinking what looked like a martini.

"We're celebrating the end of Rita's unpacking." Philip cheerfully waved his glass in my direction. "It's been a long, hard day, but she's finally got it done." He turned to Rita, and they clinked glasses. Rita beamed at Philip, and Philip beamed at me.

Okay, so these their drinks were clearly not their first.

I was not amused. Or charmed. What now?

I leaned toward Philip. "Please, I need to know. Why won't you release your financial records? Your refusal to do so is building Steve's case that you have something to hide."

"I don't." Philip waved his drink. "I've got nothing to hide."

"He doesn't," Celeste insisted.

"Philip can do whatever he wants," Rita said. "It's his life."

Were they all that clueless?

"Sure," I said, and stood to go. "If Philip wants to spend the rest of his life in prison, he can just keep his little old bank accounts to himself."

Philip just shrugged and looked away.

I saw no point in pressing the issue any further. I'd have to try again when he was sober.

Annie came out onto the porch with a tray of cheese and crackers. She shot me an oh-*you're*-back stare.

Annie. Annie was sober. And I did need to speak to her.

"Annie," I said with forced cheerfulness. "You are just the person I need to see. Could I have a word with you? Maybe in the library?"

She scrunched her nose. "Why?"

"I'm interviewing the important people in Lorna's life—and I haven't had a chance to speak to you yet."

Looking bewildered and conflicted, Annie turned to Philip as if seeking his permission to speak to me, all the while hoping he wouldn't give it.

But he just shrugged.

Celeste waved her drink. "Go ahead and talk to her, Annie. That's what I'm paying her for."

Indeed.

"But ..." Annie looked at Philip again.

"Go." Philip leaned his head back on the rocker and shot the maid a quick glance out of the corner of his eye. "We know you had the day off when Miss Lorna was killed, which means you won't be much help, and it won't take long, and then when you're done, bring me another Scotch, will you, honey."

———

I followed Annie to the library, which was on the second floor, the last room at the end of a long hall. It was as spacious and impressive as I'd expected. White oak paneled walls. Floor to ceiling shelves filled with leather-bound books and equestrian trophies. Oriental rugs covering the floor.

A large window overlooking the estate's front lawn bathed the room in light.

I smiled as I looked around. "How many books are in here?" I asked, pitching my tone as light and sunny as the room. "Thousands?"

Annie shrugged with contempt. "I guess." Her tone was snide.

"Are these Miss Lorna's trophies?" I asked.

"Yep."

Well. This was going to be a fun interview. My day so far had been nothing but laughs. Getting thrown from a horse, then having my important questions dismissed by a bunch of drunks, and now this.

So be it.

I sat down in an overstuffed chair facing the window and Annie took the one next to me, perching on the edge like a bird on a branch, ready to take off.

A bird wearing a uniform noticeably short, tight, and low cut.

Pursing her lips, she stared out the window, avoiding my eye, looking inpatient and bored. Sending me the message that she wanted to make this quick.

But I was in no hurry.

"How long have you worked here, Annie?" I asked.

She continued to stare out the window. "Two years."

"How old are you?"

"Twenty. Almost twenty-one."

"Meaning you've been here since you were eighteen?"

She sniffed. "Yep."

"How well did you get along with Miss Lorna?"

She snickered. "Fine."

"Did you like her?"

"Well enough."

"I understand she treated you almost like a daughter."

That got her attention. "Not hardly." She scoffed, giving me a sideways glance. "Who told you that?"

I didn't answer.

"I'm not Miss Celeste." She smoothed her uniform. "I'm the maid."

"How did she treat you, then?" I asked.

"Like the maid."

"How did you feel when you heard she'd been shot and killed?"

She rolled her eyes. "How do you think? I was upset."

"How upset?"

"Upset."

"Who told you?"

"Mr. Philip."

"Was he upset?"

She flashed me a look of disdain. "Of course."

"Was he crying?"

"Yeah."

"Did you console him?"

"Console?"

"You know, go over and give him a hug?"

Her mouth dropped open. "No. Mr. Philip is my boss. I can't give him no hug."

Annie was giving me no indication she felt anything for Philip, let alone that she was in love with him. So why had Steve gotten the impression that she was?

"How well do you get along with Mr. Philip?" I asked.

"Well enough." She gave an exaggerated yawn.

"Is he nice to you? Nicer than Miss Lorna was?"

She jumped up, her face growing flushed. "I don't understand why you're asking me these questions."

"Please sit back down." I pointed to her chair. "I'm just doing my job."

"Well, you're bad at it," she snapped. She sat, reached up, untied her ponytail, then rearranged her platinum blond locks into a top-of-the-head bun.

She glared at me. "Go ahead, what else you want to know?"

"I understand you're from the Pine Barrens. In New Jersey. Big woods. Near the Shore." I leaned forward. "How did you get from *there* to *here*?"

She scratched her neck. "Needed a job. This was a good one."

I waited for her to say more.

Tense silence filled the room.

I kept waiting.

She let out a long sigh. "I met Mr. Philip at the racetrack," she finally said. "He told me he needed a maid. Sounded better than mucking horse stalls, which is what I was doing. So, I said, 'sure, I'll be your maid.'"

She jumped up. "We done here, lady?"

"Not yet."

With a low moan, she sat back down and crossed her right leg over her left, exposing a lot of slim white thigh. She was not wearing any stockings, and her shoes—low-heeled pumps—were not standard maid footwear.

Why *had* Lorna put up with this minx?

"Who makes your uniforms?" I asked.

She crossed her left leg over her right. "Me," she said proudly.

"You're a seamstress?"

She lifted her chin. "I know how to sew. Had to make all my own clothes when I was a kid. We was poor."

"I admire your ambition and your gumption," I said, appealing to her pride but also meaning it. "It must have been hard growing up poor. You've come a long way. Living in a mansion like this."

"Yep."

"You have a room here?"

"On the third floor."

It's quite a different world here, from living in the woods—in what? A cabin?"

"A shack."

Again, I waited for her to say more.

She shrugged. "I was the youngest of five kids, okay? My father drank. A lot. He beat my mom. Beat me, too—whenever he dang-well felt like it. Got out as fast as I could. Quit school. Went to work at the racetrack." She jumped to her feet. "That all you need? We done here?"

"Almost," I said softly. Her story moved me, and it explained a lot. Perhaps it had been the reason Lorna had put up with this woman-child.

But it wasn't getting me any closer to finding out who'd murdered Lorna.

"Do you have any idea who might have wanted to kill Miss

Lorna?" I asked. "Any idea at all? Did she ever have any visitors who struck you as odd? Or threatening?"

She shook her head. "Nope. I'm not dumb, lady. I would have told the cops, and I would have told you. I don't know nothing. Are we done here?"

I stood up. I was beginning to understand, and forgive, her aloof, rude behavior. I felt sorry for her.

But I was also starting to feel sorry for me. Because I wasn't getting anywhere. Anywhere at all.

"Yes, we're done," I said. "Thank you for your time."

———

It had been a long day, which I planned to finish with a visit to my office in Philadelphia. I needed to type a daily report, record where I'd been, who I'd talked to, what I'd learned.

Which wasn't much that I had not already known from reading all the newspaper stories written about Lorna's murder before I'd come on the scene.

I had learned a few things, though.

I had a better understanding of the layout of Grand Gables, and its proximity to the Montague farm. But was that important?

I knew Philip was opposed to turning over his bank records, or at least stalling. But I had no idea why.

I also knew that Lorna had frequently visited a psychic medium, which the police probably did not know about. Was that important, or not?

Driving to my office, I stopped at the Chester County Regional Police Department to look at the official police report on the case. The department was housed in a modest one-story brick building with a small parking lot and an American flag out front.

When I walked into the lobby, a thin-lipped receptionist with bluish-white hair greeted me. She wore cat-eye-shaped eyeglasses and had the bored bearing of someone who'd seen it all and knew exactly why I was there.

"You want the report on the Cranston shooting, right?" She lifted a manila folder off her desk, flipped it open, and slid it around so I could read it.

How nice. I'd come in expecting to have to beg. "Thank you," I said.

"You another reporter?"

"No, private eye."

"Private eye? Huh. Well, we've had lots of reporters come by, so I'm going to tell you the same thing I tell them—you can read this, and you can take notes, so long as you stay in this room." She pointed to a metal chair against a wall. "You can sit there. Take as long as you want."

What did she think I was going to do? Sneak out the door with it?

With a shrug, I took the report and sat where instructed. Dated the day of the murder, it was three pages long, handwritten by the first police officer on the scene, Roland Murphy. The facts jived with what I already knew: Officer Murphy arrived at the stables at 10:20 a.m. after the station received a call from Francine Montague at around 10:05.

The deceased, lying face down in straw, had been shot in the back of the head. No murder weapon located. Bullet later removed from the victim's scull determined to be a .38 caliber, possibly from a Smith & Wesson Model 10, .38 Special 4-inch barrel.

The victim's husband arrived soon after with officers, who said they'd found him at the racetrack. He said had not seen his wife since around 8 a.m. The coroner put the deceased woman's time of death at anywhere from one to two hours before she was found.

Doing the math in my head, that meant Lorna could have been killed at any time between 8 a.m. and 9 a.m.

My blood chilled. Despite what he claimed, Philip did not really have an alibi if he last saw his wife at 8 a.m. He could have shot her before leaving for the racetrack. No wonder the police suspected him.

I kept reading.

The neighbor who found her, Francine Montague, claimed she had not heard any gunshots. She also said she took a shower around 8 a.m., which could account for her not hearing anything if the crime happened then. Mrs. Montague's stable man had not yet arrived for work that day because he was due to get there at noon.

The report also stated that the Cranston maid had the day off and was not on the premises of the Grand Gables estate when police arrived with the victim's husband, and that the victim's daughter, Celeste Cranston, was not home either.

The report told me a few things I had not known: the caliber of bullet, and the fact that Francine had a stable man. I had not seen him when I visited her.

I thought about asking to speak to an officer, but doubted I would learn anything more, so I returned the report and left.

I was starving, so I stopped at a diner on the way to my office, where I gobbled down a grilled cheese sandwich and French fries, washing them down with a Coke. My sweet tooth demanded something else, so I gave into a giant piece of chocolate cake. It had been quite a day, and I deserved a reward.

It was getting dark by the time I got to my office, and I was glad to see lights on in the office two doors down from mine. That meant my friend and part time receptionist, Wendy Castillo, was still working.

Did she ever go home?

Lucky for me, Wendy was dedicated to her boss, attorney Jonathan Miller. And lucky for me, Mr. Miller had agreed to let Wendy take messages for me from drop-by visitors, as well as phone calls when I was not in my office.

Since I had not been in business long, Wendy had mostly proved to be a pal I could talk to. Which I appreciated because going solo as a female private eye was proving more daunting than I'd expected and I needed a friend.

"Hi, Story." She stopped typing and gave me her warm smile. She was about ten years older than me, and I loved that she was perpetually cheerful. "How are you doing? No visitors today, no phone calls for you, I'm afraid."

"That's okay." I flung myself into the chair next to her desk. "I got a new client Tuesday. Just after I talked to you."

Wendy cocked her head. "Wow, congratulations. Is the case an exciting one?"

"Almost too exciting so far."

Wendy's eyes went big. "Tell me. How?"

"Well, today I got thrown off a horse. And I probably would have broken my neck if Steve hadn't caught me."

"Steve Evans." She beamed. "You get to work another case with that dreamboat? Fantastic."

"Not exactly."

"Huh?"

"He's sort of on the opposite sides of this one from me. You've heard of the Lorna Cranston murder, right?"

"Yeah ... who hasn't ...?"

"I've been hired to prove the husband didn't do it and Steve has been hired to prove he did." I filled her in on all that had transpired so far and swore her to secrecy.

Her eyes sparkled with excitement. "I won't breathe a word of this to a soul. I'm working for you, right? Even if you're not officially paying me, you're working a trade with Mr. Miller and someday he's going to need your services. This is so cool. Maybe you'll be in the news again. That's a good thing, right? Good for business?"

I smiled. "If I succeed."

She waved a hand. "You're good. I have faith you will."

I wished I had the confidence in me that she had. "Say, have you ever heard of a psychic named Victor Bravo?"

"Oh my God, Victor Bravo? Sure ... he tells the future and talks to dead people, right?"

My eyes widened. "How do you know about him? *What* do you know about him?"

"My friend, Joyce, went to see him once. All I know is that she was impressed. He told her things he shouldn't have known about her past. And she's really excited about what he said about her future." Wendy chuckled. "Something like she's going to meet a rich guy and marry him and they're going to have five kids—or maybe ten ... something like that."

"Wow, okay. Did she ever go back to him?"

Wendy shook her head. "He's expensive. Not sure how much he charges, but a lot. Joyce is saving up to go back." Wendy leaned toward me and whispered, "Why? What does he have to do with your case?"

"Can't tell you anything yet." I held her curious gaze. "But I need to go see him. Could you find out from Joyce where he lives?"

"Sure. I'll ask her tomorrow. Even though it's Saturday, I plan to come to the office for a few hours. So ... I'll meet you here with the information, okay?" She put her hands back on her typewriter keys, which I took as a hint that she needed to get back to work.

"Sure, thanks," I said, "I really appreciate your help."

"Hey, do me a favor." Wendy grinned. "Tell dreamboat Steve hello for me."

I laughed. "I will. When he takes me to buy a gun. Which will be soon. He's concerned about my safety. Even though we're competitors."

"Competitors?" Wendy laughed. "You two are made for each other."

I felt my cheeks go warm.

"Hey, do me another favor," she added. "When you see Victor Bravo, ask him about that. Ask him if he sees a future for you and Steve."

Nine

When I returned to my office the next morning Wendy handed me Victor Bravo's address, then informed me Steve had just been there and left.

"He was hoping you'd be here since he wants to take you gun shopping today. I told him I'd give you the message."

"I hope you didn't tell him about Victor Bravo."

"No. Why?"

"Not sure. It's just ... I don't want him interfering with my leads. I need to work this one myself."

I took Victor's address into my office and pulled my trusty map of Pennsylvania out of the top drawer of my desk. The psychic lived on a rural road just outside West Chester, the county seat of Chester County, and according to the map, about ten miles north of Grand Gables.

From my office in Philly, the 35-mile trip would make a pleasant road trip on this sunny summer day, so I decided to take the chance he'd be there.

Top down, breeze ruffling my hair, not much traffic, I made good time.

Victor Bravo lived in a small gray cottage not far from the road. The house was barely visible from the street because the front yard was a jungle, a wild riot of trees, bushes, weedy looking things, flowering plants, and vines.

A mailbox with his name on it told me I'd come to the right place, so I pulled in, drove up to the house, and parked.

I half expected to see a sign somewhere indicating his profession, but didn't, so I went up to the door. It was ajar and through a screen door I could see into the living room. Modest furnishings. Sofa, two chairs, wall to wall carpet.

From somewhere in the back of the house I heard someone singing. I knocked and called, "Hello?"

A bald, heavy-set man wearing a loose-fitting bright red shirt and baggy black pants came to the door. "Hello," he said, giving me a cheerful smile. "Can I help you?"

"I hope so. Are you Victor Bravo?"

"I sure am." His smile widened. "Have you come for a reading?"

He looked so hopeful that I hated to disappoint him. "No ... I'm here to ask you some questions about one of your customers. Or maybe you call them clients? Lorna Cranston."

His smile vanished. He opened the screen door and ushered me in. "Lorna was my client, yes. And a dear friend." He waved for me to take a seat on the sofa. "How can I help you, sweetheart? You know, of course, that she was murdered. I assume that's why you're here?"

I nodded. "I'm a private investigator." I took a card out of my purse and handed it to him. "Lorna's daughter, Celeste, hired me to find out who killed her. Lorna's friend, Francine, told me that she visited you often."

He studied my card. Holding it in the palm of his hand, his eyes narrowed, fixing on it so intensely that I wondered if he was getting some kind of vibrations from it or something.

Spooky.

He looked over at me, his eyes wide and bulging. Then he smiled and they crinkled around the edges. "Nice to meet you, Story Smith. How interesting that you are a detective. And how brave. But how can I help you? Lorna's murder—such a tragedy. I'd been hoping the police would have made an arrest by now."

"Have the police been to see you?"

"No. Why would they come see me?"

"Same reason I'm here. To find her killer."

His eyes bored into mine. "They probably already have him identified."

"Her husband?"

"Exactly."

I held his penetrating gaze. "Why do you think that? You knew Lorna well. She probably confided things to you. Was she worried about her husband? Did she feel threatened?"

He set my card on a table beside him. "Normally everything a client tells me is confidential, but in this case ..." He sat back in his chair. "Since she is dead ..."

I sat forward. "Yes?"

"I don't see the harm in sharing some information." He shrugged. "She seemed happy with her marriage. She came to see me to communicate with her beloved mother because they'd been very close, and she missed her dearly. But lately, during readings, her mother began to warn her that she was in danger."

I sucked in a breath. "In danger from whom or from what?"

"Sadly, that was unclear."

Was this guy for real? I didn't know much about people who claimed to speak to the dead, but surely if Lorna's mother had truly been trying to warn her daughter of danger, she could have been more clear. I asked, "Did Lorna seem concerned? Did she have any idea what those messages meant?"

"She had no idea, which was frustrating. I just kept hearing her mother say, 'tell her to look out, tell her to beware.' I also sensed a dark energy around Lorna in the past month, which I conveyed to her. Sadly, I couldn't tell her anything more specific."

I nodded, not knowing what to believe. Lorna had believed this man had supernatural powers. But that hadn't saved her.

Was he telling me the truth? I had only his word for that. Maybe Lorna's deceased mother *had* communicated through him. Or maybe he was just making it up now, to make himself look good.

From what I'd learned, Lorna had not acted like her life was in danger, had not confided to anyone that she was worried about her safety. Death had taken her completely by surprise.

"You say you can connect with people in the spirit world," I said.

He looked at me, his expression deadly serious. "I can."

"So, that means you should be able to connect with Lorna, right?"

He squinted at me. "Yes." His lips formed a sly smile. "I know what you are going to ask me next."

"The obvious question, Mr. Bravo. Have you connected with Lorna since she died?"

"Of course."

"And did you ask her who killed her?"

He stared at me. "Of course."

"And ...?"

"I hear her say, 'Philip'. That's all. 'Philip.'"

Goose bumps popped up on my arms. A cold chill grabbed the back of my neck. It couldn't be. I didn't want to believe it. Should I?

Shaking my head, I held the medium's gaze in tense silence, then asked, "Did you ever think about calling the police? If you care about Lorna, and want to see justice for her, you might want to talk to them."

He shook his head, then sighed. "I doubt they would take me seriously."

I chewed the side of my lip. "Still ..."

"I also wouldn't want to become one of their suspects."

"What? Why would you?"

"Because my dear ..." He held my gaze for a few seconds, the stood up. He held up a finger. "I'll be right back."

My eyes nervously followed him as he left the room. He came back a minute later holding a document in his hand and handed it to me.

Puzzled, I glanced down at it. Shocked, I saw that it was a will. A handwritten one. I started reading. It couldn't be. Lorna's will?

My eyes moved to the bottom of the page. To her signature. And the date: June 1, 1955. A mere few weeks before her death.

Confused, I looked up at the psychic.

"You are reading it right, my dear. She spells out that in the event of her death, she is willing all her horses to me."

I clutched the paper in my hand. "But why?"

"She knew her daughter didn't care about them, and she didn't like the way her husband treated them, and she loved them, more than anything in her life. So ..." He shrugged. "She left them to me."

Okay, motive.

He had motive.

If the will proved genuine, it meant Victor Bravo had inherited horses that were probably worth a fortune. No wonder the man was worried about becoming a suspect.

As far as I knew, Philip and Celeste didn't know about the will. Neither had mentioned the psychic's name to me, let alone a will. And, to my chagrin, I had not asked if she had left one.

"I didn't ask Lorna for this," Victor Bravo said. "You see where I live. I have no room for horses here. And I know nothing about them."

"But why?" I shook my head. "Why did Lorna write this?"

He reached over and took the will back from me. "It happened after a particularly emotional session. When her mother came through from the other side, once again warning of impending danger. Lorna became frustrated at the vagueness and the darkness of the message. She asked me for a piece of paper and a pen." He waved the will. "Then she wrote this. Told me to keep it in a safe place. Said she didn't have a will, but that now she did. Just in case."

"This is her signature at the bottom?"

"Yes, and I got two neighbors to witness her signing it. They didn't ask questions and we didn't volunteer anything. They know me, know that I'm a little quirky. And they're good friends."

"But there's nothing on this that addresses anything but her horses."

He shrugged. "I assume it's because her father, Arthur McKay, owns Grand Gables and most everything else on the estate."

I nodded. "Philip did tell me that. And that her father gave them monthly allowances. Generous, no doubt."

"No doubt. She could easily afford me every week." Victor clutched the will in his hands. "You're the first person who knows about this. I suppose I'll need to get an attorney."

I stared at him. I would need to tell Celeste and Philip about the will. And then what would they do? Call the police? And then what would the police do? Start looking at the psychic as a suspect?

Philip, in any case, would surely contest the will. His concerns about money had already led him to try to get Lorna's life insurance money. He would not accept losing his prize thoroughbreds to this exotic soothsayer. Did Philip even know about him?

"I agree that you should get a lawyer before you do anything with the will," I said. "I don't think Philip will take this well."

"I am certain he will not."

"Did Lorna tell Philip about you?"

"As far as I know. She said he didn't care what she did with her money—as long she didn't question what he did with his."

"Do you want the horses? You said you don't have—"

"No! Yes!" He jumped up and started pacing back and forth. "Lorna wanted me to have them. So, I need to honor her wishes. Only I have no idea what I would do with them. Sell them? Give them away to someone who will take good care of them?"

My eyes followed him as he paced. "I think that's something you'll need to discuss with your lawyer."

He sank back in his chair. "Yes, you're right."

I felt sorry for the horses. Which was silly. They needed to be the least of my worries. "I'm going to need to tell Celeste and Philip about this will," I said. "If I were you, I would hire an attorney soon. Before the police come knocking at your door."

He ran a hand over his bald scalp. "Yes, I will." He stared at me. Then his eyes suddenly turned big and bulging. They were the most mesmerizing thing about him. They changed size, shape, intensity in an instant with his thoughts and moods. "There's something else you should know," he said, his tone ominous. "Something else you need to tell your clients."

I braced myself. "What?"

His eyes went squinty. "Lorna also frequently visited a tarot card reader."

I blinked. "A what?"

"A tarot card reader."

I shook my head. "Don't they predict the future? I thought you did that."

He spread his hands apart, palms up. "Lorna was fascinated by the occult."

"What do you mean?"

"I think she was looking for advice. From the cards."

He'd lost me. "Tarot cards give advice?"

"Some people believe they do. There are more things in heaven and earth, Horatio, than are dreamt of in your philosophy ..."

"Shakespeare," I said. "Hamlet."

He gave me a sly grin. "Very good."

"So, what are you saying?"

"That some tarot card readers predict the future, or claim to, by reading the cards. But they also help people find answers to questions about their lives. Questions about love. Questions about their health. Questions about their relationships."

"Questions about any danger they might be in?"

"Exactly."

I ran a finger across my lips, trying to think. This case was going in bizarre directions. I could hardly believe how bizarre. But I needed to follow this eerie trail of tips. Like it or not.

What else did I have?

I asked, "Do you happen to know the name of Lorna's tarot card reader?"

"I do. It's Zelda Buttinsky. She goes by Madame Z." He widened his eyes to bulging. "But look out for her, my dear. Her reputation is shady. I tried to warn Lorna about her, but she didn't listen. She believed Madame Z could protect her."

Oh boy, was this going to be fun. "Do you happen to know her address?"

He stood, held up a finger, left the room, and came back with a piece of paper and a pencil. He sat back down, scribbled an address and crude map on the paper, then handed it to me.

"She lives about five miles from here," he said. "Not far. But if you go see her, beware. Beware of Madame Z."

———

Madame Z, to my disappointment—and relief—was not home.

She lived in a modest duplex near downtown West Chester, and as soon as I pulled up, I figured it had to be the place. Her half of the house was painted bright blue, and the other half, bright yellow.

A woman opened the yellow door when I knocked on the blue door and got no answer.

"Can I help you?" She stepped out on her front porch, which was separated from the other porch by a wooden railing. She had long dark hair, heavily streaked with gray, and pale green eyes.

"I'm looking for Zelda Buttinsky," I said. "She also goes by Madame Z ...?"

"She ain't home." The woman was dressed in an ankle-length shapeless shift that covered all but her boney arms. "She's working the circus," she added in a reedy, raspy voice. Reeking of cigarette smoke, she stared at me, like I should know what that meant.

"The circus?" I pursed my lips. "What circus?"

"You ain't a client?"

"Not yet." Which technically could have been true.

She smiled, revealing a mouth of gaping holes where some teeth should have been. "Oh, then, let me introduce myself." She reached over to shake my hand. "I'm Bertha, Zelda's sister. You can call me Madame B."

Her hand was warm and dry and scaley. "Are you a Tarot card reader, too?" I asked, struggling to keep my tone light and conversational.

She tilted her head. "I read cards. But mostly I use a ball. You know, a crystal ball. "She squinted at me. "Why? You needing your future told?"

"Uhm. No, not really. I wanted to ask Madame Z about one of her former clients, Lorna Cranston. Did you by any chance work with—"

"No. Not that one. Not that unfortunate woman." Madame B jerked her fingers out in front of her forming the shape of a cross. "Zelda warned her. Warned her, warned her, warned her."

"To no avail," I half-whispered.

"To no avail," she hissed.

"I would like to speak to your sister about that." I cleared my throat. "When will she get back from the circus?"

Madame B shrugged. "Maybe in a week."

"A week? You mean she lives there?"

"Travels with them, right, deary. Summertime. This time a year."

That complicated my investigation. "Where do they travel?"

"Around the state, Delaware, New Jersey, too. All over. By truck. In a big caravan."

"Barnum and Bailey?"

"No." She cackled. "Not that big a circus. Romiani Brothers Circus. They got a polar bear and a guy who can jump over a herd of elephants and a lady who can juggle while riding a horse standing up. Backwards."

I swallowed hard. I couldn't even ride a horse sitting down. Facing forward. "Sounds fun," I said, forcing a smile. "Do you happen to know where they are now?"

"Not sure. Delaware, maybe? They got an office in Philly where you can buy tickets. Should be in the phonebook. You know, the Yellow Pages. They could tell you."

"Okay," I said. "I'll look them up. Thank you."

Her green eyes glinted. "Before you go, you want your fortune told, deary? I'll give you a bargain rate."

This woman did not strike me as dangerous, only slightly creepy. But I did not want my fortune told.

What if she warned me that I was in danger? Like Steve had. No thanks. I'd known, when I'd decided to become a private eye, what I was in for. And it wasn't for sissies.

"No thank you," I told her. "But I appreciate the offer."

TEN

"Hi, ready to go gun shopping?" Steve, sitting cross-legged outside my office door, flashed me a flirty grin as I strolled up.

My office was locked, and since it was a Saturday, no one was in the building. Not even Wendy, who'd apparently gone home.

It was now around one-thirty, and I'd driven straight there from West Chester to type up notes about what I'd learned from Victor Bravo and Madame B.

"I guess I'm ready." I give him a brave smile, hoping to mask my nervousness. Guns made me uneasy, but I had convinced myself I would get over it when I became a P.I.

I should have bought a gun by now, but I'd been procrastinating.

Steve bounded to his feet, looking good, as usual. *Great*, as usual. Slightly in need of a haircut, some of his dark brown hair was beginning to curl over his ears, which was awesomely cute. He was wearing a white T-shirt, dark blue shorts, white sneakers, and a too-charming-for-my-good smile, putting my already quivering nerves into overdrive.

I unlocked my office door, and we went in. "I was planning to write a quick report on the day's happenings, but that can wait. Thanks for coming by. I hope you weren't waiting long."

"Hours." He gave me a teasing grin. "But you're worth it, and you're welcome."

I shoved the map that Victor Bravo had given me into my top drawer, along with some notes I'd scribbled to myself at a diner, where I'd stopped for a quick lunch. I looked around, seeing my modestly furnished office through Steve's eyes. Compared to his spacious office, on the top floor of a swanky high-rise building overlooking the Delaware River, my small digs were sparce indeed. "Guess that's it," I said. "I'll type up what I got later."

"What did you get?" His eyes gleamed. "Where'd you go? Who'd you talk to? Any leads on an alternate suspect to the fine, upstanding, and surely innocent Philip Cranston?"

I batted my eyelashes at him. "Wouldn't you like to know? Except, oh wait, you're my competition."

"Oh, so you *have* located an alternate suspect?" Steve took a step closer to me, which in my tiny office put us way too close. "Come on, spill."

"No." I lifted my chin. "I don't think I should."

"Why? Will this information exonerate your client in the eyes of the police? If so, I need to know. You owe me that, Story."

Steve stepped closer. His expression suddenly serious. "If you've found somebody out there who's confessed to shooting Lorna, and there is credible proof they really did it, then I need to tell the insurance company. Now."

I shook my head. "It's nothing like that. I wish."

"Then ...?" Steve raised his eyebrows. "What'd you find?"

I wanted to tell him. I really did. Victor Bravo and the Madams Z and B were too juicy to keep to myself. Anyway, what could Steve do with the information I'd learned about them? Nothing that wouldn't make Philip look better by comparison.

So, I spilled. Told him all about the psychic medium, the fortune tellers, Lorna's will, and the supernatural warnings from Lorna's deceased mother.

He stared at me, then burst out laughing. "Amazing. I can't believe you. What you get yourself into ... what a gumshoe. Way to go."

"Thanks ..." I said, "I guess?"

"I mean it. Philip Cranston looks so guilty the police are probably planning to swoop in and arrest him at any moment, and you've managed to cough up a couple of suspicious characters nobody else seems to know about, along with a secret will? I am truly impressed."

"Thanks." I matched his amused smile.

"If it all checks out." He dropped his smile.

"Don't worry," I said. "I'm going to tell Philip and the police about the will and see what happens next. Maybe Victor Bravo did murder Lorna for her horses. If so, I'll have done my job."

Steve narrowed his eyes and stared at me. "Something tells me you don't believe the psychic did it. Do you?"

I sighed. "I've got to consider the possibility. Maybe he's a convincing con artist who led Lorna to believe she was in danger, then talked her into putting him into her will, then murdered her, figuring the police would suspect her husband." I groaned. "If that's the case, though, he's got me fooled. He seemed like a nice guy. Weird, but nice."

"And the Tarot card reader?"

I pressed my lips together. "Hmmm ... I don't know enough about her yet. Victor Bravo claims she's shady and dangerous, but if he is a con, maybe he's just saying that to deflect suspicion from himself. I need to track her down."

"At the circus?" He sounded dubious.

I shrugged. "If need be."

"Do you think she really could be dangerous?" Now he sounded worried.

"Maybe. I guess I'll find out."

"I know you—so I'm sure you will." Steve reached for my hand. "I don't know how much trouble you can get into at a circus, but come on, let's go buy you that gun."

We were inches apart. I could tell by the spark of desire in his eyes that he wanted to kiss me. I did *not* want him to kiss me. I *did* want him to kiss me. I *could not* let him kiss me.

I was squeezing his hand so hard he must have sensed how jangly and confused I felt.

Or else I was hurting his fingers. With a gentle smile, he dropped my hand. "Come on, kid," he said. "Let's go."

———

"A Smith & Wesson snub-nose .38 Special." Steve glanced at me out of the corner of his eye as he drove us in his beige Bel Air sedan to a pawn shop in South Philly. "Trust me, Story, that's the gun for you."

Steve's car was the opposite of mine. Unobtrusive, blend into the background, and perfect for his profession. When I first met Steve, he was working as a bodyguard for a wealthy woman, so the only automobile I had ever seen him drive until recently was hers.

Now, I liked his Bel Air. It made me smile. Even if it was boring. Of course, I would never tell him that. It would hurt his feelings.

"A Smith & Wesson? If you say so," I said. "I know absolutely nothing about guns."

"That model is a good size and weight for you. It'll be easy to learn how to use. But you're going to have to practice."

I blew out a breath, trying to blow away my fear of guns. Of course, I'd have to practice. "I know," I said.

"Practice drawing, practice shooting."

"I know."

"It's not going to do you any good if you don't practice."

I let out a loud sigh. Okay, already. Like I didn't know that getting good at something took practice, and lots of it? "I promise, I'll practice," I said. "I'll go to a shooting range to do that. But first I need you to teach me *how* to shoot."

Steve pulled up to Pete's Pawn & Jewelry and parked. He smiled. "You've got yourself a deal."

The shop looked pretty much like I'd imagined a pawn shop would look like.

On the ground floor of a five-story building, the place clearly catered to a range of customers and their needs.

Behind the front window I could see everything, including a kitchen sink—really, who pawned their kitchen sink? Also, musical instruments, wrist watches, cameras, radios, and jewelry—lots of jewelry.

No guns in the window, though. They were behind a glass case, next to a long counter where the cash register sat. So many weapons. In all shapes and sizes.

Then Steve surprised me. He'd obviously been there and chosen a gun for me.

As we approached the counter, a bushy-bearded man behind it waved to Steve, like he recognized him. Then he bent over and pulled out a gun from under the counter. "Here it is, Mr. Evans," he said, putting it in Steve's hands. "I set this beauty aside for you, just like I promised."

"Thanks, Pete." Steve turned to me and held out the weapon. "This is what I was talking about, Story. Smith & Wesson. Five-shooter. Two-inch barrel. This one—practically brand new."

My eyes went big. It was chrome-plated, with a walnut handle. Shiny. Compact. Powerful. I couldn't believe I was doing this.

Pete nodded at me. "This the little lady?" He asked Steve.

I bristled. Yes, guns scared me, and yes, I was genuinely grateful to Steve for his help, but I resented being called a little lady.

I held my hand out to Steve. He put the revolver in it. It was heavier than I'd expected.

"How much?" I asked Pete.

He stroked his beard. "Fifty bucks."

Hmmm, okay. I could afford that, thanks to the thousand dollars from Celeste.

"I'll take it," I declared, then added, "But I'm not Steve's little lady."

"What?" Pete watched warily as I turned the gun over and over in my hand. Like he was afraid it might go off. I didn't blame him. I didn't trust myself with it either.

"I'm not Steve's little lady," I said again. "We're friends."

"Colleagues," Steve said.

"Business competitors," I said. "We're both private eyes."

A corner of Pete's mouth lifted in a you're-kidding-me grin. "A female P.I.? Now I see why you need a gun."

"And I'm paying for it, too." I put the weapon down on the counter, reached into my purse, counted two twenties and a ten, and handed him the money.

Pete whipped out a box, placed the gun in it, then put the box in a paper bag and handed it to me.

I couldn't believe it was this easy. Maybe I should I have haggled the price down. I'd never been to a pawn shop before. Was I supposed to do that? Too late now.

"Congratulations," Steve told me. "Now all you need is ammunition and a holster." His eyes went to Pete. "Can you help us out there?"

Pete gave a happy nod. "Sure thing." Reaching back under the counter, he pulled out a box of bullets and a leather belt with a gun holster attached. The belt looked kind of big and bulky.

"This is on me." Steve handed over a twenty before I could protest.

"Thanks," I said. "But I'll probably just carry the gun in my purse."

Steve gave me a funny look. "You will, will you?"

"I really appreciate your help with this," I said as we left the shop. "You made it easy."

"Glad to help. Maybe I can stop worrying about you. Now I need to teach you the basics to get you started."

"You said my gun's a five-shooter." I bit down on my lip. "Uhm. What does that—"

"Five bullets. It means you can fit five bullets in the chamber. Which means when you start shooting, you only get five shots before you need to reload."

"Which means I better be a good shot."

He grunted. "If you want to live."

Steve opened his front passenger side door for me. I slid in and placed the bag on my lap. Learning how to use my new gun suddenly felt urgent. "Where can we go where you can teach me how to shoot?" I asked when he got in behind the wheel.

"Out in the country would be best."

"Where in the country?"

He glanced over at me. "How about my parents' place? Birdsong. It's not far from Grand Gables."

I gripped the bag and stared at him. "Your parents? Birdsong?"

He nodded. "Birdsong is the name of my family's estate. Big place, more than a hundred acres, lots of birds. My grandfather named it, and it fits." He started the car. "Let's go there, we'll find a spot where nobody will hear the gunshots."

My heart started beating faster. I'd known that Steve had grown up in privilege. Upper class. Private schools. But for some reason meeting his parents made me more nervous than shooting a gun.

He saw the look on my face and laughed. "Don't worry. My mom and dad are not home right now—they're in Europe for the month. Although they'd love to meet you if they were home." He gave me a teasing smile. "They're used to me bringing girlfriends around."

I felt my chest go hot. "Very cute, Steve."

He winked. "I know."

———

On our way out of Philly we stopped at a bar to trash pick some beer bottles for target practice.

Forty minutes later, with about fifty brown bottles stashed in Steve's trunk, we arrived at the entrance to Birdsong. Steve turned into the long drive leading to the estate's three-story white mansion, neatly tucked away behind tall trees, barely visible from the road.

The gently rolling-hilled estate, framed by miles of pristine white fence, occupied a beautiful slice of the Brandywine River Valley. In the distance, horses were grazing, and I could see cows and sheep on the other side of a large red barn.

"It's lovely," I said, embarrassed at how awed I sounded. "What a wonderful place to grow up."

He smiled. "Yes, it was. I consider myself lucky." He drove closer to the house. It was as lovely as the land it sat on, rivaling Grand Gables in size and splendor.

"Is anyone home?" I asked.

"No, but we have an estate manager who lives above the barn and takes care of the animals. His name's Lloyd. Let's drive over and let him know we're here—so he doesn't wonder who in tarnation is shooting off guns."

Lloyd was outside the barn when we pulled up. Dressed in denim overalls and a plaid shirt with his sleeves rolled up to the elbows, he welcomed Steve.

Not sure what to do, I stayed put, rolled my window all the way down, and waited.

Lloyd looked to be around thirty, with a mop of light brown hair and a pleasant, ruddy face.

Steve brought him over to me and introduced us.

"Glad to meet you, miss," Lloyd said. "Steve tells me he's going to give you some shooting lessons. That's nice." His gaze flicked to Steve. "Where are you wanting to practice? Over by the woods?"

"That's what I was thinking." Steve pointed to a line of trees far off in the distance, beyond the fields. "There's some old fence over there so we'll be able to line our bottles up on it and fire away."

Lloyd nodded. "Okay. Won't spook the animals over there. Shouldn't bother nobody. Be nice and private." His eyes met mine and for a few seconds he didn't say anything, like he was trying to figure me out. I wondered how many of Steve's girlfriends he had met.

Bidding him goodbye, we headed toward the woods along a narrow dirt path.

The road was pitted with holes. Steve focused his attention on going around them or inching through them, so he didn't blow a tire. I was glad we'd taken his car and not my T-Bird.

When we finally reached a section of old wooden fence, Steve cut the engine, scrambled out, popped open the trunk, then started lining some the beer bottles up along the flat top rail.

"Have you done this before?" I asked as I grabbed more bottles out of the trunk.

"Used to practice shooting out here growing up," he said. He stepped back, and with his hands on his hips, squinted at the bottles, about a foot apart.

Nodding at a grassy spot a few feet away, he told me to put the rest of the bottles over there.

"How quickly we'll need to put out more will depend on how accurate you can get," he said.

"Who taught you how to shoot, Steve?" I asked after all the bottles were out of the trunk.

He grinned. "My dad. He wanted a hunting buddy, but I'm afraid I was a huge disappointment in that department."

"Really? Why?"

His smile turned wry. "I was his only boy—and his only boy didn't have the heart to kill animals. So instead, we practiced target shooting with bottles. Which was great. I got fast. I became more and more accurate. And I gained confidence. Skills which come in handy now."

Now it was my turn to smile. Steve didn't have the heart to hurt animals. That made me love him even more than I already secretly did.

Thanks to him and his gun, we had survived my first case when things went bad.

But I couldn't count on him being there the next time I encountered danger. I had to ignore my flushed face and the rapid beating of my heart and concentrate on learning how to save my own skin.

"Ready?" Steve asked, an eager glint in his eye.

"As ever," I said, then hurried to the car to grab my revolver.

"First, the bullets." He showed me how to open the chamber and insert them.

I nodded. "Easy enough."

"Now ..." With his hands on my shoulders, he backed me up about fifteen feet from the bottles. "Stand here."

Squinting at my targets, I took a deep breath. "Okay ..."

He pointed to the bottle furthest to the left. "We'll try for that one first."

My heart racing, I gripped the gun in my right hand. "Okay ..."

"We'll start with your stance. When it comes to shooting, your stance is important. When you're in self-defense mode, it's vital."

"Okay, okay." A dribble of sweat ran down my face.

"Lean in, not back, keep your weight forward, your head in front of your shoulders, your shoulders in front of your hips.'

I did what he said.

"That's good. Keeps you stable and less likely to be thrown off balance by the gun's recoil."

I swallowed hard. "Recoil?"

"That'll happen when the gun goes off. You'll need to be ready for it."

"Sure, sure."

"Now, bend your knees slightly—that helps keep you balanced and stable. Never lock them."

I bent my knees. Slightly. Took a deep breath. Nodded.

"Now, for your grip. Think of your gun as an extension of your arm. When you take aim, your movement should be fluid and smooth. Keep your hand tight and strong. Never go limp at the wrist."

I nodded, but I must have gone limp at the wrist because Steve moved closer to show me how to do it right.

"The recoil will be stronger if your grip is weak," he said, going behind me. With his rock strong abdomen up against my sweat-drenched back, he put his right arm over my arm, his right hand over mine.

Oh, my God.

Focus, I told myself. *Focus.*

"Make your grip strong," he said, his words tickling my ear, the heat of his body stealing my breath.

Focus, I told myself. *Focus, focus.*

"Now bring your left hand up and use it to support your right hand. Now, wrap your right hand around the gun ... aim ... and ... squeeze."

I squeezed.

Boom. Missed the bottle—but now knew what he'd meant by recoil.

Steve backed away from me. "Try again," he said.

Boom.

Missed again.

I took a deep breath. Aimed better. Squeezed the trigger.

Boom.

Pieces of glass flew up in the air.

Yes!

Two more bullets. I aimed at another bottle.

Boom. Got it!

Then another.

Boom! Got that one, too.

I turned to Steve—the huge grin on my face matched his.

"I did it!" I shouted, jumping up and down. "I can do this!"

I ran over and gave him a hug.

He pulled me closer and held me tight. Which felt wonderful and right. I was suddenly no longer afraid of guns, or of my feelings for Steve. I could master both, and I'd be okay.

We stood together, hugging each other, for what felt like a very long time—how long, I have no idea, because time vanished.

Then, Steve let me go. He stepped back. Our eyes locked. "We've got more bottles." His voice was husky, his lips formed a wisp of a grin.

"Yes, we do." I slow-grinned back.

"So ...?" He lifted an eyebrow.

"So ... I guess I should blow them to smithereens, too." I looked at my gun, then back at him, giving him a cocky, confident smile. "Just to prove I can."

ELEVEN

It was late afternoon by the time I'd disposed of all the bottles.

A better shot than I'd ever dreamed possible, I felt mighty proud. But I was also feeling increasingly anxious about getting back to Philip and Celeste with the news about Lorna's will.

"Grand Gables is near here," I told Steve. "Do you mind driving me over?"

"Mind?" His eyes sparked. "I can't wait to see the look on Philip Cranston's face when he finds out some weirdo has inherited his horses. Or claims to have. Whatever happens, this stuff about the will is going to be good."

I stowed my revolver in Steve's trunk and fifteen minutes later we pulled up to the Cranston mansion.

Where it was clear that Philip already had company. Two Pennsylvania state police cars were parked by the front door. Yikes. Did that mean he was about to be arrested?

I looked over at Steve. "Uh-oh."

He nodded. "What did I tell you?"

"Celeste must be beside herself," I said. "I better get in there."

Steve parked next to one of the cop cars. "I'm coming with you."

We ran up the steps to the front door, which was ajar about an inch. We heard voices coming from the living room. Knock or just go in?

I knocked.

Annie opened the door. She stared at me, then at Steve. Her usual haughty air gone, she looked flustered, upset, and confused. Flushed cheeks. Watery eyes. She was biting down on her lower lip to keep it from trembling. "Are you here to see Mr. Philip?" Her eyes went to me, then to Steve, then to me, as if she was trying to figure out which one of us had come to see him, and why.

"I need to speak to Philip and Celeste," I said. "Steve's here because he gave me a ride."

"Oh ..." She waved us into the vestibule. "I'm not sure—"

"I see the police are here," I said. "I need to talk to them, too, so ..." I pointed toward the living room. "Can we go in?"

"Uhm ... I don't know ..."

In no mood for that answer, I skirted around her, followed by Steve.

Two blue-uniformed, armed police officers stood side by side in front of the fireplace, facing Celeste and Philip, who were sitting on the sofa, with their backs to us, when we entered the room.

One of the officers had a long face and short cut gray hair. His younger, baby-faced partner sported a sandy blond crew cut. Both had their arms crossed in front of their chests, with almost identical, serious, no-nonsense expressions on their faces.

"Can we help you?" Crew Cut called over to Steve and me, clearly annoyed that we'd just barged into the room, interrupting whatever was going on.

Celeste and Philip turned around and Celeste gasped. "Story ... Steve?"

Philip's eyes widened. "How did you get in, did Annie let you in?"

"I need to talk to you." I moved toward Philip, then nodded at Celeste and the police officers. "Actually, I need to talk to all of you. It's important. I have important news."

"But why is *he* here?" Philip stood and jabbed a finger at Steve. "I don't want *him* here."

"Let him stay." Celeste grabbed her father's arm. "For heaven's sake, what difference does it make at this point?"

"What do you want, miss?" the older officer asked me. "We are having an important, private discussion here. Perhaps it would be best if you—"

"She's my private investigator," Celeste cried. "Let her stay. Please."

"Private investigator?" The older officer furrowed his brow, then looked at Steve. "And you, sir? Who are you?"

"An investigator hired by Mr. Cranston's life insurance company." Steve cleared his throat. "If you don't mind, I would like to be part of this meeting, too."

"The more the merrier," Crew Cut said. "I'm Officer Romano, and my partner here is Officer Olson. We'll let you stay—just make this quick."

Celeste stood up and stared at me, her eyes wild and pleading. "What is your important news, Story? I'm so scared. I'm so worried that these men plan to arrest Father. Please—he can't go to jail. Please, please, please ..."

I announced, "There's a will."

Silence. No one moved. Celeste and the officers and Philip gaped at me like I was holding a bomb.

"A what?" Philip's asked, his tone incredulous.

"Do you know a man named Victor Bravo?" I asked him.

"Mother's psychic." Celeste rolled her eyes and flopped down on the sofa. "Your news is about him?"

"That crackpot." Philip scoffed.

"Apparently, Lorna visited him often." I looked back and forth between Philip and Celeste. "And then one day, not long before she was killed, she asked him for a piece of paper and scribbled out a will, leaving him her horses in the event of her death."

"What?" Celeste shook her head. "Are you saying mother thought she might die? And why would she want to leave her horses to her psychic? That's ridiculous. They're worth a fortune."

Philip blinked at me like he thought I had lost my mind. "I agree. Why?"

I hesitated, knowing that whatever I said about the psychic medium communicating with Lorna's dead mother would sound crazy to the cops.

But before I could say something that sounded halfway sane, Romano held out his hand. "Where is this will?" he asked me. "Bring it over here. I want to see it."

"Yes, please," Philip said.

I walked up to the officers, holding my hands out, palms up, to show them I didn't have the will. "Mr. Bravo would not give it to me,"

I said, "but I do have his address. He told me he would be happy to show it to the police or whoever wants to see it."

"Who is this person, exactly?" Romano asked.

"He calls himself a psychic medium, claims to be able to communicate with dead people and predict the future." I nodded to Celeste. "He told your mother that she was in danger. That *her* mother was warning her from heaven to beware. Of what, she didn't say."

Steve walked up and stood next to me. "Lorna was apparently worried about her horses, which is why she wrote a will. Celeste, your mother knew that you don't care for horses, and she didn't like the way your father treated them—breeding them and racing them."

"Outrageous," Philip said. "Lorna had no such objections."

"Wait." Olson narrowed his eyes at Philip. "You said you had a wonderful marriage. No problems. This surprise will, if it truly exists, casts doubt on that claim."

"We did have a wonderful marriage." Philip glared at Steve. "Stay out of this, you fool. And I'm saying it again—get out of my house."

"I'll leave when I'm good and ready," Steve said.

"Why are we just hearing about this will now?" Romano asked me.

"Mr. Bravo told me he was afraid to call the police because he didn't want to be considered a suspect."

Celeste gasped. She grabbed her father's hands. "Maybe he murdered Mother. For her horses."

Philip smiled. "Yes ... that makes sense." He beamed. "Yes, that's who murdered her. That's who killed my wife. He's the culprit." Philip stood and dramatically shook his fist at the police officers. "Go arrest that man. Go arrest him, now."

"Not so fast, Mr. Cranston." Romano spread his feet apart. He put his hands on his hips. He gave Philip a hard stare. "We'll pay the psychic a visit. We'll look at that will. In the meantime, sir, we believe you murdered your wife. For a million dollars. You remain the most obvious suspect."

———

"No!" Pressing her hands together as if in prayer, Celeste shot Steve a please-help-me look. "Steve ... you know me. You know my family. Tell them—my father would never, ever—"

"Mr. Philip."

We turned. Annie had slipped into the room. Clutching the frilly apron around her waist, she was twisting its hem so hard her knuckles were white. "Excuse me, Mr. Philip," she said, "but I was wondering if our guests would like something to drink?"

"No. These guests are just leaving, Annie." Philip pointed to the police officers. "Please show them out."

She curtsied. "Yes, sir."

"We'll be back in touch soon, Mr. Cranston," Olson said. "In the meantime, do not leave town. We're warning you. *Do not* leave town."

"They have some nerve," Philip said after they left. "Just where do they think I'm going to go?"

Steve blew out a breath. "You might want to get yourself a good lawyer, Cranston."

Philip ignored him and turned to me. "Take me to see Victor Bravo. I've never met the man, and it's time I did. I want to meet the guy who thinks he's going to get his hands on my prize stallions. Just let him try."

That didn't strike me as a good idea. I shook my head. "The police might be headed there now. I don't think—"

"I don't care about the damned cops." Philip turned to Celeste. "You hired Story. That means you're her boss. Tell your P.I. she needs to take me to see that psychic. Now."

Philip was acting like a childish brat. Where had his smooth, easy charm gone? The sudden change in him made my chest grow tight with apprehension but I told myself it was because he was afraid.

"Story." Celeste pressed a hand to her forehead. "Please, please, just do as he asks. Take him to see Mother's medium. What harm can it do?"

"Well ..." I glanced at Steve, but he just shrugged, as if to say this was my case and my decision.

"Take me now," Philip demanded. "I'd like to get to him before the police do."

I sighed. What choice did I have? Anyway, what would be the harm of Philip seeing the will with his own eyes?

He and Victor might get into an argument about it. But ... so what?

They might even get into a fight over it. But ... so what?

I had a gun now.

"We'll take my car." Philip waved for me to follow him. "Let's go."

Uh-oh. My gun was in Steve's trunk.

"Wait, Philip, I need to get something—"

"No," he snapped. "I'm in a hurry."

My chest went tight. A lot of good my gun would do me now. I needed to learn to carry it in my purse.

Steve and I exchanged anxious glances. He was thinking what I was thinking. "What about Steve?" I asked. "Can Steve come with us?"

I knew the answer, of course, but it was worth a try.

"No." Philip was clearly in no mood to argue. "Let him wait here."

"Yes, he can wait here with me." Celeste winked at Steve. "We have a lot to catch up on. It'll be fun."

TWELVE

I was on edge as I hopped into Philip's shiny silver Cadillac.

My gun was in Steve's trunk, a stupid place for it.

Steve was staying behind with Celeste, and who knew what might happen there, given his reputation with women and her continued infatuation with him.

It was also growing late, and would soon be dark, and I just wanted to call it a day.

Nibbling on a thumb nail, I told myself that Victor Bravo's place wasn't far, and that we wouldn't be there long, and that I should stop being such a worry worm.

I fixed a fake smile on my face as Philip pulled out of Grand Gables and headed down the road. "I'm surprised you never met Lorna's psychic," I said, trying to sound cheery and conversational. "Weren't you curious about him?"

He glanced over at me shrugged. "Not really. He made Lorna

happy and that's all I ever cared about." He tightened his grip on the steering wheel. "Until now."

"Do you think he really can talk to dead people and predict the future?"

He snorted a laugh. "Of course not. The man's a charlatan. Which I never worried about—since I always thought he was a harmless charlatan—until now."

"Hmmm."

"So, what do you think?" Philip glanced back at me, resuming his usual charming grin. "Do you believe this Bravo guy is real or fake?"

"I don't know. I try to keep an open mind about such things."

"Do you think the will is real?"

"I can't say without knowing what Lorna's handwriting looks like. But you do. Maybe this trip is a good idea after all."

He chuckled. "Glad you think so."

"He lives outside West Chester, about ten miles from here," I said as we approached a stop sign. "Make a left here."

He turned right.

My heart jumped. "Wait ... didn't you hear me? I said go left."

He grunted. "I heard you."

My heart started to pound. What was he doing? Where was he taking us? "Philip," I said, my voice tight. "We're going the wrong way. This is not the way to Victor Bravo's."

He gave a small ugly laugh. "I've changed my mind."

Panic rushed through me. I shook my head in disbelief. "Changed your mind about what?"

"We're not going to go see Bravo." He turned to look at me and I saw fear, raw fear, in his eyes. "You're going to help me go into hiding."

The hair on the back of my neck stood at attention. "Hiding? Why are you going into hiding?"

He sped up. We were on a rural road that I didn't recognize. Headed where? I willed myself to calm down, so I could think. "Where are we going, Philip? Please, tell me where we're going. You're scaring me. This is a bad idea."

"I'm not going to jail. I am not going to let them put me in jail."

"So, where are we going?"

He clamped his lips together and didn't answer.

I was in full blown panic now. I needed air and rolled down my window. We passed a herd of cows, an old red barn, row after row of corn.

I wanted to jump out of the car, but we were going too fast.

"Please don't think I'm criticizing you, Story ..." Philip reached over and patted my shoulder, his hand lingering with the last pat. The car swerved. He grasped the wheel just in time to avoid running us into a ditch, then chuckled. "It's just that while you have been working oh so very hard to clear my name, the police have been making plans to arrest me and I will not let that happen."

"But this will make things worse for you," I said. "Can't you see that? This makes you look more guilty than you already do."

"I didn't murder my wife."

"And I'm trying to find out who did."

"I shouldn't have to rot in jail in the meantime."

"But going into hiding is *not* the answer."

"It's the only thing I can do." He jerked the wheel, making a hard right onto a four-lane road. Ahead a sign declared: "Welcome to Delaware."

Delaware? We were leaving the state when the police had warned

Philip not to leave town. A wave of trepidation washed through me. This was going to lead to big time trouble. For Philip, and for me.

"Delaware …" I snapped the word out of my mouth. "Where are we going in Delaware?"

Philip glanced over at me. "Don't worry your pretty little head about it. I have an idea. Just trust me."

"Trust you? To do what? And for the record, I'm plenty worried. The police told you not to leave town and I don't want to be charged with the crime of helping you escape from the police. You're putting me in legal jeopardy."

He gave a low, throaty laugh that made my already racing heart do double time. "Relax, doll, you won't get into any trouble. I'm going to check myself into a hotel in Wilmington under a fake name and stay there till you find Lorna's murderer. The only thing you need to do is tell everyone, including Celeste, that you have no idea where I am."

"What? I can't do that. That's a crime."

He smirked. "Just do it."

"Let me out," I said in a low throaty growl. "Stop and let me out of this car now."

He sped up, passed a line of cars, then gave me a tight-lipped smile. "It will be better for everyone if you just do what I say. Better for Celeste, especially. She can't get into trouble if she really, truly doesn't know where I am."

I could not believe this was happening. "But what about me?"

"I'm going to check you into the hotel as my wife."

My blood froze. "You can't do that …"

"Yes, I can."

"But I won't let you. I won't go along with this."

"I didn't say I was going to force you to stay with me. Just for the night. Then in the morning you can drive my car back to Grand Gables. You will tell everyone, including the police, that you have no idea where I am. You will tell them that I promise to come out of hiding after Lorna's killer is arrested."

He reached over and stroked my cheek with the back of his hand. "I'll come back when you find her killer and I have complete faith that you will."

His hand was icy. My heart was pounding against my ribs. I jerked my head away, determined to make a run for it when I got the chance. Maybe at a red light. Or the hotel.

But, then what? Report that Philip had kidnapped me? He would be arrested and that would end my case. I'd have to return most of Celeste's money and this scared-to-death man would likely go to prison for a murder I believed in my heart he did not commit.

It wasn't just about the money, or the challenge of this important, high-profile case. It was also about justice, finding justice for Lorna Cranston. I decided to put that ahead of my personal or professional risk and try to talk sense into Philip once we got to the hotel.

It was dark when we turned into the parking lot of a gray-stone, multi-story building, where a lighted sign above the entrance said we were at The Cosmopolitan Hotel.

Philip parked, came around, and opened my door. "Please don't do this," I said. "I'm making progress with my investigation. It won't be long before I find out who shot your wife. Let me go do my job."

He shook his head. "No."

"Please, Philip, we can just go back to Grand Gables. We've been gone awhile, but we can just tell everyone we took a ride in the country so we could talk. No one will know we left the state."

"No."

"You're afraid, that's why you're doing this. But it's going to make things worse."

"We're not leaving," he snapped.

Fear iced my veins. It was no use. He was not going to listen to reason, and I didn't like the look in his eyes. "Then just give me the car keys now," I said. "You can stay, but I'm leaving."

"Spend the night with me," he crooned, shoving the keys into his pants pocket. "It's late. You can leave in the morning."

"No. I'd rather leave now." I veered away as he reached for my arm.

"Not yet." He grabbed my hand and yanked me toward him. "We are going to check in as man and wife."

"But why?" I tried but failed to get out of his grip. "There's no need for this."

He yanked me to a stop. "Why fight me, Story? Most women find me attractive. Don't you?"

What? "What are you talking about, Philip?" I said in a low hiss. "Your looks have nothing to do with this."

"Are you in love with that idiot Steve Evans?" He pulled me toward the hotel door, then opened it and shoved me inside, whispering, "That man is nothing but trouble. Just ask my daughter."

"Steve has nothing to do with this," I whispered back. "Just give me your car keys. I'll go do what you've asked. You can stay here by yourself."

"Just one night." He steered me toward the registration counter, where a clerk watched us with a curious expression.

I wanted to run. But I was frozen with fear and confusion. I would just have to talk sense into him once we got to the room, and then get my hands on those keys.

I watched stupefied as Philip signed us in as Mr. and Mrs.

Benjamin Lively, with no check-out date, telling the clerk we were on our honeymoon and were not to be disturbed.

The clerk handed him a key to room 202, second floor.

Gritting my teeth, I walked with Philip to the elevator while plotting my escape. It would be quiet. No drama. All I had to do was get my hands on the keys to the Cadillac and I'd figure out the rest later.

He opened the door.

We went in.

He closed the door.

And then I knew with gut-clenching, queasy certainty that I was in more than legal danger.

Panic gripped me as I gaped at the large bed in the center of the room.

Philip shoved me onto it.

I rolled all the way across the bed and landed on my feet on the other side. "I don't know what you think you are doing." I spit the words out through my teeth. "Just give me the keys to your car and we'll forget this happened."

Philip's lips twisted into a leer. "Come on. Women love me. Most women would die to be you right now."

Die. What an unfortunate choice of words. I shook my head. "I don't think you are in your right mind right now, Philip. You're scared and not acting rationally. Just let me leave."

"You don't know how many women I've had to fend off," he said. "But now I'm a widower. I'm a free man. And I want you."

"You won't be free much longer if you don't let me go."

"Come on." He was whining now. "Just one roll in the hay."

"No!"

We stared each other down. The situation was absurd. I wished I had my gun. I also wished I knew karate. I made a mental note to sign up for classes at the first opportunity. "This is making you look really bad, Philip," I said, aware of how terrified I sounded. "I'm beginning to wonder..."

"Wonder what? If I'm capable of murder?"

"Yes, the way you're acting now."

"I'm just acting like this because you turn me on, Miss Private Eye. I've been wanting you since I first laid eyes on you."

Oh. My. God. Beads of sweat trickled down my back. I stared at him from across the bed. Then something in his eyes hit me with a truth so profound my stomach lurched. His faithful husband act had all been a pretense. A lie. A complete lie.

"You want me as another trophy on your shelf, don't you?" I said, narrowing my eyes at him. "Lorna won trophies for jumping horses, while you spent your marriage collecting trophies of another sort. By successfully luring women into your bed."

I could tell by the gleam in his eye that I'd hit a nerve.

"How many trophies have you collected over the years, Philip?" I was taunting him, not caring if that put me in more danger. This man was not going to win me.

With a low growl, he launched himself across the bed and grabbed for my arm.

I dodged his grasp.

He rolled onto the floor. Landed on his back.

With every ounce of strength in me, I jumped on his stomach, knocking the breath out of him, then jumped off, outside the range of his grasp.

"You bitch," he wheezed.

Gasping and coughing, he struggled to sit up.

I kicked him in the face. Hard.

He fell back. Blood streamed from his nose. He put his hands to his face, groaning, gagging, gasping for air.

Perfect, just where I wanted his hands.

I leaned over, snatched the car keys sticking out of his pocket, then backed away.

"I'll be going now," I said, dangling the keys as I moved to the door. "I'm going to pretend this never happened. I'm going to tell Celeste, the cops, Rita, and anyone else who wants to know that you gave me your car and then ran away from me into the night."

He moaned.

"It's far more than you deserve, Philip," I said. "But I'm doing this for Celeste. Because she believes in you. Maybe she should. Maybe she shouldn't. But I'm after the truth. And I'm going to find it."

Then I opened the door and bolted.

Thirteen

S teve ran out to Philip's Cadillac when I pulled up to Grand Gables, alone.

He stared at me through the driver's side window with an expression of relief, quickly followed by confusion. "What took you so long? Where have you been? And ... but ... where's Philip?"

I opened the door and got out as Celeste and Rita dashed out of the mansion to the car. "Where's my father?" Celeste cried. "Story, did you drive here by yourself?"

I'd been rehearsing what I would tell them, hoping I could make it sound believable, given the length of time I'd been gone. How long had it been? It felt like days, but it had probably only been a few hours.

I met Celeste's anxious gaze. "Your father went into hiding," I grimaced. "He doesn't want to be arrested. He's afraid of going to jail. He told me to tell you that he plans to hide out until your mother's murderer is found."

"What?" Steve looked at me, then at Celeste, then at Rita, then back at me. "How did this happen?"

"We never went to Victor Bravo's. He changed his mind. He drove around and around, telling me that he wanted to run away. Then he pulled over to the side of the road, got out, handed me the keys, and ran off."

The story sounded ridiculous, even to me. I wished it were true, and I could tell by the expression on Steve's face that he didn't believe it.

"He drove around and around—where?" Steve asked. "You've been gone a long time."

"I lost track of time. What time is it?"

"Close to ten o'clock. Where'd you go?"

"Uhm. I think we drove into Delaware."

"You *think*?"

"Okay, I know we drove into Delaware. We drove around for a long time. Country roads ... you know. I kept trying to talk Philip out of running away. Told him he'd look more guilty. But he kept getting more and more upset. I couldn't stop him. I didn't know what to do. When he ran off, I just drove back here."

"He ran off into a field?" Rita sounded as unbelieving as Steve.

I pressed my lips together and nodded. I hated lying, but it was better this way. I would stick to my story. For now.

"Where did he plan to go?" Celeste sounded on the verge of hysteria. "Where will he stay?"

"He told me he had plenty of money in his wallet—so he'll probably hole up in a hotel somewhere." I reached into the car for my purse and hugged it to my chest. "I wouldn't be too worried about him," I said, allowing myself to sound as weary as I felt.

I turned to Steve. "Meanwhile, I need to keep plugging on this case. It's been an incredibly long day and I need to go home and get some sleep. Can you drive me back to my car?"

"Of course." He divided a look between Celeste and Rita. "I don't know what's really going on here, but believe me, I plan to find out. Just not tonight. Story's right—it's late and we're all tired. I'll be back in touch. Soon."

Celeste ran over and threw her arms around Steve. "Thank you so much for being here. You can't imagine how much it means to me to have you back in my life."

He hugged her back, then awkwardly stepped away. "Depending on how this works out, Celeste, you might not be thanking me later," he said, his voice tight. "Things are not looking good for your father right now. Even though Story is trying her best."

I was touched by his support. Support I sorely needed.

"Come on." Steve took my arm and guided me toward his car.

I waved to Celeste. "I'll call you tomorrow."

She waved back. "Please do."

Steve was quiet as we drove away from Grand Gables. "I'm glad you're okay, Story," he said. "I was worried. Couldn't imagine why you and Philip were gone so long."

If he only knew. "Thanks," I said.

"But—what really happened?"

"What? What do you mean?"

"That hogwash about Philip running off into a field ... somehow I can't picture that dandy getting cow dung on his shoes."

I sighed. "People do strange things when they're afraid."

"Philip has good reason to be afraid—but you haven't answered my question." Steve sounded exasperated. "I trust you have a good reason."

"You trust right." I put my head back and closed my eyes. I was tired. So tired. I'd be able to think clearly in the morning. Come up with a plan for what to do next.

Steve reached for my hand and squeezed it. "I'll let this go for now," he said softly. "But only for now."

Fourteen

A good night's sleep was indeed what I'd needed.

When I woke up around ten o'clock, sweat drenched and tangled in my sheets, I was able to think clearly about my case. Unfortunately, mulling it over in the clear light of that hot, humid summer Sunday morning, I had to admit it looked mighty bleak.

The man whose name I had been hired to clear looked increasingly guilty, and the more I investigated, the guiltier he looked. Standing to gain a million dollars upon his wife's death, he hadn't even waited until after her funeral to try to collect the money. He was refusing to turn over his bank records over to Steve. And now that he'd gone into hiding from the police, he was swearing me to secrecy about his whereabouts.

Would keeping his secret cost me my private investigator's license? I could conceivably be charged with accessory after the fact by helping him escape.

Anyway, should I be helping him keep his stupid secret at all, now that I knew the kind of man he was? A womanizer, who had tried to rape me.

What would have happened if I had not escaped his clutches?

With a shudder, I threw off my covers and rolled out of bed. At least now I had my gun. When Steve dropped me off the night before, I had made sure to take it out of his trunk, and for now was safely securing it on the top shelf of my bedroom closet. It still made me nervous, and I didn't want to store it in my purse.

Shuffling over to the closet, I pulled out my pink chenille bathrobe, slipped it over my summer nightgown, then padded barefoot out to the telephone on a table by my living room sofa.

I live in a small ground-floor, one-bedroom apartment in the Manayunk section of Philadelphia and my telephone shares a party line with the Pratts, an elderly couple living in the apartment above me.

The chances were good they were at church, meaning my conversation with Celeste would not be overheard by Mrs. Pratt, a shameless gossip who was always on the phone, chatting with one of her friends about the latest neighborhood scandal. She would always hang up when I interrupted to ask if I could please use the phone, but sometimes I suspected she would pick back up and listen in.

Now, plopping down on the sofa, I picked up the phone and lucky me, I got a dial tone. I dialed Celeste.

She answered on the first ring. "Story ..." she squeaked, sounding frantic. "Have you heard from Father?"

"No." I pushed my hair off my face. "But I need to speak to your grandfather. Could you arrange a meeting?"

Silence, then a sniff. "What? What did you say?"

"I need to speak to your grandfather. Arthur McKay. It's important."

I nibbled on a fingernail as I waited for her reply. I had been meaning to interview Arthur McKay, and now I couldn't stop thinking about what he'd said to me at the funeral: *I'm not so convinced that my son-in-law is innocent, dear, so good luck.*

Why had he said that?

It suddenly seemed important that I know. Especially since it wouldn't be long before the world learned that his son-in-law was hiding from the police.

"Why do you want to speak to grandpa? He won't know where Father has gone." Celeste sounded on the verge of tears. "They don't get along."

That was no surprise, but it helped to hear her confirm it. "Your grandfather whispered something to me at the funeral that I can't get out of my mind," I said. "It's something I need to investigate, and I need to speak to him privately without going into it now. Could you help me arrange a meeting?"

"I guess." She didn't sound happy about it but didn't press for the reason.

"Good, thank you."

"Tomorrow. I'll ask him to come over tomorrow. Is that okay?"

"Perfect. Arrange for him to come in the morning, so I can get an early start on my day."

"After that, are you going to search for Father?"

No, since I knew where he was, but I wasn't going to tell her that.

"Everything depends," I said, "on what I learn from your grandfather."

It was too late for me to make church, but unless I had a good excuse, my mother always expected me to come over for Sunday supper, and I was starving.

She always started serving around one in the afternoon, so I took a shower, washed my hair, put on a nice dress, and was ready to go.

I hoped my brother Rob and his new wife, Piper, would be there. They often were, and I planned to pick his brain about my case.

After many years as a private investigator, Rob—my role model and mentor—had just taken a job as an agent with the F.B.I. I hoped he could offer me valuable advice about Philip and what I'd uncovered so far about Lorna's death.

"Story!" My mother enveloped me in a hug when I walked in the house, which was filled with the heavenly smell of roast beef, potatoes, and my favorite, sliced-almond-topped green bean casserole. "I was hoping you would make it today. I've been worried about you."

"She's always worrying about you," my father called from the dining room.

I smiled when I saw Rob and Piper were there, too. My father was seated at the head of the table, with Rob and Piper to his left. To his right, places were set for my mother and for me.

A starched white tablecloth covered the table, set with my mother's finest China and gleaming silverware. The homey setting warmed my anxious heart. No matter what happened in my life, I could always count on this.

"Mom keeps wishing you would quit being a detective," Rob said. "She blames me for giving you the idea."

Piper, her blonde hair pinned up in a pretty bun, gave me a

welcoming smile. "Hi, Story. So glad you could make it. We can't wait to hear about your latest adventures."

"And I can't wait to tell you," I said, then hurried into the kitchen to help my mother carry in the hot plates of food.

Hopefully no one could hear the ravenous gurgling noises my stomach was making as I sat down, smoothed my napkin on my lap, then dug in. Everyone made small talk while I savored my mother's home cooked meal and the camaraderie of a normal family.

But that couldn't last. They all knew my life was far from normal and were eager to hear about it.

"Are you close to finding Lorna Cranston's murderer?" Rob picked up his glass of water, took a sip, then smiled at me from across the table. "Come on, tell us. Everything we're hearing on the news says Philip Cranston is about to be arrested any day."

I put down my fork and cleared my throat. "Unfortunately, that's true." I needed to be careful about what I revealed. But this was my family, and if I couldn't trust them who could I trust?

"What I'm about to say is confidential." I met Rob's gaze, then looked around the table. "Promise me that what I tell you never leaves this room."

"Of course, dear, we all promise that." My mother dabbed her mouth with her napkin. "But now you're really scaring me. What have you been up to?"

I gave them a rundown of everything I had accomplished so far and everyone I had interviewed, leaving out the part about being thrown from a horse. I also mentioned Steve was working for Philip's life insurance agency.

"Steve helped me buy a gun," I blurted out when I finished. "And he taught me how to use it, so now I feel like a real private eye."

"A gun?" my mother squeaked. "I can't believe my little girl has a gun. Where is it—did you bring it here?"

"Don't worry." I said, annoyed at the alarm in her voice. "I left it at home. In my bedroom closet."

"Good for you for arming yourself." Rob's eyes sparked approval as he leaned toward me. "But a gun is not going to do you any good if you keep it in a closet. Do you have a holster?"

"Steve bought me one, but it's too bulky for my taste. I plan to keep it in my purse."

"That sounds better than in your closet," my father muttered.

Rob jabbed his fork into the pot roast. "What's your next move?" he asked as he sliced off a piece of meat. "You seem to have a lot of loose ends and Lorna sure had some kooky characters in her life. But what now?"

I grimaced. "I haven't told you everything. Philip was not a faithful husband. He apparently cheated on his wife with many women. Collected them like trophies. And I'm afraid I don't know the half of it yet."

"That has not been in the news," my father murmured. "That sounds bad."

"How do you know?" Piper stared at me, her eyes wide and unblinking.

"He went after me." I took a deep shaky breath and told them what had happened. I had to tell someone. It was weighing on me.

"Oh, my God," my mother clapped a hand to her mouth.

"Don't worry." I reached over and patted her shoulder. "I got away before anything happened."

She let out a screech-moan from behind her hand. Not the kind of sound any dutiful daughter wants to hear her mother make.

"I'm okay, I'm fine," I said. "I can't tell you the name of the hotel where I left him because he swore me to secrecy." My eyes met Rob's. "But I don't think I can keep it a secret for long."

"Not if the police demand to know where he is, you can't. You would be arrested for helping him leave town." Rob shook his head. "You've got yourself a complicated case, Story. But so far, good job."

"Good job?" My mother pushed back her chair and stood up. "I should say not." She frowned down at me, her face full of fury, hands on her hips. "You need to quit this job and right now, young lady. Come to your senses before you get yourself killed."

My eyes met her tear-filled ones. "I can't, Mother. This is my life, the one I've chosen for myself, and you need to accept it."

"June, please sit down," my father told her. "Calm yourself."

She shook her head and jabbed a finger at my father. "No, Ralph. I will not *calm* myself." She looked back at me. "Why can't you just find yourself a good man and get married and have children, like your friend, Brenda? Why can't you do that?" Raising her voice with every word, she'd ended the question with a shout.

I stared down at my plate and closed my eyes, hoping everyone couldn't see the puffs of steam coming out of my ears.

Brenda was my best friend in high school. We'd kept in touch but had little in common anymore. She'd married her high school, star-football-player-boyfriend, Allan, shortly after graduating. While I had gone on to college and then a career in journalism before switching to private investigating.

Brenda, a housewife at age twenty-six, and Allen, now an accountant, had three children.

While I had a gun.

"I'm not Brenda," I said through clenched teeth. I turned and looked my mother in the eye. "I'm Story. I love my life. And I'm going to be me. And I'm going to find out who killed Lorna Cranston. And I'm not going to give up until I do."

"Yay!" Rob applauded, stood up, and came over to me. "Could I have a word with you, Story? Alone?"

I shrugged. "Sure." I stood and faced my red-faced mother. With a sigh, she sat back down and bowed her head. I looked over at my father and Piper. "Please excuse us. We'll be right back."

Pretty certain I knew what Rob wanted, I followed him to the living room. "I admire your guts and grit," he told me. "But you want to make sure you don't get arrested for accessory after the fact by helping Philip pull his stupid disappearing act. And you might want to track down that tarot card reader."

"Oh, don't worry, I plan to," I said. "I've also got other avenues to work."

"You're doing the best you can. But a word of warning ..."

So, yep, *here it comes*. "What ...?"

"Steve Evans ..."

I huffed a loud sigh. I welcomed Rob's career advice. But not his advice on my love life. "I knew you were going to bring him up, Rob."

"He's back in your life, Story."

"So?"

"So, I'm warning you again. Watch out. He's broken many a woman's heart. Don't let him—"

"—break mine." I rolled my eyes. "I *know*."

FIFTEEN

"It's about time we connected, young lady." Arthur McKay toasted me with what looked like a Bloody Mary—celery-stick-stirrer and all—when Celeste led me into her living room Monday morning. "I've been waiting for your call," he added, addressing me the way an impatient teacher might snap at a laggard student.

He was seated in one of the soft leather armchairs by the fireplace and didn't bother to stand. Instead, he pointed for me to take a seat in the armchair facing him.

"Thank you for meeting me here." I lowered myself into it with a forced smile. I was not going to let this older gentleman intimidate me. He believed that his son-in-law was guilty, which meant he probably considered me an enemy of the truth. So be it.

I glanced at Celeste, who looked most unhappy as she remained standing, as if waiting for her grandfather to give her permission to stay.

"You may go," he told her.

She shook her head. "I'd rather not. I'd like to hear what you are going to tell Story."

"You're not going to like it."

She gave a petulant shrug. "I still want to hear it."

Confused, I looked back and forth between them. "I don't understand. What is Celeste not going to like, Mr. McKay?"

He stirred his drink with the celery stick, clinking the ice cubes against the glass. "I'm upset that Celeste hired you, Miss Smith." He waved his glass in my direction. "And I don't like that she's using money from the trust fund I gave her to do so."

"You told me that you believe your son-in-law is guilty." I leaned toward him. "That's what I need to talk to you about. Why do you believe that?"

"He never liked Father." Celeste glared at him. "That's why he believes that."

"Go." Arthur McKay glared back at her. "I told you that I would speak to your detective if we could meet privately, and you agreed." Downing the rest of his drink, he handed the empty glass to her. "Please give this to Annie and tell her we do *not* want to be disturbed."

I watched Celeste stomp out of the room, then asked in a loud whisper, "Is it true that you've *never* liked Philip?"

He sighed deeply. "Sadly, yes."

"Why?"

"I knew the minute I laid eyes on him that he was a good for nothing scoundrel." He pursed his lips into an expression of disgust. "He'd dated Rita, then dropped her for Lorna—what man does that? It was clear from the beginning he couldn't be trusted. Next thing I know, he proposes to Lorna, hurries up and marries her against our wishes, and then we're stuck with him. For Lorna's sake and for Celeste's sake—who came along exactly nine months after they were married."

I asked, "Is that why you gave him a monthly allowance?"

"My wife and I decided it was the best way to avoid the scandal of divorce, to preserve our family's reputation. Because Lorna claimed to be madly in love with him, even though he didn't have a dime to his name. And he certainly never intended to dirty his hands by taking a real job."

"Real job?"

Arthur McKay's eyes bore into mine. "He let the world believe he was a big deal breeder of thoroughbreds and the owner of champion racehorses." He grunted. "Nothing could be further from the truth. You want to know the truth? It was all for show. A hobby. An expensive hobby. Which I financed."

"So, he let the world believe he was wildly successful, and he was anything but ...?"

"None of the horses on this estate ever belonged to him. I paid for them and gifted them to my daughter, Lorna. Who let her beloved husband have his fun racing and breeding some of them. Unfortunately, the expenses of that enterprise always far outweighed any winnings or profits, which Lorna chose to ignore." He sniffed loudly. "Look where that got her."

Indeed. Maybe Lorna had been more concerned about her husband's expensive hobby than she had let on. Which would explain why she had left the horses to her psychic medium.

I asked, "I assume you've heard about Lorna's will?"

He waved a hand. "The one where she supposedly left her horses to her spiritual advisor ... sure ... what of it?" He sounded bored by the whole idea.

I was confused. Victor Bravo, a spiritual advisor? He was kidding, right? "You mean her psychic medium?"

"Yeah. That Bravo guy."

"Do you think the will could be real?"

He leaned toward me, narrowing his eyes, and asked through clenched teeth, "Who cares? What difference does it make? My daughter is dead. Bravo might as well get her horses. Maybe he's a total phony, or maybe he does have a direct connection to heaven—either way, he made Lorna happy."

"You don't think he could have murdered—"

"No ...absolutely not."

"Did you ever meet him?"

He grunted. "Once. Struck me as a total fruit cake. A harmless flamboyant."

"So ... you're fine with a harmless flamboyant inheriting your daughter's valuable horses?"

He barked a laugh. "Better than her lazy, good-for-nothing husband, who should be in prison by now. Even if he never spends a day in jail, it'll mean goodbye to his so-called profession as a racehorse owner and breeder."

"True ..."

"And now I've cut off his allowance. He'll never get another penny from me." His tone was defiant, but the deep sadness in his eyes touched my heart.

He cleared his throat. "That's the reason he tried to cash in that huge life insurance policy he had on my daughter's life. Which I'd known nothing about."

I didn't know what to say to that. What could I say? In this grieving man's opinion, I was working for the enemy. I wanted his help, but I was walking a tricky path.

"Did Lorna seem happy to you?" I asked. "With her marriage? Did she ever give any indication that she was troubled by anything?"

"You mean the jerk's philandering?"

I widened my eyes and held his gaze. "Philandering?"

"Don't pretend you don't know about that, Miss Smith." His voice dripped with sarcasm. "You call yourself a detective, but it doesn't take a detective to see that my son-in-law was a cheating son-of-a-bitch."

I dropped all pretense of pretending. "You're right. I have uncovered evidence of that," I said, although I held back how I'd discovered it. No sense adding fuel to his bonfire. "Only ... it leaves me wondering if Lorna knew."

"How could she not?"

"What do you mean, sir?"

He leaned closer to me, half-whispering, "You've seen that maid, Annie. Let's start with her."

"What about her?"

"You tell me."

I remembered what Steve had said, that Annie was in love with Philip. I had not seen that. But now? Maybe Steve was right. Maybe Annie was one of Philip's trophies. I felt sick. Annie, so young and vulnerable, living under the same roof, would have been an easy win.

"The way she dresses, and carries herself, you may be right," I said. "Still, cheating on your wife doesn't make you a murderer."

"No ..." Narrowing his eyes to slits, he studied me for a moment. "Why did you come here today, Miss Smith? Why did you ask to speak to me? You're working for Celeste, and you know what Celeste wants. Another suspect. Which I can't provide."

"You're wrong." I lifted my chin. "I am working for the truth. To find the truth."

"Are you?"

"Yes. And I think you might be able to help me with that."

I was groping my way through an increasingly murky case, but I'd glimpsed a faint light up ahead. An illusion? Maybe. But it was something I needed to explore.

"The racetrack," I said. "As a thoroughbred racer and breeder, Philip must have spent a lot of time at the racetrack."

"Yes, he did. Garden State Park. Over in New Jersey. Why? You think he's hiding from the cops there?"

"No. But he may have friends there, or enemies. People I need to speak to. Who may be able to guide me closer to the truth. Whatever it is."

Arthur McKay nodded. "I know Garden State Park well. Often frequent the place myself."

I smiled. "Could you take me there? Give me a tour? Introduce me around?"

"Sure." He seemed taken aback by my request, but then returned my smile with a glint in his eye. "There is no time like the present, young lady. Let's go now. I'll have my driver take us in my Packard."

———

Garden State Park racetrack in Cherry Hill, New Jersey was far larger than I'd envisioned.

And grander.

It reminded me of a football stadium, with seating for thousands, only instead of facing a football field, the seats faced a wide, packed-dirt racetrack, which was empty when we arrived just before noon.

Even so, the place reeked of money, glamour, excitement.

"The first race doesn't start until one-thirty, by which time this place will be packed," Arthur McKay said as he led me toward the brick clubhouse, connected to the stadium, where he assured me we would find the people I needed to speak to.

The clubhouse was clearly the place to be during the races. Entering the dining room, I was struck by the view of the track beyond the huge floor-to-ceiling window.

A dozen tables, adorned with white linen tablecloths, set with fine China, silverware, glasses, and goblets, were ready for the action to begin.

But only one table was presently occupied. In the middle of the room, next to the window, three men and a woman were enjoying an early leisurely lunch.

"Regulars, usually the first ones here," Arthur McKay whispered in my ear as he guided me over to their table with the easy air of someone who was often one of them.

The three men looked so much alike they could have been brothers. Dark haired, middle-aged, dressed in expensive-looking suits. The woman, a red head, wore a navy-blue dress with a scalloped white collar. A perky hat matching her outfit sat atop her curls.

In my pale blue sleeveless blouse, white pedal pushers, and white sneakers, I suddenly felt terribly underdressed. This was my first visit to a racetrack, it was a hot day, and it had not occurred to me that one needed to dress for the occasion.

Then again, I told myself that I'd probably fit right in among the cheap-seat crowd in the stadium. Stuffing my inferiority complex, I reminded myself why I was there.

"Lady and gentlemen, this is Story Smith, a private eye hired by my granddaughter, Celeste," Arthur McKay said as the men stood to greet me, polite curiosity filling their eyes.

He waved a hand at the woman, who remained seated. "This is Adele McMaster, and ..." he nodded at the man closest to her, "her husband, Bruce." Then he gestured to the other two men. "Chester Moore and Ed Green. All friends of Philip's."

"A private eye?" Mrs. McMaster remarked coolly. "I don't understand."

"I've been hired to solve Lorna Cranston's murder," I said as the men sat back down. "As I'm sure you all know, your friend, Philip, is considered the prime suspect right now by police, but his daughter doesn't believe he could have done it. Since he spent a great deal of time here, I'm hoping to dig into his life, investigate other possible angles, see if maybe he had any enemies who may have wanted revenge."

Everyone looked at me in stunned silence.

Then Chester Moore turned his gaze to Arthur McKay and asked, "Arty, Is this some kind of a joke?"

I squinted at him. Joke?

"Arty—you old dog," Chester Moore continued, his eyes lit with amusement. "You know Philip Cranston is no friend of ours. Why are you filling this young lady's head with such nonsense?"

I turned to the man who had brought me here in his chauffeur-driven sedan. Raising his gray eyebrows at me, he flicked me a wry smile. "So, I might have exaggerated. These good folks know my son-in-law. Quite well, as a matter of fact. But I'm afraid he doesn't have any real friends."

"Lorna was my friend," Adele McMaster declared. Raising her dainty chin, she gave a sad pout. "She had lots of friends."

"Who do you think might have murdered her?" I asked.

"Why ... I have no idea." She stared at me, unblinking, for what felt like forever. Then, "I just hope it wasn't her husband."

"Who was deeply in debt," Bruce McMaster said. "We all know that. It's common knowledge. The way that guy threw money at the bookies— there was no parimutuel betting for him. No siree, he played it big time."

"Parimutuel betting?" I had no idea what that was.

"That's when you bet legally," Bruce McMaster explained. "You place a bet at the track window for win, place, or show. That was too small change for Philip. He wagered big bucks with the off-track bookies."

Glancing back at Arthur McKay, I realized why he'd brought me here. His sly smile hinted that he was giving me more proof of his son-in-law's guilt. Great, just great.

"Is there anyone else here at the racetrack I could speak with?" I asked him, inwardly wincing at the pleading in my voice. "Maybe in the stables? Someone who works with the horses? Even if Philip didn't have any friends over there, an enemy or two would do."

The foursome at the table regarded me with pity in their eyes. Then, "That sounds like a good idea, honey," Ed Green said. "Can't hurt."

"I suppose," Arthur McKay murmured. "We came all this way. Guess we could head over there. Philip did spend a lot of time at the stables."

"Good luck, missy," Ed Green told me. "Philip Cranston is no pal of mine, but I wouldn't want to see an innocent man go to jail. If somebody else killed his wife, you need to find them—and I have faith you will."

———

Ed Green's kind, encouraging words echoed in my mind as I followed Arthur McKay into the stables.

High expectations and drama filled the air. It was getting close to the first race, and the stables—a huge extended barn on the opposite side of the track from the stadium—was bustling. Stable boys were putting saddles on horses. Colorfully dressed jockeys were leading thoroughbreds out of their stalls.

Arthur McKay halted and pointed to a stable boy brushing down a sleek black thoroughbred. "Hmmm ... I think that kid over there might have worked with Clear Winner." He touched my elbow. "Come on, let's go ask him."

"Sure," I said, stepping around a pile of fresh horse dung. "But Clear Winner? Is that the name of—"

"Yes ... one of Lorna's stallions. One of the horses that I bought her which she handed over to her husband to race. He named the horse, not her."

"Rather presumptuous name for a racehorse," I mumbled. No wonder Philip didn't have friends at the racetrack, if indeed that was true.

"Excuse me, lad," Arthur McKay called to the sandy-haired stable boy.

The kid turned at the greeting. "Yes, sir?"

"What's your name, boy?"

He looked at me, then back at the older man asking the question. "Jethro, sir."

"Jethro, have you ever worked with Clear Winner?"

He blinked, looking confused. "Yes, sir. A fine horse, sir."

"So, you know his owner? Philip Cranston?"

Blinking again, he said, "Mr. Philip? Yes, sir."

Clutching a horse brush in one hand and the reins of the thoroughbred he was grooming in his other, Jethro was clearly nervous. I needed to put him at ease. "I'm a private investigator," I said, "investigating the murder of Mr. Cranston's wife. Could I speak with you for a moment?"

That seemed to make him even more nervous. He swallowed hard, causing the Adam's apple in his skinny neck to bob up and down. "What?" he squeaked. "I don't know nothing about no murder."

I smiled. "That's okay. I'm not accusing you of anything. I just want to ask you a few questions about Mr. Philip."

"Mr. Philip?" He shook his head. Holding my gaze, his eyes looked panicked. "But I can't leave Best Boy here." He waved the brush he was gripping. "I got to get this horse ready to race, lady. I got no time—"

"I'll help!" Another stable boy ran over. Taller and older than Jethro, he reached for the reins and the brush. "I heard what this lady said. Murder? That sounds important, Jethro. Go on, talk to her."

"Uh ..." Jethro didn't look so sure he wanted to talk to me. "I don't know, Ned."

"Go!" Ned said. "If anybody asks, I'll just tell 'em you're on a break."

"I'll make it quick," I said, gesturing to Arthur McKay to stay where he was and for Jethro to follow me into Best Boy's stall. The racehorse's name was carved in cursive over the top of the entrance, and the stall, its floor lined with hay, looked spacious and clean. As good a place as any.

I lowered myself down onto a big block of hay, bound with rope, and gestured for Jethro to take a seat on another block beside me.

"I don't know how I can help you." Jethro glanced at me, then away. "I don't know Mr. Philip all that good." A pink blush was spreading from his neck to his cheeks.

"I understand. I just want to know how he treated his horses. Did he treat them well?"

He furrowed his brow. "Sure. Real nice."

"Was he nice to you?"

He shrugged. "Sure. Real nice."

Where was I going with this? I wished I had a clue. "Was Mr. Philip nice to everyone, as far as you could tell?"

Another shrug. "Sure, I guess."

"How so?"

He stared at me as the flush deepened. I sensed that he wanted to help me but didn't know how. "He tipped good." He grinned. "Real good."

"He tipped you?"

"Yeah. Mr. Philip has a lot of money. I mean, all the owners here do, but he likes to show it off, if you know what I mean."

"No, what do you mean?"

"Whenever I was finished grooming Clear Winner or his other racehorse, Showoff Sam, Mr. Philip would pull out his wallet and hold up a bunch of bills and count some out for me and hand them to me. But you know ... real slow ... like he wanted the other boys to see."

"The other boys?"

"The other stable boys. And the jockeys, too, I guess. He liked to show everybody he had money and we liked to see his money. And get some of it." Jethro's grin widened, as if he was starting to like this conversation.

A thought came to me. "What about stable girls? Are there any stable girls here?"

He chuckled. "No. Girls? This ain't no place for a girl."

"What about Annie Leeds? Do you know her? She's Mr. Philip's housekeeper now, but she told me she used to work as a stable girl at the track."

Jethro put a hand to his forehead, like he was thinking. Then, as if a light bulb went off, "Annie Leeds? A stable girl?" He laughed, like he found that incredibly funny. "No ... if Annie was ever a stable girl, I never heard tell of it. No, she was the girlfriend of Mr. Paul for a while ... then, let's see ... Mr. Jeff ... then Mister ... uhm, I think she was just the track's party girl, if you know what I mean."

My heart bumped. "I don't know what you mean. Tell me."

"She made herself available for dates is what I mean. Went to parties with some of the owners. After the races. Where the winners go to celebrate."

"Where?"

He shrugged. "Mostly in the clubhouse, I think. Maybe bars, too?" His grin was even bigger now. Gossiping about the owners was clearly fun for him, giving him a feeling of power.

"Did you know that Annie is now working as Mr. Philip's housekeeper?" I asked.

He shrugged. "Nope. Never knew what happened to her, where

she went. Never cared, tell you the truth. That pretty girl never looked my way. Cause I didn't have no money. She liked men with money."

I pressed my lips together and thought about what I'd just heard. Maybe I'd been wrong about Annie. Maybe she wasn't one of Philip's trophies. Maybe he was one of hers. But what did that have to do, if anything, with Lorna's murder?

I couldn't think of any more questions for Jethro. He needed to get back to work.

And I needed to get back to Grand Gables.

I thanked him for his time, then told Arthur McKay I was ready to leave.

The first race was set to begin, but I didn't need to hang around for that.

I had more questions for Annie Leeds.

Sixteen

Unfortunately, Annie Leeds was busy when I got back to Grand Gables, meaning my questions had to wait.

When Arthur McKay dropped me off, he told me to tell Celeste goodbye for him and instructed his chauffer to take him home.

Since I was eager to speak to Annie, I let myself in and found her in the dining room serving lunch to Celeste, Rita, Francine, and Steve.

Steve?

"Hi, Story." He greeted me with that smile of his that always made my legs go weak. That slightly lopsided grin that twinkled his eyes and grabbed my heart.

"Hi." I gave a tight smile back. "What's going on? What are you—"

"Story—where's Philip?" Rudely interrupting, Francine jumped to her feet, peering behind me, as if expecting him to follow me into the room.

I frowned. Hadn't anyone one told her? I shrugged. "He's staying in a hotel somewhere because he's tired of talking to the police."

I glanced at Steve, still wondering why he was at the luncheon, then cut my eyes back to Francine. "Philip is fine. Why do you ask?"

"*Why*?" She pressed a hand to her chest. "I'm worried about him —that's *why*."

Steve rolled his eyes. "Since Philip elected to go on vacation during his wife's murder investigation, I was hoping Celeste might be able to give me his bank records." He turned to Celeste, seated beside him, and gave her gave a dramatic sigh. "Unfortunately, she says she is unable to help me, although she did kindly ask me to stay for lunch."

Celeste reached over and patted Steve's hand. "Now, now, you know I would help you if I could. But I can't. Since my name is not on Father's bank accounts—and I have no idea why he isn't cooperating with you." She leaned toward him, her lips quirking into a flirtatious smile. "I know Father has made a mess of things, but I'm glad you're here. Thank you for understanding."

I suppressed a groan. Celeste wasn't being a bit subtle about wanting Steve back and it was becoming more than a bit tiring.

But surely Steve knew she wouldn't or couldn't give him the bank records. He was probably using that dubious request as an excuse to visit Grand Gables. But why? To learn the status of my investigation?

Wishing I had news that was worthy of announcing, I watched Annie come in from the kitchen carrying a large glass bowl filled with a yummy looking lettuce and tomato salad. She set it down in the middle of the table. I must have been staring at it with longing eyes because Celeste told me to grab a chair, insisting there was plenty of food for all.

Grateful, I accepted her invitation, and pulling a chair away from the wall, wedged myself in between Steve and Rita. I was famished. And anyway, I needed to hang around so I could question Annie alone.

"I understand my father took you to the racetrack." Rita gave me a polite smile. "Did you learn anything interesting there? Anything that will help Philip?"

Annie was back with a platter of chicken salad sandwiches. Stiffening at the word "racetrack," she stared at me before slowly setting the platter down next to the salad.

Naughty-me was tempted to blurt out what I'd learned at the racetrack about Annie's party-girl past. Professional me held back. Avoiding Annie's tense gaze, I told Rita, "Well …I found out a few things that I'll need to check out. Talked to a few of Philip's acquaintances, had an interesting chat with a stable boy, but that's all I'm going to say for now."

"I don't understand why Philip ran away." Francine sniffed. She sounded like a whiny little girl who'd just lost her puppy. "He needs to come back."

"Why?" Rita asked. "He's probably better off staying away, at least until Story solves this case. Right, Story?"

Rita's faith in me was touching. And sounded genuine, which was heartening.

Steve cleared his throat. "Since all clues lead to Philip, Story might have a problem solving this case any time soon if she ignores that unfortunate truth."

"Gee, thanks," I said.

"Not that you're not good at what you do …" He gave me an encouraging grin. "It's just that you're not a miracle worker. Or a magician."

"I have faith in Story," Celeste said with a huff. "That's why I hired her."

And to get back in touch with Steve, I thought, but kept that to myself.

"What's your next move, Story?" Celeste looked over at me with a pleading expression in her eyes.

Something told me not to divulge my desire to interview Annie again. Not until I knew more. Annie had gone back in the kitchen, but I had no doubt she was listening, and I wanted to keep all my cards to myself.

Then I remembered a lead I had yet to investigate. The tarot card reader, the elusive Madame Z.

"Your mother's tarot card reader," I told Celeste. "I need to track her down. She travels from circus to circus, but maybe she's home by now."

Steve reached for a sandwich and put it on his plate. "That's a long shot."

I gave him a one-shoulder shrug. "One I need to take."

"I'll go with you," Celeste said. "I want to meet this woman."

I nodded. "Sure. Good idea."

"But what about the police?" Francine jumped to her feet, her eyes misting up, her lips trembling. "Am I the only one here worried that the police might coming to look for Philip? Don't you think it looks suspicious that he ran away?"

"Yes ..." Steve said under his breath. "Quite."

Annie brought me a plate, napkin, and silverware. As she put them down in front of me, I noticed her hands were trembling.

"Does that mean you know where Philip is?" Francine asked me, sounding more desperate than before, like a mother who'd lost a child.

Or a woman who'd lost her lover? Oh, my God. Was Francine another one of Philip's trophies?

"I have an *idea* where he might be," I told her, forking salad onto my plate. I reached for a sandwich and gave her a serene smile. "But I can't tell you, or anyone else, because he swore me to secrecy."

Annie was staring at me. Then her eyes moved to Francine. Like Francine, the maid seemed unusually anxious. Her face was pale and large sweat marks were blooming under her arm pits, forming half-moon shadow-shapes on her uniform.

"May I have some iced tea, please?" I asked, waving my hand to bring Annie's attention back to her job.

She blinked, blinked again, then gave a stiff nod. "Of course, miss," she said, her tone polite. Aloof. Deferential. That of the ideal housekeeper. One who knew her place.

But the look she gave me just before turning to go into the kitchen was jarring.

"Crap, did you see that?" Steve whispered to me.

"Yeah," I whispered back.

"Annie looked like she was about to throw up."

"I know. She's upset about something. I need to talk to her."

Someone rapped on the front door. Loudly. Then again, louder.

"Annie!" Celeste called. "Could you get that, please?"

"I'll go," I said, then hurried to the door and yanked it open before anyone could stop me.

I knew who it was, maybe we all did.

Yep, it was the police. Two uniformed officers, the same ones who had demanded that Philip not leave town. Officers Romano and Olson.

"Philip Cranston ..." Olson said. "We're back and need to speak to him again. May we come in?"

I braced myself for trouble. "Uh ... I'm afraid he's not here. But, by any chance, were you able to interview that psychic, Mr. Bravo, about that will?"

"We're here for Mr. Cranston," Olson snapped. "Where is he?"

"Uhm ..."

Celeste ran up to us. "My father went for a drive, officers. Perhaps you could stop by later?"

Romano frowned. "A drive *where*?"

"We're not sure," I said.

"He wasn't supposed to leave town," Romano said tightly. "Where did he go?"

Celeste shook her head. "We don't know."

Olson patted the revolver on his hip. "How long ago did Mr. Cranston leave?"

Celeste and I exchanged glances. I gave a nervous shrug, silently cursing Philip. What was I supposed to do now?

I felt Steve's hand on my shoulder. "Officers, please come in," he said.

Motioning for me and Celeste to step aside, Steve waved them into the vestibule, then signaled for everyone to follow him into the living room.

Rita, Francine, and Annie ran in to see what was going on.

"Oh, no," Francine whimpered. "What did I tell you? What did I tell you?"

Both officers fixed their eyes on me. "Where is Mr. Cranston?" Olson demanded. "Tell us now."

I opened my mouth, then closed it. The jig was up. Philip should not have done what he'd done. He'd made things much worse for himself, not to mention me.

"Story, tell them what you know," Steve said.

Both officers raised their eyebrows and waited.

"He's staying in a hotel in Delaware. I think ..." I pressed my hands to my head. "He doesn't want to be arrested and taken to jail."

"What hotel and where in Delaware?" Romano asked.

"Uhm, I'm not sure. Not sure if he's still there. He ran away from me."

Romano raised his eyebrows. "Ran away?"

I heaved a shaky sigh. "He told me he wanted to go see the psychic, Victor Bravo. To confront him about the will. I told him it wasn't a good idea, but he insisted, so I got in his car to take him there—but then he suddenly changed his mind and drove to Wilmington instead." I swallowed hard. "He checked us into a hotel. As man and wife."

Annie gasped. Francine gasped. Rita gasped. Celeste murmured, "No, no, no."

"What?!" Steve yelled.

I stared down at the floor, unable to meet Steve's eye as I thought of a plausible story to avoid the whole truth—that Philip had tried to rape me. To protect Philip from additional charges, not that he deserved it. "I was upset," I said. "And I didn't want to stay in the hotel room. So ... we went for a ride. In the countryside. And then, then Philip suddenly pulled over and jumped out of the car. Told me to take it. Then he ran off. Into a field full of cows."

"Cows?" Francine whispered.

I glanced at her and then at Steve, who was looking at me with concerned suspicion, like he knew there was more to my story. And that it wasn't going to be good.

"Quite a tale," Romano remarked, the police officer's tone as skeptical as Steve's frown. "The suspect didn't just leave town, he fled to another state."

"Let me call some hotels in Wilmington," I said. "Philip probably ended up there. I'll tell him to come home. Tell him to take a cab."

"Tell him he has twenty-four hours," Olson said. "We'll be back this time tomorrow and he'd better be here."

"And if he's not?" Celeste pressed a hand to her mouth.

Olson pointed to me. "We'll arrest her. For helping a known suspect escape the law."

———

"Call that hotel now," Steve told me the minute the police drove away.

Celeste pointed to a telephone sitting on a desk by the wall. "Yes, over here," she motioned me over. "What was the name of the hotel that he checked you into as his wife?" She lifted the receiver.

"The Cosmopolitan Hotel. Downtown Wilmington." Heat rose to my cheeks as I met Steve's eyes. "I'm sorry I didn't tell anyone sooner. But Philip swore me to secrecy. He thought that if Celeste could say she honestly didn't know where he was, she couldn't get into trouble."

He obviously hadn't been worried about me.

Celeste dialed the long-distance operator and asked for the Cosmopolitan in Wilmington, then handed me the phone. "I have the front desk clerk on the line. A woman."

"Hello?" I took a deep breath, wondering what to say next, given that Steve, Celeste, Rita, Francine, and Annie were all keenly watching me. And listening. "I'd like to be connected to Philip Cranston's room, please."

Silence, then, "Philip Cranston?" The clerk sounded confused. "There is no one by that name here."

I gripped the phone harder, pressed it to my ear. Darn. Philip had used another name to check us in. What was it?

"I'm so sorry," I blurted. "Forgive me, but I got confused for a moment. Could you please connect me to the room of Mr. Benjamin Lively? Room 202."

Out of the corner of my eye I could see the surprise on Celeste's face. I didn't dare look at Steve.

"Thank you," the clerk said. "I'll ring the room now."

The phone rang and rang and kept ringing. Philip was either not there or just not answering.

I hung up. "He is still checked in, or the clerk would have said otherwise," I told Celeste. "But if he is in the room, he is not picking up the phone."

"Call back," Steve said. "Ask the clerk if she has seen him."

Celeste dialed long distance again and got the clerk back on the line for me. The clerk had not seen Mr. Lively coming or going—and couldn't remember the last time she had laid eyes on him. Or his wife.

"This is his sister," I said. "If you see him, could you please give him a message from me?"

"Certainly."

"Tell him that he needs to come home. Now. To hire a cab. Because it's important. His daughter, Celeste, needs him. Can you tell him that?"

"Goodness, of course. I'll leave a message at the desk if I'm not here, dear. I hope it's not an emergency?"

"Not yet," I said. "But if he has any questions, tell him to call home."

I hung up and looked at Celeste. "I don't know what else we can do."

"I hope you don't get it in your head to drive to the hotel to get him." Steve narrowed his eyes at me. "Because if you're planning to do that, I'm going with you."

"I'm not going to do that." I lifted my chin. "If Philip wants to keep hiding from the police, that's his choice."

"Benjamin Lively?" Steve ran a hand through his hair. "That's the name he's using?"

"Yes. He checked us in as Mr. and Mrs. Benjamin Lively."

"You and I need to talk, Story," Steve said, his tone grave. "In private."

I nodded. I'd known this was coming, and I was ready to tell Steve what had happened in the hotel room. But I didn't want Celeste to hear it. Yet. What if she didn't believe me? Her beloved father—accost a woman? She might accuse me of lying and fire me on the spot. No, better to keep that from her for now.

"I hope Philip gets the message," Francine whimpered. "I hope he comes home."

"Yes," Rita said. "I agree."

Twisting the hem of her apron, Annie turned and rushed out of the room. This was my chance to talk to her, privately.

Excuse me," I told Steve. "I'll be right back."

I found Annie in the kitchen. She was at the sink, getting a glass of water, and turned when she heard me come in.

"I need to talk to you," I said, noticing her eyes were red and puffy.

"About what?" She gulped some water and lowered the glass to the counter.

"Mr. Philip. And you."

"What about us?" She shot me a hostile, defensive glare.

"How did you two really meet? You weren't shoveling horse manure in a stable when you were introduced to him, were you? I bet you were on the arm of a high roller at a party."

She pursed her lips in a haughty manner. "What of it?"

"You lied to me."

"I did not. So bloody what if I was working as an escort when I met Mr. Philip? I was mucking stables before that. Being an escort paid better."

"Probably more than being a housekeeper. So why the job switch?"

She folded her arms across her chest. "I needed a place to live. This is a nice place."

I couldn't argue with that. "Has Mr. Philip ever made any advances on you?"

She widened her eyes. Her cheeks flushed. "Advances?"

"You know, tried to touch you in an inappropriate way?" She knew what the word meant but it didn't hurt to spell it out.

"No," she whispered. "No. He would never do that. And I wouldn't let him."

"Do you think he's attractive?"

Her eyes went bigger, her cheeks pinker. "Mr. Philip? No. He's old."

"And up to very recently, was married."

Annie shook her head. "I'm done talking to you. Your questions are stupid."

I nodded. "Okay. I just have one more."

"What?"

"You seem upset that he ran away. As upset as Mrs. Montague, it seems. Why?"

Her eyes shot daggers at me. "That's your dumbest question yet, lady. I'm worried about losing my job, okay? I like it here."

"So, why do you think Mrs. Montague is so upset?" I'd lowered my voice and changed my tone from inquisitor to confidant.

She wasn't fooled. "You said one more question and I done answered it and anyway I got no idea why that fool woman is upset. Ask her."

I shrugged. "Okay," I said. "I will."

———

Steve was waiting for me when I left the kitchen. "Like I said, Story, you and I need to talk." He took my arm. "Let's step outside."

I pulled back. "I need to talk to Francine."

"That can wait."

Frustrated, I protested, "I'm trying to do my job."

"And I'm trying to help you."

"I don't need your help, Steve." I bit down on my lip. Too harsh. He didn't deserve that. Still ...

"It will just take a minute," he said.

We went back into the living room, where Celeste was huddled together with her aunt and Francine. They were having a whispered conversation. "Steve and I will be right back," I said. "He wants to speak to me about something."

Before anyone could comment, we went out the front door and headed down the drive.

"What happened in that hotel room?" Steve asked.

I didn't answer right away. I kicked a pebble and watched it roll. "He tried to grab me."

Steve reached for my arm and pulled me to a stop. "That monster. I knew it."

My eyes met Steve's. "Nothing happened. Because I got away. I jumped on his stomach when he fell to the floor, knocked the breath out of him, then grabbed his car keys and escaped."

Steve tightened his grip on my arm. "Unbelievable. I cannot believe what you keep getting yourself into."

"I can take care of myself." I couldn't pull my eyes away from Steve's, but I did manage to free my arm. "You don't have to keep worrying about me. I'm not your problem."

"Why didn't you tell Celeste what her father did?"

"What good would that do now? She might not believe me, and then she might fire me, and I need this case."

"He's guilty, you know."

"No, I don't know that."

Steve looked angrier than I'd ever seen him. Not only angry, worried beyond belief. Then his eyes went to my lips. Like he wanted to kiss me.

Kiss me?

No. No, please not that. I suddenly couldn't breathe. I took a step back. "I've got work to do," I declared. "Please, believe me when I say nothing happened between Philip and me. And that I can take care of myself."

Steve blew out a breath. "Oh, yeah? What's your next move, then, Miss Superwoman Private Eye?"

"I'll just have to wait for Philip, hope he comes home," I said, hating that it sounded so powerless.

"He has twenty-four hours."

"Yep."

"So, you're just going to sit in Celeste's living room, twiddle your thumbs, and wait for him to walk in the door?"

I gave a deep sigh and lifted my chin. "No."

"So?"

"So ... I'm going to go find that tarot card reader, Madame Z. Tomorrow morning. I'll get an early start. Take Celeste with me, like she wants me to do."

Steve sighed. "I get it. Action helps allay anxiety. Always."

I nodded. "Yes, that's it."

"But someone will need to hang around Grand Gables to greet Philip when he shows up." Steve grinned. "*If* he shows up."

"Oh, right."

"I'll do it," Steve offered. "I'll wait for him. Be glad to. I need to talk to him anyway."

"Thank you, I think." I chewed the side of my lip. "But please ... be nice."

"Nice?" Steve gave a harsh laugh. "That, my dear, is not what I have in mind. And if he tries to run off again, I'll hold the jerk at gunpoint until the police arrive. I won't let you go to jail because of him."

SEVENTEEN

The next morning, I finally got a break.

Madame Z answered her door when Celeste and I arrived at her house.

At least I assumed the woman eyeing us with glittery green eyes was the tarot card reader.

Dressed in a striped, ankle length caftan that had to include every color of the rainbow, she was an older, scarier, heavier version of her sister, Madame B. Long, stringy gray hair, sharp pointed chin, with a calculating gleam in her eyes that sent a chill through my veins.

I flashed back to Victor Bravo's warnings about her—to beware—and forced a smile. "Madame Z?"

"Yes …" Her voice was deep, like a man's. "And you are?"

"Story Smith, private eye." I handed her my card. "And this is my client, Celeste Cranston, daughter of—"

"Lorna Cranston." She beamed a smile that transformed her face from eerily scary to eagerly welcoming and opened the door. "Please, come in, come in."

We stepped into her living room. Which was tiny, crowded, and cluttered. Every inch of space taken up by *something*. A large maroon sofa, overstuffed chairs, vases, candles, rugs all over the floor, and in the middle of the room, a long table.

In the middle of that table sat several packs of cards. Tarot cards, I presumed.

"I see a resemblance to your mother," Madame Z boomed, narrowing her eyes at Celeste. "Although not a strong one." She flicked her gaze to me. "You must be here about Lorna. If so, how can I help you? Perhaps you would like a reading?"

"Not exactly ..." I looked around the room. "Perhaps we could sit down?"

"Certainly." She waved a hand at our various options. I took one of the chairs, sinking into its over-stuffed-ness. Celeste sank into another, and Madame Z settled herself on the sofa.

"I'm investigating Lorna's murder," I said. "Her psychic medium, Victor Bravo, told me that Lorna came to see you often."

"That's true." She gave a heavy sigh. "I don't care for Mr. Bravo personally, but his vague warnings from the other side did send Lorna to me, so I have to thank him for that."

"Warnings that she was in danger?"

"That's right."

"So, what were you able to do for her? About those warnings? What could you tell her?"

She gave a deeper, louder sigh. "Every reading I did for her confirmed what Victor said, unfortunately." She squinted at Celeste and then back at me. "Do either of you know anything about tarot cards?"

We shook our heads.

"Each card in the deck means something. When a card appears for you, it advises you about a direction you need to take. Lorna kept drawing the Ten of Swords—a card that represents the end of something. It scared her, and I didn't blame her."

Celeste widened her eyes. "Why?"

"Because it coincided with the warnings from her mother, from the beyond, according to what Victor told her. It was not good."

I leaned forward. "What other cards did she keep drawing?"

Madame Z's eyes bore into mine. "The Devil and The Hanged Man. The Hanged Man usually indicates that you will not—in all likelihood—be able to help yourself out of whatever dilemma you are facing. Your energy is blocked. Always bad, always bad."

Blocked energy did indeed sound bad, although I had no idea what this woman was talking about. The way she was looking at me now was beginning to make me nervous. And was it my imagination, or was the room growing darker?

I glanced at Celeste. She gave me a let's-get-out-of-here look.

No way. Not yet. I shook my head. "If Lorna's energy was blocked, what could she do?" I asked Madame Z. "Were you able to give her any advice?"

Her lips slowly formed a mysterious grin. "Yes, of course. That's one reason she kept coming to see me. Some tarot card readers can communicate with angels, you see. But I am unique. I can communicate with evil forces. And keep them at bay."

"Oh ..." I stared at her. "How?"

"By lighting special candles and incense and chanting for them to grant mercy." Her grin grew wider. "Expensive candles and rare expensive incense, and long, long chants."

Astonished, I looked at Celeste then back at the gray-haired woman. "But ... but ... they didn't work. Lorna was murdered."

"That's because she stopped paying," Madame Z snapped. She waved a crooked, boney finger at Celeste. "She stopped paying for the candles and the incense and my time. And then she *died*."

I could not believe what I was hearing. But why was I surprised? Victor Bravo had warned me about Zelda Buttinsky, and here it was. She had been bribing Lorna to keep evil spirits at bay, and apparently Lorna had believed her and paid the money. Until, for some reason, she stopped.

Celeste was gaping at me in horror, a hand to her mouth, tears welling in her eyes.

"Why did she stop paying you?" I asked.

"I don't know, she refused to say."

"Did you murder her?"

"Certainly not. Although I warned her that her life was in danger, and she didn't listen."

Celeste started to sob. "You murdered my mother," she hissed in a ragged whisper. "I know you murdered her. Because she wouldn't pay you anymore. You evil woman." She jumped to her feet, eyes tear-filled and desperate. "Story, we've got to go. Now. We need to call the police."

"Wait!" Madame Z shouted. "Sit back down, Miss Cranston, unless you want to meet the same fate as your mother."

Celeste froze.

I jumped up. "What are you talking about?" I suddenly remembered my gun, which was still in my closet. A lot of good it was going to do me there. I really needed to remember to start carrying it in my purse.

"I have the power to keep the evil away from you, Miss Cranston," Madame Z cooed. "If you pay me for the candles and the incense that those spirits love so much—as well as for my time—I can protect you."

Ludicrous. If the situation wasn't so sad and so serious, I would have laughed. I looked over at Celeste.

She was not laughing. She was furious. "You'll never get a dime out of me—you witch," she screamed. Running for the door, she waved for me to follow. "Come on, Story, we're done here. If you don't call the police, I will."

———

"We're not going to look for a pay phone," I told Celeste as we drove away in my T-Bird. "I'm betting that by the time we get to your house the police will already be there looking for your father. We can tell them about Madame Z then."

"I know she did it." Celeste sniffed. "They better go arrest her."

I was right. Romano and Olson were waiting for Philip when we got back, with Rita playing hostess in the living room as Annie served them glasses of lemonade.

I wondered where Steve could be.

"See, here are Miss Smith and my niece, Celeste, now." Rita, clearly flustered, jumped up when we walked in. "I told you they'd be back soon."

"With Mr. Cranston, I hope?" The older officer, sitting on one of the leather chairs before the fireplace, stared at me, glass halfway to his mouth.

"You're early," I said, then bit down on my tongue. That was dumb. They weren't that early. Philip still had another couple of hours, but he was pushing his luck.

"Where is he?" asked Romano, who was sitting in the other leather chair. "Is he on his way?"

"I ... ugh ... I'm not sure." I went and stood before the fireplace, facing them and Rita, who was on the sofa. "Rita," I said, "has Philip called?"

Pressing her lips together, she shook her head.

Annie scurried out of the room. Was she trying to avoid being questioned? Or going to fetch me and Celeste some lemonade? Based on the look on her face, I wasn't counting on any lemonade.

"He should be here any minute, I'm sure he will be," I said, hoping it was true.

The front door squeaked open, then slammed shut. Everyone looked to see who'd come in.

Philip?

No, Steve.

"Where were you?" I asked, relieved to see him.

"Outside looking around." He ran a hand through his hair. "I thought I heard a gunshot earlier, but maybe it was my imagination. Everything's quiet out there as far as I can tell."

"Gunshot?" Olson stood up. "Do you think maybe Mr. Cranston shot himself?"

"No!" Celeste ran over and grabbed Steve's arm. "No. Father would never do that." She looked at me, then at Steve, then at the officers. "In fact, Story and I can prove he didn't shoot Mother. It was her tarot card reader ... tell them, Story."

All eyes focused on me. "Ugh, we can't exactly prove anything," I said. "But Madame Z did threaten us, or rather, Celeste, and admitted to fleecing Lorna out of money to keep evil spirits away." I swallowed hard. "Although ... she didn't exactly call it *fleecing*, she called it *protecting* ... and she claimed Lorna died because she stopped paying for the candles and incense that the spirits liked." With a weak smile, I glanced over at the police officers, who were eyeing me with a mixture of shock and ill-concealed amusement.

Romano cleared his throat. "We'll look into that," he remarked dryly. "In the meantime, we're more interested in speaking to Mr. Cranston." He pointed a finger at me. "Or else."

"Or else what?" a voice called from the vestibule.

The front door slammed shut again and Philip sauntered into the room.

"I'm here," he announced with glee, as if we were all there to throw him a surprise birthday party. "Have you been waiting for me?"

Eighteen

"Where have you been?" Olson jumped to his feet with a scowl, clearly in no mood for Philip's innocent little-boy act.

Philip gave a nonchalant shrug and smirked. "What difference does it make? I'm here now."

"Answer the question—where have you been?" The furious officer stared him down.

"I was staying in a hotel. Needed to get away."

Romano stood and took a step toward Philip. "We told you not to leave town. How did you get here just now?"

"What do you mean?"

"How did you get from your hotel to here? Did you drive?"

Philip glanced at me, then quickly away. "No. Took a cab."

"Where did it drop you off?"

Philip frowned. "At the end of my drive. Why?"

"We didn't hear a car pull up, that's why." Brandishing handcuffs from somewhere on his uniform, Romano held them out. "Mr. Cranston, you are under arrest for the murder of your wife."

"No ..." Philip stumbled back. "No. I didn't do it. Didn't you go see that psychic? Bravo? He murdered her. For her horses."

"We questioned him, and he gave us the will, which we plan to have analyzed by a handwriting expert." Olson put his hand on the revolver at his side. "Mr. Bravo says he's not sure he even wants the horses. He has no idea how to care for them. Doesn't have the land or facilities needed for them. And probably couldn't even afford to feed them. Sure, he could sell them, but for how much? Enough to make murder attractive?" He scoffed. "You, on the other hand, Mr. Cranston, stood to gain a million dollars."

"Turn around," Romano said. "Put your hands behind your back."

"No!" Celeste cried. "What about Madame Z? She's the one you should arrest."

"Don't worry, we plan to pay her a visit," Olson said. "But your father had the motive, and his alibi is weak, and we're taking him in."

"No," Rita whimpered.

"No," Annie cried in a hoarse whisper.

I turned to look at Annie. I had not heard her come back into the room. Her eyes were wide and unbelieving.

Philip glanced at her, then quickly bowed his head, turned, and keeping his eyes on the floor, put his hands together behind his back.

Romano snapped the cuffs on and then he and his partner walked him to the door.

"This is a mistake," Philip muttered in a low growl. "You have the wrong person."

"I'll get you out of this, Father," Celeste cried. "Don't worry—you won't have to stay in jail for long."

Steve met my anguished gaze. I couldn't help feeling like I'd failed, even though I knew Philip's arrest was not my fault. He looked as guilty as a cheating husband could, and the cops didn't even know about the cheating part.

"You tried," Steve told me.

"And you better try harder," Celeste said, her voice ice cold serious. "Or you're fired."

"I'm doing my best—and I'm not nearly done," I said.

I went to the door and watched the officers put Philip in the police car and then drive away. An empty, gaping hole filled my chest, but I told myself to buck up. The truth was out there somewhere, and I was going to find it.

Turning, I walked back to the living room. Celeste and Rita were huddled together, crying. Annie, her hands to her mouth, her eyes huge and unblinking, stood watching them.

Steve walked over and gave my shoulder a sympathetic pat.

"Guess Philip won't be collecting that million dollars any time soon," I told him. "The insurance company has won, for now, anyway. Congratulations. It's a victory for you."

He gave me a wry smile. "It also means they won't be needing me anymore. Going to have to look for another—"

"Help! Somebody, help!"

Someone—a man—was pleading for help from the front yard.

Steve and I ran to the still-open front door.

"Help, someone, help!" he screamed. He dashed up the front steps, his face red, his mouth agape in shock, then bent over to catch his breath.

"What's wrong?" I shouted.

"It's Miss Francine." He straightened up and looked at me, his eyes wild and bulging. "I'm her stableman. And I just found her dead. In the barn. Somebody shot Miss Francine dead!"

———

Francine Montague—dead?

"What?" Steve asked. "Are you saying Francine Montague has been shot?"

The man moaned. "Yes. She's dead ... I'm sure she's dead. Come see. Come help ... please."

"Gus!"

I turned to see Celeste and Rita behind me, still clutching each other. "Gus," Celeste shouted again over my shoulder. "What are you talking about?"

"I took the truck out to run some errands and when I got back, I couldn't find Miss Francine anywhere." He swallowed hard. "So I goes into the barn. And there she was. Laying face down. In some hay. Then ... blood. So much blood."

"Have you called the police?" Steve asked, his voice tight.

"No, sir. I didn't know what to do, so I ran here. Fast as I could."

"Celeste and Rita, call the police," I said. "Steve, we'll go with Gus. We can take my car."

Ten minutes later, we pulled up to Francine's red brick mansion and ran to the barn.

It was just as Gus had described. Francine's white stallion was still in its stall. In an empty adjacent stall lay Francine, sprawled out, face down, blood pouring from the back of her head. Most definitely dead.

She was also half naked, from the waist down. Gus had forgotten to mention that part.

"Oh, my God." I stepped closer, my legs shaking.

Steve grabbed my arm and pulled me back. "No, Story. This is a crime scene."

"It's just like Lorna. It looks like what happened to Lorna." I looked at him wildly. Except ..."

"Lorna was fully dressed," Steve said grimly. "At least according to the police report."

Steve and I stared at each other as we listened to the screeching siren of a police car. Seconds later, a uniformed cop ran up to us, followed by a man in a suit.

"Officer Sanford," the cop said, flashing his badge. "And this is Detective Brown, Homicide."

Steve introduced us and hurriedly explained how Gus had found Francine.

"Francine Montague," I said. "She was the best friend of Lorna Cranston. Her neighbor. Who was also shot in the head. Murdered. Just like this. Not long ago." I was blubbering, but I couldn't help it. This didn't seem real.

Then I remembered. "Lorna was murdered on a Tuesday," I said. "And now ... Francine has been murdered on a Tuesday."

Steve somberly met my gaze. "Coincidence, or planned? Either way, around here, it seems Tuesday means trouble."

Nineteen

"Please get back." Detective Brown motioned for me, Steve, and Gus to move away from Francine's body. "Only don't leave. We have more questions."

Another police car pulled up and an officer with a camera jumped out, followed by another officer in uniform.

I watched morosely as the photographer snapped photos of Francine's corpse from every angle, then, after getting more shots of the area where she lay and the barn's interior, he nodded to the detective that he was finished.

The officer who had arrived with the photographer started testing the area for fingerprints, although it wasn't an ideal location for getting anything of much use.

Who could have done this? And when? Feeling sick to my stomach, I dropped to my knees. Could Philip have killed her? And if he did, why?

But he couldn't have—could he? If he was telling the truth about a taxi picking him up at his Delaware hotel and letting him out at the end of his driveway, it didn't seem possible.

Except now I knew Philip well enough to know that he lied with ease. And could easily be lying now.

So where did that leave me? He'd just been arrested and hauled off to jail for murdering his wife, and now his wife's best friend was dead? Killed the same way and in eerily similar circumstances. Moreover, I couldn't get the idea out of my mind that Philip and Francine might have been having an affair.

Detective Brown was leaning over Francine's body. He lifted sections of her hair around the bloody area where it appeared she'd been shot, then motioned for two of the officers to turn her over.

I closed my eyes and took a deep breath, embarrassed for the dead woman whose privates were now exposed to the men surrounding her.

I opened my eyes and looked up at Steve and Gus. Standing side by side, they were also staring down at the naked body, clad from the waist up in a silk lavender blouse, half unbuttoned to expose a white lace bra.

What had Francine been wearing from the waist down? I glanced around.

"Look, over there." Steve pointed to what appeared to be a dark skirt on top of a small pile of hay. About five feet away from the body, it looked as if it had been tossed there. Along with nylon stockings, a garter belt, and her shoes. High heels. Spikey high heels.

"High heels?" I hiss-whispered. "Who wears high heels into a barn?"

"Just what I was wondering," Steve whispered back. "She didn't come in here to go riding. Which means, what was she up to? And who was she meeting?"

Detective Brown had also seen the clothing strewn on and around the hay pile and gestured for the forensics officer to get fingerprints.

Good idea. Maybe fingerprints belonging to someone besides Francine's were on those items.

I stood up and glanced over at Gus. His face was flushed and there was a look in his eyes that sparked my curiosity.

"Gus," I whispered, "do you have any idea who Francine might have come here to meet?"

His eyes grew big as he kept them on the crime scene. He swallowed hard. "Uh ..."

"Hey!" Detective Brown waved a hand at Gus. "I need to talk to you first. You're the one who found her, right?"

"Yessir."

"Over here." The detective motioned for Gus to follow him to another stall, far enough for privacy and out of my listening range. Disappointed, I watched Gus go, sure he had been about to reveal something important. Now I bet he would be telling the detective what he knew.

Steve leaned toward my ear. "What are you thinking, Story?"

I kept my eyes on Francine's body, unable to pull my gaze away. I whispered, "She was meeting a man."

"And I bet you have an idea who."

"Unfortunately. And I don't think she was raped. I think this was a prearranged meet-up."

Steve gave a low grunt. "Philip had time to do this—if he was lying about taking a taxi here from Delaware."

I nodded. "I think he and Francine might have been having an affair. She knew he was staying at the Metropolitan in Wilmington. She heard me call there on the phone. She could have gone and picked him up. But then, why would he murder her?"

"No!"

We turned to see who'd screamed.

Celeste and Rita were running toward us. Rita screamed again and Celeste pulled her to a stop and made an awkward attempt to cover her aunt's eyes. "Don't look, Aunt Rita, don't look!"

Rita yanked Celeste's hand away from her face. "I can't believe it. Francine's dead! Who killed Francine? And where are her *clothes*?"

Officer Sanford came over, flashed his badge again, and said we all needed to leave the barn. "Immediately."

"Where's Gus?" Celeste grabbed Steve's arm. "What's going on?"

As we all backed out of the barn under the steely gaze of Officer Sanford, Celeste tightened her grip on Steve, wailing, "Who killed Francine? I don't understand. What happened?"

Once outside, Steve peeled Celeste off him and faced her. "It seems someone shot her in the back of the head. We don't know who. The police are questioning Gus first and then they want to talk to Story and me."

"Oh my God, oh my God." Rita clapped a hand over her mouth. "Who would have shot Francine? She was such a nice person. She was my friend ..."

"It's not looking good for Philip," Steve said. "Let's just put it that way."

Rita blinked at him, then her eyes bulged in disbelief as she glared at Steve like he was some kind of mad man. "What did you say? Philip? Why would he kill Francine?"

"Yes, why?" Celeste grabbed Steve's arm again and shook it. "What are you saying about my father?"

Anguished, Steve looked at me, as if pleading with me to join the conversation.

I gave him a look like I wanted to strangle him. Why did I have to go and open my big mouth and tell him my suspicions about Francine and Philip? It was just a hunch I'd had, nothing more, which I should have kept it to myself, at least for the time being. The last thing I wanted to do now was incur Celeste's wrath. She might fire me.

"Francine was crazy about your father," I told Celeste. "I think that's what Steve is saying."

"Right." Steve cleared his throat. "Is it at all possible that Francine and your father ... you know ... were ..."

"Lovers?" Rita narrowed her eyes at him. "Is that what you're asking?"

Steve lifted his shoulders in an anything's-possible shrug.

"No." Rita shook her head. "No. That's not possible. Philip loves me. He's in love with me."

We all stared at Rita in shocked silence. Which I finally broke. "What are you saying, Rita?"

"He dated me before Lorna. He married her, but I think he always knew he'd made a mistake. Because he loved me more." Rita's voice was so soft that I thought I'd misheard her.

Then I looked at Celeste and knew I hadn't. Celeste had the expression of someone who had seen a ghost. Pale. Shocked. Disbelieving. "That's not true, Aunt Rita," she whispered loudly. "You know that's not true. Take that back."

Rita lifted her chin. "No. I'm sorry, Celeste, but it is true."

"What?" I asked Rita. "Are you saying that you and Philip are lovers?"

"No." She shook her head at me, clearly shocked I could possibly think such a thing. "Of course not. I would never have betrayed my sister like that. But when she died, I realized that now was my chance. My chance to prove to Philip that I was the one he should have married— and was now free to marry."

"Did you murder Lorna?" I blurted out. Was this a confession?

She gave me a haughty stare. "Of course not. How ridiculous of you to even suggest that."

"It would have been ridiculous for Story to *not* ask that," Steve said quietly. "She's just doing her job."

"And now what?" Celeste looked about to cry. "What's going to happen now? Steve, do you think the police are going to suspect Father killed Francine, too?"

He gave a reluctant nod. "They might."

"But, why? Because he's handsome and charming and women are drawn to him, even if he can't help it?" Celeste glared at her aunt, leaving no doubt she meant to include her in that unfortunate group of misguided women.

It took everything I had not to shout out that her beloved father used his looks and charisma to woo women, and that I knew that because he'd tried it with me.

"Your father will probably be a prime suspect," Steve told Celeste. "Until proven otherwise."

To my surprise, Celeste brightened. A determined, calculating expression spread across her face, replacing the anguish I'd seen seconds before. "Then I want to hire you to work with Story to prove his innocence," she told Steve. "Is that possible? Are you available?"

Steve looked at me and I looked at him and my heart suddenly lodged in my throat.

"As a matter of fact, I am." He smiled. "I'd love to work with Story again."

Twenty

I couldn't believe it. Steve and I. Together again. Working a case. My case.

I should have been upset. Insulted. Because I was perfectly capable of succeeding solo.

But secretly, I was thrilled. Because being in Steve's company made me happy. No matter how hard I tried to ignore that, being with him made me feel like everything was right with the world, that everything in it was wonderful, magical, enchanting.

But dammit, that was an illusion, and a dangerous one. Which was why I struggled to keep my feelings secret even though my heart was beating wildly in my chest when Steve and I met at Francine's estate the next morning.

We had agreed to rendezvous there at nine o'clock to go over the crime scene together after it had been cleared by the police.

Now, as I climbed out of my T-Bird and spotted him waiting for me at the entrance to Francine's barn, my heart wasn't the only part of me acting weird. My mouth was dry, and I'd broken out into a sweat.

In my defense, it was a blisteringly hot summer day. And knowing that it would be, I had dressed accordingly in a sundress and sandals.

Still.

It wasn't the weather that was making my cheeks burn as I walked over to Steve.

Looking breath-stealing-good in khaki trousers and a pale green, short-sleeved shirt, he watched me approach with a curious expression that slowed me in my tracks.

Where was his usual bewitching grin? Instead, he was giving me a twitchy, nervous smile.

I smiled back. "Hi, Steve."

"Hi." He reached for my hands, but then, changing his mind, lowered his hands to his side. "Here we are again." He widened that awkward grin. "*Partner.*"

"Right ..." I grinned back. "Partner."

"You know do know why Celeste hired me to help you, don't you?" He raked his fingers through his hair. "I hope you're not taking it the wrong way. As an insult to your competence, I mean. I'm not trying to steal your case."

So that's what this was about. "Oh, I don't mind," I said breezily. "Really. You're an excellent detective. The best."

"You're not upset about this? You're not taking it personally?"

"Of course not." I waved a hand. "I get it. Celeste wants to keep you around—because she wants you back."

Steve puffed out a breath. "Yes, she does."

"And?"

'And I'm going to let her have that fantasy, so I can work with you."

"Wow. Okay."

"Do you think that's wrong?"

"Wrong? No. Why would I think—"

"I was afraid you might think it makes me a cad. Given what you believe about my so-called reputation."

"Oh, no. I mean, I guess it's okay—so long as you don't ..."

"Lead her on romantically? I never led Celeste on. We only went out a few times."

"I believe you." I shrugged. "It's not your fault that women find you irresistible."

Steve tilted his head. A spark lit up his eyes. "Are you one of those women?"

Uh-oh. "I'm trying not to be." I lifted my chin. "Because your reputation proceeds you, sir."

He frowned. "Story—"

I felt heat rise to my cheeks. "Anyway, we're working together again, Steve. I have *my* reputation to protect."

"You can trust me." He sounded hurt. "You know I will never let you down."

"I know."

"And that I would never hurt you."

That I didn't know.

It wasn't that I didn't trust him—I wished I could say that. The problem was that I didn't trust myself with him. If I let myself get hurt, I'd only have myself to blame.

"Maybe you'll want to date Celeste again," I said, eager to get the conversation off me. "You never know. Celeste is pretty and she's sweet and—"

"And she's not my type, Story." Our gazes locked. You are."

My heart felt like it was melting down to my toes. I knew he'd say that. And I believed he meant it. For now. But what would happen if I surrendered my heart and soul—and body—to him and then he grew tired of me? How could I let myself believe that I was different from the other women who'd fallen for him?

"We need to get to work, Steve," I said, hating how shaky my voice sounded. I cleared my throat. "Let's go and see what the police may have missed."

———

Francine's body was gone, removed by the medical examiner, but a lot of dried blood was still visible in the stall where she had fallen—on clumps of straw and on the dirt floor.

We were going on the theory that she had been killed by one bullet, which was probably lodged in her skull, but Steve and I carefully searched the area just to be sure.

"Nothing here, no stray bullets," I said, not surprised.

Nodding, Steve glanced around. "If there were any, the police would have found them. We need to try to get a police report today."

The police had questioned us separately yesterday after they'd finished with Gus.

I'd told Detective Brown what I knew about Francine but didn't mention her crush on Philip or his womanizing. He was my client, so I was keeping that to myself for now.

Steve told me he had done the same, since Philip was also now his client.

After the police told Steve and I that we were free to go, we'd gone looking for Gus but hadn't been able to find him anywhere.

"Let's go look for Gus now," Steve said, brushing pieces of straw off his pants. "Find out what he told the cops."

I had a feeling we shouldn't go just yet. "Let's look around some more first," I said. "Maybe we can find something that will give us a clue as to who she was with yesterday." I circled the stall, carefully nudging the straw and dirt on the floor with my foot.

Nothing.

Frustrated, I glanced up. And yikes. Spider webs, giant ones, dangled from wooden beams above my head.

"Ahhheee!" I screamed, stumbling back.

Steve ran over and grabbed my arms. "What's wrong?"

"Spiders ..." Panting, I pulled away and pointed up.

He looked to where I was pointed, then gave a low chuckle. "Oh yeah? Where?"

I looked again, then felt silly. "Uhm ... never mind ... just webs, just webs. Sorry, sorry."

"You're afraid of spiders?" Steve's eyes glinted and his lips curved into that annoyingly cute grin of his that always made my heart do flips.

"Well ... yeah." I pressed my lips together, trying to look embarrassed, trying to stop myself from giggling.

But I couldn't help it. I started laughing. I couldn't stop laughing.

I told myself that this was a murder scene, that tragedy had happened here, that I shouldn't be laughing. That I needed to stop.

I pried my gaze away from Steve's equally amused expression, looked down at my feet, inhaled deeply. Exhaled.

And that's when I saw it. Something shiny. Sticking out from under my sandal. I moved my foot, bent over, and picked it up.

"Wow, this could be important ..." I handed it to Steve.

Nodding, he said, "Looks like a man's cufflink." He handed it back to me.

"Sure does." I turned it over in my palm. It was silver, and grimy. I rubbed it with my finger. "It has some initials." I sucked in a breath. "You'll never guess ..."

"PC?"

"Yep."

"Philip Cranston. Son of a gun." Steve shook his head. "What do we do now?"

"Easy," I said. "We go visit him in jail, show him this, and demand to know what he was doing with Francine in the barn. Then we turn the cufflink over to the police."

"I can tell you what he was doing in the barn," a voice called out.

Steve and I froze, then turned.

Gus walked up to us. "Miss Francine and Mr. Philip were lovers. They met here, regular-like, for what they called their fun time." His face growing red, he shrugged a shoulder. "You know ..."

I widened my eyes and shook my head, waiting for him to go on.

Steve narrowed his eyes and stared at the stableman. "Know what ... know what? Spell it out for us, Gus."

Gus blinked his eyes, swallowed hard, took a deep breath. "Miss Francine and Mr. Philip used to get naked and do their thing," he said, his cheeks now the color of a ripe tomato. "They used to call it their rolling in the hay time. Those two—they loved making love in the hay."

———

Steve and I gaped at Gus.

Then we both blurted the obvious question at the same time: "How do *you* know?"

Gus sniffed. "Saw them together." He sniffed louder. "One day when they thought I wasn't around. I heard noises. Snuck up. Saw them. Then they saw me—they knew I knew."

I could only picture it. "When was this?" I asked, trying to banish the lurid and totally believable image from my mind.

He pressed a finger to his chin. "Don't know. Two years ago, I reckon. Maybe three?"

Steve shook his head. "Lorna's husband and best friend ... I wonder if she knew?"

Gus shrugged. "I got no idea."

"You kept their secret, then?" I asked.

"Didn't want to lose my job, so yeah I did." Gus looked down at his feet. "Wasn't any of my business."

"How often?" Steve asked.

"How often what?" Gus looked up and met Steve's steely gaze.

"How often did they get together for these rolls in the hay?"

Gus ran a finger over his lower lip. "Not sure but I'd say maybe a few times a week. Maybe more."

"How about yesterday?" I asked. "Were they together yesterday?"

"Can't say ..." Gus looked at me, then at Steve. "Didn't see them together anyhow. Only time I saw Miss Francine yesterday, she was dead."

I had a bad feeling about this. Really bad. "Did you tell the police about this hay rolling, Gus?"

He turned his eyes back to me. "Sure did. I didn't want no trouble with those cops. Didn't want them to think I killed her. Heck, why would I? Now that she's dead, I'm out of a job."

Twenty-One

Philip was being held in the Chester County jail in downtown West Chester, and I almost didn't recognize him when a guard led me to his cell.

Dressed in a black and white striped prisoner uniform, his uncombed hair was askew, his unshaved face stubbly. It was immediately obvious that his aura of cocky confidence was gone, replaced by a look of dull, unbelieving defeat.

Hunched over and staring down at the floor, he jumped off his cot when he saw me, came over, wrapped his fingers around the gray iron bars separating us, and hissed. "Get me out of here—now."

Then he saw Steve, coming up behind me, and his tired, bloodshot eyes widened. "What's *he* doing here? Bad enough they're treating me like a common criminal—but does this jerk have to witness it?" He jabbed a finger at Steve. "Go away. Leave me alone. I need to talk to Story, not you."

"Celeste hired me to help Story." Steve stepped up next to me and offered Philip a sarcastic, aren't-you-glad grin. "Which means I'm not going anywhere. Which means whatever you've got to say to Story you'll also need to say to me."

"Well then—get me out of here." Philip glared at Steve, then at me, then back at Steve. "Now."

"We're working on it," I said, then looked around to see if any guards were around who might overhear us. The one who'd brought us to Philip was down the hall, talking to a prisoner in a nearby cell.

Good.

I whipped the cufflink out of my purse, showed it to Philip, then quickly stowed it back in my purse. "Recognize that?" I whispered.

Philip blinked at me. His cheeks flushed. He opened his mouth, closed it, swallowed hard. "Where'd you find that?"

I took that as a yes. He recognized it alright.

"Found it in Francine's barn," Steve said, pausing to let that sink in. "Next to the stall where they found her body yesterday."

Philip's eyes bugged out of his face. "Her body?"

"Didn't you know that she'd been murdered?" I leaned closer to him. "Gus, her stableman, came to tell us she'd been shot just minutes after you were arrested and taken away."

Philip's mouth hung open as he continued to stare at me. I couldn't tell if he had known Francine was dead, or if he was just hearing about it now. He didn't say anything, just shook his head back and forth. Slowly, as if in shock.

"We know you and Francine were lovers," Steve whispered loudly. "Gus told us all about your long affair and your rolls in the hay."

Philip gripped the bars so tight his fingers went white, but he didn't say anything.

"Gus found Francine half naked, lying face down, shot in the back of the head, just like your wife," Steve said. "Which means, if the police are not looking at you as a suspect in Francine's murder, too, it's a good guess they will soon."

"Oh my God." Philip let go of the bars and slowly backed up to his cot. Collapsing onto it, he put his face in his hands and moaned. "I can't believe this ... I can't believe this. No, no, no ..."

"I'm assuming the police haven't questioned you about this yet?" I asked.

Keeping his face in his hands, he shook his head.

I was confused, and suspicious. Philip was either truly surprised to learn that Francine had been murdered and was genuinely distraught at the news. Or he knew he wasn't a good enough actor to pull off pretending not to know—hence the moaning, mumbling, and face covering.

One thing for sure—the cufflink had him rattled. I put my face between two bars and hiss-whispered, "Did you murder Francine?"

He looked over at me. "No."

"Were the two of you having an affair?"

He gave a loud sigh. "Yes. But we haven't been together recently. I was hiding out in Delaware, remember? I have no idea when I lost that cufflink. I have many cufflinks. Didn't even notice that one was missing."

"We're going to have to hand it in to the police," Steve said. "We just wanted to show it to you first."

Philip shot up, came over and grabbed the bars again. "No. Please, no." He looked at Steve, then at me. "No. Just give it to Annie. She knows where it goes. In my bedroom, in the small wooden chest on my dresser, where I keep all my cufflinks."

"Annie?" I stared at him. "You want her to get involved in covering up evidence of a possible crime?"

Philip nodded. "Sure. She'll gladly do it for me."

"You're asking a lot," Steve said. "She'd be breaking the law for you."

I decided to play along, to pretend that Steve and I would really do such a thing. "You might get that innocent girl in trouble with the law," I said. "Is that what you want? Is that fair to her?"

Philip cracked a tiny smile. "She won't mind," he said. "She'll do anything for me."

———

"Guess we won't be taking the cufflink to the police just yet," Steve said as he and I headed to my car.

"Guess we won't." I smiled grimly. "Not until we see how Annie reacts to Philip's instructions about it. What do you think she'll do?"

Steve slowed as we approached my T-Bird. "Mind if I drive again?" he asked, the corners of his eyes crinkling as he flashed me a please-please grin.

He sure did love driving my convertible. We'd left his Buick behind at Francine's barn so we could go visit Philip together and discuss the case on the way.

I loved having the power to make Steve happy. "Sure." I tossed him the keys. "As long as you put the top down."

"Always." He winked. "Whenever the weather allows. Today's hot —but it's a beauty."

"What do you predict Annie will do when we show her the cuff link?" I asked again as Steve opened the passenger door for me and I climbed in.

He got behind the wheel, loosened the levers to lower the top, and glanced over at me. "I think she'll hide her feelings and just do what her boss instructed." He got out of the car, folded the top down, then hopped back in. "Will she be upset when we tell her where the cufflink was found and then confide to her that she'll be hiding evidence? That will be interesting to see."

"If nothing else." I fished my sunglasses out of my purse and slipped them on. "Do you think she knew about Philip's affair with Francine?"

Steve shrugged. "Hard to say, but I'm betting not. I told you from the get-go that I sensed Annie was in love with Philip. I still believe that. Why else would she be so willing to do anything he asks?"

"Why indeed?" I put my head back and smiled as Steve started the car and we headed to Grand Gables. "This should be fun."

———

Steve and I agreed that we needed to get Annie alone.

Fortunately, when we arrived at Grand Gables after stopping at a diner for a quick lunch, we learned that Celeste was out shopping.

"And Miss Rita's up in her room," Annie informed us, holding the front door open only far enough to talk to us, signaling that she wasn't going to let us just breeze in.

"It's you we've come to see," I said. "This won't take long."

"Again?" She pursed her lips at Steve, obviously and rudely avoiding my gaze. "I already told you everything I know about Miss Lorna getting shot."

"This is about Miss Francine getting shot," I said. "We've just come from visiting Mr. Philip in jail, and the police might be charging him with that, too. Because, in case you don't already know it, she's dead. Mr. Philip told us to come see you. Said you could help."

"Me?" Annie kept a tight grip on the door. She shook her head, looking visibly paler than she had a few seconds ago. "I don't see how."

"Mr. Philip instructed us to come see you," Steve said, his voice firm. "And since Miss Celeste has now hired me as well as Story to help him, we're doing what he said. *Can* we come in?"

With a loud sigh, Annie opened the door, watched us enter, then shut it. "Okay. You're in. Now what?"

"Let's go up to Mr. Philip's room." I pointed to the stairs. "We need privacy, and we have something to show you in that room."

Rolling her eyes, Annie nodded unhappily and beckoned for us to follow her.

When we got to Philip's room, I pointed to his dresser. "Over there."

With a puzzled frown, Annie trudged over to the dresser. Steve and I followed.

I whipped the cufflink out of my purse, held it out to her in the palm of my hand, and watched for a reaction.

She looked at it but didn't make a move to take it from me. Just shrugged. "What is that?"

"Take it," I said.

She plucked it out of my hand and held it up to her eyes in an exaggerated, mocking squint. "Okay, I'm looking at it. Still don't know what it is."

I ignored her rudeness. "It's Mr. Philip's cufflink. His initials are on it. Steve and I found it in Miss Francine's barn, near where her body was found. The day after her body was found."

Annie handed it back to me, her face stiff and emotionless. "I don't understand. What does Mr. Philip want me to do? Hide it?"

"He wants you to put it in the box with all his other cufflinks." Steve pointed to the masculine mahogany jewelry box on top of the dresser. "Can you open that please, and let us see the other cuff links in there? We want to see how they're organized."

She shrugged and opened the box.

Steve and I peered inside. It held about ten pairs of cufflinks, coupled together in little separate compartments. Gold, dark blue, dark purple, black.

The silver one, with initials, sat by itself.

Steve picked up the cufflink I was holding and gave it to Annie. "Philip wants you to put this back where it belongs," he told her. "But I must warn you that if you do, you'll be breaking the law. Hiding evidence in a crime. Are you willing to do that?"

Annie shrugged, dropped the cufflink next to its twin, and shut the box. "There." She sniffed. "Done."

Okay, now Steve and I had to get it back. "Wait," I said, as if something important had just occurred to me. "I don't want to get into trouble with the police, do you Steve?"

With an exaggerated frown, he shook his head and met my gaze. "No ..."

I pulled the box toward me and flipped it open. "We need to turn the cufflink into the police, as evidence." I snatched up the one I had found in the barn and shoved it back in my purse. "Sorry to bother you, Annie, but we've changed our minds."

"What?" Annie dropped her blasé attitude and grabbed for my purse. "Give me that back."

I stepped out of her reach and shook my head. "No. Steve and I could lose our P.I. licenses if we were to get caught hiding evidence in a murder investigation."

"No," Annie said. "You're not going to get caught. I won't tell."

"Tell what?"

We all turned.

Rita came into the room, her limp more pronounced than I'd noticed before. "What's going on here?"

"Nothing," Annie snapped. "This is private."

I didn't see any reason not to tell Rita about the cufflink. Or that Philip had confessed to having an affair with Francine. After all, Gus wasn't keeping it a secret any longer.

I was also curious as to how Rita would react to the news. It was entirely possible that she'd murdered Lorna and Francine to get them out of the way so she could marry Philip.

So, I told her. About the cuff link.

And the hay rolling high jinks.

And she had an emotional meltdown.

"Lies, lies, everything you just said is a lie," Rita screamed at me. "None of it can be true. It can't be true. Because Philip loves me."

"Story's telling the truth," Steve said softly, obviously trying to calm Rita down. "Philip is not the man you think he is. He's a womanizer."

But Rita was not having it. "No." She covered her ears and shook her head back and forth. "More lies. I don't want to hear any more. Stop, just stop."

"Philip enjoyed the hunt," I shouted. "He loved seducing and charming women so he could capture their hearts so he could win their bodies." I shot a quick glance at Annie. "While married to Lorna, he collected women like trophies."

Annie gave a loud gasp.

Rita limped toward me. "How do *you* know, Miss Private Eye?"

I met Steve's gaze. "Because Philip tried it with me."

Annie made a strange gagging sound.

Rita gave a harsh laugh. "You? When?"

"In the hotel room in Delaware. When he checked me in as his wife. I wasn't swayed by his charm, and I defended myself, but other women were not so lucky. If he didn't try to get you into bed, Rita, consider yourself the fortunate exception."

I looked at Annie.

Steve looked at Annie.

Annie's face was now eerily pale. As rigid as a statue, she stared into space at nothing, her eyes unblinking, her chest not moving, as if she'd stopped breathing.

Rita stepped toward Annie. "Tell Story that you don't believe a word she's saying." Rita grabbed the maid's arm and shook it. "Tell her, tell her ..."

Annie blinked. Looked at Rita. At me. At Steve. And then, with a whimper, ran out of the room.

———

I wasn't finished with Annie. I ran after her.

Steve called to me, "Where are you going?"

"I forgot to ask Annie a really important question," I shouted back. "I want to do it in private. Wait there."

I found the maid in the kitchen, at the table, leaning over it, her face pressed into her arms.

I walked over. "Annie."

She didn't move or look up. "Go away."

"I just need to ask you one more question," I said, taking a seat across from her. "Just one more question for you, then I'll leave you alone."

She kept her face in her arms. "No. No more questions. Go away."

I knew what she was thinking. She was afraid I was going to ask her if Philip had charmed her into bed. But that wasn't what I was going to ask. Because I was pretty sure I knew the truth about that. And that she would just answer me with a lie.

No, the one question that I needed to ask her now was far more important. And I was mad at myself for not asking it before.

"Just one more question, Annie," I whispered. "I'm just going to sit here and wait ..."

She slapped her hands hard on the table and glared at me. "What?"

"As I recall, you had off the day that Miss Lorna was murdered."

She looked confused. "That ain't a question, lady. But yeah. I did."

"So—where were you that morning?" I asked. "You live here at Grand Gables, so were you up in your room?"

She smirked, held up two fingers. "That's two questions, lady."

I sighed, held up one finger. "Where were you that morning?"

She shrugged. "Down the Shore."

Down at the Shore? The New Jersey Shore? I sat back in my chair, surprised. The closest New Jersey Shore town was at least a two-hour drive away by car. "How'd you get there?" I blurted. "Who'd you go with?"

She shook her head again and gave me a deeper smirk. "You said one question."

I pressed my lips together. Hard. I blew out a breath. "Please, please tell me, who did you go with? I love going to the Shore myself, Annie. It's one of my favorite things to do. And honestly, I'm just surprised you had a way to get there. I didn't think you had a car."

She stared at me with narrow-eyed distain. "I have friends."

I spread my hands. "Okay. And ...?"

She gave a grunt-sigh. "I went with my friend, Marie—okay? She picked me up—okay? Real early that morning—okay?"

"Marie? She sounds like a nice friend to have. Where does she live?"

"Outside Chatsworth."

"Where's that?"

"Pine Barrens."

I shook my head, confused. "The Pine Barrens, in New Jersey? The Pine Barrens are nowhere close to here. It's probably an hour and a half drive."

She shrugged. "So?"

"You're telling me that Marie drove from the Pine Barrens here, picked you up, and then drove to the Shore? Where at the Shore?"

"Wildwood." She gave me a sullen stare. "I already told the police all this."

I didn't recall seeing it in the police report. Maybe I'd skimmed past it. "I'd like to talk to Marie," I said. "What's Marie's last name?"

Annie's eyes went big. "You gonna go see her?" She sounded surprised, but not upset by the idea.

"I might. You grew up in the Pine Barrens, right? Is she your childhood friend?"

"Yep. She's a Piney, like me." For the first time ever, Annie graced me with a smile. It was a tiny flicker of one, but she was no longer acting sullen.

Then I realized that she found the idea of me going to find her friend in the deep woods of New Jersey rather amusing.

And that smile gave me a tiny chill.

"Hale. Marie Hale." Annie's friendly grin widened, then turned sarcastic. "Won't Marie love it when you show up looking for her? You, a real-life private eye? Marie will be so excited. Nothing exciting ever happens in Chatsworth. Yes, siree."

I pressed my lips together and held Annie's amused gaze. Not sure what to say, I decided to press my luck and keep going. While I was nosing around her neck of the woods, why not look up her family? Maybe they'd find me just as exciting. What did I have to lose?

"I think I *will* take a drive to Chatsworth," I said. "I would like to meet Marie and confirm your alibi. And while I'm there, maybe look up your folks. You know, just to say hi."

She squinted at me, suddenly sullen again. "Okay, lady, yeah, go check out my alibi if that's what you need to do. Cause it's true. I was on the beach and boardwalk in Wildwood all day that day with Marie. She'll tell you."

Then her smile came back—and so did my chills. She leaned across the table. "Bert and Mattie. My parents are Bert and Mattie Leeds. And please tell them hello for me. They'll get a big kick out of that. My brothers, too. I got a bunch of brothers."

I raised my eyebrows. "Okay, thank you. I will. And thanks for answering my questions. *All* my questions."

She gave a one shoulder shrug. "Sure, lady. The woods are pretty. Enjoy the drive."

The way she said that gave me pause, because her snarky tone said, *I hope you crash into a tree and never come back.*

I decided to ignore her sarcasm and veiled threats—if that's what they were. Because I had gotten far more information out of her than I'd expected. A trip to the Pine Barrens might lead me nowhere in my investigation. Might end up being a complete dead end. But it was worth a shot.

Because a fluttery feeling in the pit of my stomach told me there was something off about sly, sad, sullen Annie Leeds. And I needed to find out what it was.

Anyway, I didn't intend to go alone because Steve would go with me. He would love that road trip—especially if I let him drive my car.

I left the kitchen smiling.

Twenty-Two

I was proud of myself.

For once, I'd remembered to pack my gun. It was in my purse, tucked by my feet, on the passenger side floor of my T-Bird as Steve and I traveled through Southern New Jersey's deep pine forests.

Yesterday, Steve had agreed to accompany me to the Pine Barrens. After meeting up at my office, where he left his car, we'd gotten ourselves off to an early morning start.

"So glad you finally remembered to bring your gun." Steve glanced over at me, then put his eyes back on the two-lane road that for miles had been taking us through beautiful wilderness.

No houses. No towns. No stores. No gas stations. Just trees, trees, and more pine trees.

"This is the kind of place where you want to be armed," Steve added. "We're not that many miles from Philadelphia or New York City, but it feels like we've left civilization far behind."

"Sure does," I agreed, admiring the view. As Annie had said, the woods were pretty.

And romantic. With the convertible top down. A balmy breeze blowing my hair. The sweet, earthy scent of pine delighting my nose. And the handsome guy next to me wearing a contented grin as his strong hands gripped the wheel.

The woodlands, known as the Atlantic coastal pine barrens, stretched across seven New Jersey counties. The sandy, acidic soil didn't allow for farming, but it did support interesting flora and fauna in addition to pine trees—orchids, carnivorous plants, and large patches of rare pigmy pitch pine trees.

The area's many bogs, streams, and waterways were also ideal for growing cranberries, an industry that employed many residents. Their ancestors had been carving out lives for themselves in these rural backwoods since the 1700s. I'd heard that during the American Revolution, most Pineys had sided with the British, making them traitors in the eyes of their patriot neighbors after the war.

"What do we know about Marie?" Steve glanced over at me. "I'm still amazed that Annie was so willing to fork over information to you about her friend."

I raked my fingers through my hair. "The only thing I got out of Annie was Marie's first and last names and the name of the town where she lives. I was happy to get that much, although it probably just means Marie will confirm Annie's alibi. Why else would that sex kitten housekeeper have been so helpful?"

"You think Annie really spent that day in Wildwood?"

"Sounds plausible."

"So why track Marie down?" Steve grinned. "Because it's a good excuse for a road trip?" He laughed. "Not that I'm complaining—definitely not complaining."

"I want to find out more about Annie." I reached down for my purse, fished a cotton hair tie, grabbed hold of my windswept locks, and pulled them into a messy ponytail. "I also want to hear Annie's alibi from her friend's lips," I said. "See if Marie knows anything about the men in Annie's life. Because I think you're right. I think that little maid is in love with the master of the house."

"Strange that the police report didn't mention anything about where Annie claimed to be that day," Steve said. "Did they ask her about it, then forget to put it in the records?"

Steve and I had stopped at the police station to hand in the cuff link and look at the report on Francine's death before heading to the Pine Barrens. The report didn't contain much that we hadn't already known. It also confirmed what we'd suspected—that she was killed with one bullet to the back of the head. Same type and caliber as the one that had killed Lorna.

While at the station, we'd also taken another look at the report on Lorna's murder but saw nothing significant about Annie except that she'd had the day off.

"I think the cops were so focused on Philip that they never seriously considered anyone else," I said. "He also didn't do himself any favors by trying to collect on her million-dollar life insurance policy so quickly. Can't say that I blame the police for zeroing in on him as the obvious suspect."

"No." Steve shook his head. "But let's go over who else could have done it." He drummed his fingers on the wheel. "There's Victor Bravo. He could have murdered Lorna to inherit her horses. Only he doesn't seem to want them."

"Right."

"Then we have Madame Z, who could have murdered Lorna for revenge." Steve glanced at me, then back at the road. "Only that would have meant killing the goose that laid the golden eggs. Which would have been incredibly stupid."

"Right."

"Then there's Rita, who could have murdered her sister out of lust for her husband. Except she doesn't strike me as the type."

"No, she doesn't. But you never know."

"It's also possible that Francine shot her friend, Lorna, and that someone knew it and killed Francine in revenge." Steve shook his head. "But that just doesn't make any sense, especially given how Francine died."

"I agree."

Steve frowned. "Then we have Annie. How does she figure in on all this?"

"I think she's involved. I just have that feeling. But nothing more."

Steve pointed to a sign ahead that said, Chatsworth, ten miles. "Hopefully we'll get more, Story. Looks like we're getting close."

———

Ten miles of pine trees later, we pulled into town.

If you could call it that. Centrally located in the Pine Barrens, and one of the area's few towns, Chatsworth was far smaller than I'd expected. A traffic light, several blocks of houses, a couple of stores, a gas station, and a café.

"Everybody here must know everybody here," I told Steve. "Marie Hale should be easy to find."

He nodded and parked the car in front of the Chatsworth Café.

It looked cozy and welcoming, the kind of place where you could get a nice home cooked meal. Red and white checked curtains on the windows, a wide wooden front porch, red geraniums in pots by the door. It took up the first floor of a historic building from the Victorian era, now painted pale blue with white trim. The second story appeared to house apartments.

We climbed the steps to the porch and opened the door.

It was a bright, cheery eatery.

Sunlight poured in from the large window facing the street. Tables were covered with white tablecloths. But—no customers.

A bald man wearing a dark red apron around his big belly stood behind a cash register, counting dollar bills.

A young woman in a cherry-red dress and white apron was sweeping the floor with a whisk broom.

Both stopped what they were doing when Steve and I came in and closed the door behind us.

"Can we help you?" the man asked with a questioning smile.

The woman, a pretty brunette, pointed to a clock on the wall. "It's ten o'clock, so we just closed for breakfast. We open again at eleven for lunch. Maybe you can come back then?"

I looked at Steve. "That's tempting."

"Actually, we're looking for a woman named Marie Hale," Steve said. "Do you know her?"

The woman stared at him, then beamed. "I sure do. That's me."

Then her wide smile faltered, and a cautious look crept into her eyes. "Wait ... I'm not in any trouble, am I?"

I couldn't believe our luck. I quickly shook my head. "No, no. Not at all."

Clearly Annie had not called her friend to tell her I was coming. Or maybe Marie was confused by Steve's presence. She was looking Steve up and down like he was a movie star. With stars in her eyes, and a hesitant, shy, flirtatious smile.

Steve was dressed in jeans and a gray cotton shirt and old sneakers. Nothing special. Nothing fancy. Clothes that would make most men blend into a crowd.

Most men, not Steve. As far as Marie Hale was concerned, I was suddenly invisible.

Great.

I cleared my throat. "We're private investigators. From Philadelphia."

She tore her eyes away from Steve and looked at me. It seemed to take a minute to sink in. "What? Private investigators? You mean you guys are detectives? Real life detectives?" That wary look in her eyes came back. "Wait ... you're here to see me?"

I nodded. "About your friend, Annie Leeds. I was talking to her yesterday and she suggested I come talk to you."

"What about?" the bald man asked, his voice sharp and alarmed.

Frowning, he came out from behind the counter, wiping his hands on his apron. "Marie is my daughter. I'm Sam Hale, owner of this place, and I have a right to know what you want to talk to my girl about."

"Are you aware of the recent murder of Annie's employer, Lorna Cranston?" I asked.

"Yes, of course, we know all about it." Marie gave her father a let-me-handle-this glare. "I was down the Shore with Annie the day it happened. Shook Annie up real bad, I tell you."

"And how many times do I have to tell *you* to quit being friends with Annie Leeds?" Sam Hale snapped at his daughter. "That girl's been nothing but trouble since she was a tot. Whole family's nothing but trouble. For God's sake, everybody knows they're related to the Jersey Devil."

"The Jersey Devil?" Steve gave a throaty chuckle. "Are you talking about that myth—"

"Ain't no myth, son." The café owner shook his head. "Everybody around these parts knows the Jersey Devil is real."

"Sure, sure." I shot Steve a let-me-ask-the-questions look. "It's sort of New Jersey's version of Bigfoot or the Abominable Snowman. From what I've heard, the story goes that about a hundred years ago a woman named Mrs. Leeds had ten or so kids and didn't want any more. Is that right?"

The Hales nodded.

"Then," I said, "when she gave birth to her eleventh child—or maybe it was her thirteenth—she took one look at him and screamed because he looked like a monster, not a human baby. Hairy, with wings, she declared him a child of the devil and threw him out the window, into the woods, where he flew away. He survived and thrived, and many people claim he still haunts the woods today."

I looked back and forth between Marie and her father. "Did I get it right?"

Sam Hale smirked. "Close enough. Anyway, everybody knows Annie Leeds and her folks are descended from one of those other kids of Mrs. Leeds. And that they all got some of the devil in them. Cause they sure act like it."

"Fascinating," Steve muttered.

"Yes." I turned to Marie. "I would love to ask you more about the

Leeds family, and Annie in particular, especially regarding that day trip you two took to the Shore. Could you give us a few minutes?"

She gave the wood floor another quick swipe with her broom, then leaned it against the wall under the clock. She looked at her father. "Dad, don't you have a lot of work to do to get ready for lunch? These detectives are here to talk to me, not you, so ..."

He took the hint and pointed to the kitchen behind the counter. "Okay, okay. But make this quick, Marie. I'll be needing your help."

When her father was out of her sight and out of her mind, Marie waved us over to a round table in the corner. Then she went over and locked the door and came back and sat next to Steve. "So ..." Marie gave him that fawning, googly-eyed gaze again. "You haven't told me your names."

"I'm Story Smith," I said, "and this is Steve Evans."

Marie turned her eyes to me. "I can't believe you're a lady detective. So cool."

"Annie thought you would think so." I put my elbows on the white tablecloth and leaned across the table to put less distance between us. "It sounds like you've been friends with her for a long time?"

Marie shrugged. "Since first grade. My dad never liked Annie because he didn't like anybody in the Leeds family. People around here don't have a lot of money, but the Leeds never seemed to have any. They live on the edge of town, half in the woods, in a rundown cabin. I always felt sorry for Annie, though I tried not to let her know it."

"She left town a couple of years ago, right?" I picked up a salt-shaker and moved it back and forth in front of me. "To work at the racetrack?"

"Yes. I was happy for her. We kept in touch. Wrote letters back and forth. Then one day, she told me she got a job as a maid, in Pennsylvania. Working for rich people. Meaning she got to live in a mansion, so I was even more happy for her. After that, we got to sometimes talk on the phone."

"So, these rich people, the Cranstons, let her use their phone?" Steve asked.

"Yep. Even though calling me was long distance. My family lives upstairs." Marie pointed to the ceiling. "In an apartment above our café, and we have a phone." She said the word phone with pride. I got the feeling that the Hales were better off financially than many of their neighbors.

"Long distance is expensive," I said, sliding the peppershaker next to the saltshaker.

"Annie said Miss Lorna and Mr. Philip didn't care how much it cost. She loved working for them, thought they were nice." Marie pressed a hand to her forehead and looked forlornly at Steve. "And now ... I still can't believe Miss Lorna is dead."

"Speaking of which ..." I used my now-let's-get-down-to-business voice, compelling Marie to look at me. "Do you remember what time you picked Annie up that day to go to the Shore?"

She shrugged. "Around eight, I think."

I nibbled on my thumbnail. "Are you sure it wasn't any earlier?"

She scratched her head. "Yeah, I'm sure. Because I had to leave here around six-thirty in the morning to get there by then. After I picked her up, we still had a more than two-hour drive to Wildwood."

"Do you own a car?" Steve asked.

"My dad lets me borrow his truck sometimes." She smiled at Steve. "He didn't ask who I was going to the Shore with, but I think he knew. Annie and I have a tradition. At least one day every summer we go to the Shore. As shoobies. You know what that means?"

She'd directed the question to Steve, but I answered. "Shoobies are day-trippers who bring their own lunch, sometimes in a shoebox, to save money. It's a derogatory term of sorts."

She nodded. "Anyway, we packed our lunch in sacks and spent the day on the beach and then went to the boardwalk. I think I dropped Annie back at her place around eight-thirty that night. I didn't go in with her, so I didn't hear about the murder till later."

I clicked the salt and pepper shakers together. "What did you and Annie talk about while you were on the beach?"

Marie cocked her head, as if thinking it over. "Uhm ... Annie talked about her job a lot. How much she loved it."

"What, cleaning toilets?" Steve raised his eyebrows at me.

"What did she love about her job, Marie?" I flashed Steve a warning frown, to please cut the sarcasm and let me do the talking.

Marie looked at Steve and giggled. Okay, so she found him funny. *Fine.*

"Annie said Mr. Philip was the nicest man she ever met," Marie said. "He not only let her use the phone whenever she wanted, he let her swim in the pool."

Oh. My. Lord. I swallowed hard, then stared at her. "Swim in the pool? When?"

"Whenever Miss Lorna and Miss Celeste were out shopping, or whatever. Mr. Philip bought her a real pretty bathing suit. She wore it on the beach at Wildwood. Got a lot of looks from the boys there. Lots of whistles, you know? I was jealous."

"Because ...?" Steve let that question linger as he met my gaze.

"Because it's ... you know ... low cut. It fit Annie ... well." Marie glanced at Steve out of the corner of her eye and blushed. "You know what I mean, right?"

"Did Annie go swimming in the Cranston pool alone?" I asked before Steve could answer.

"I don't know." Marie narrowed her eyes at me, and a look came over her that told me she was becoming uncomfortable with the turn of our conversation. "Why?"

"Just wondering," I said, "if maybe Mr. Philip went swimming with her?"

She looked down at the table. "I think maybe ... probably. Why?"

"Just asking."

Marie turned back to Steve. "Annie loved swimming in the pool, is all I know. She told me she loved lollygagging around, relaxing in the sun. That she really liked that kind of life." Marie blinked at Steve and smiled, as if she'd suddenly thought of something else that he might like to hear. "I think Mr. Philip taught Annie how to swim. Yeah. That's right. She did tell me that. She didn't know how to swim, and he taught her, so she wouldn't drown."

Wow. This was getting better and better. Juicier and juicier. But sad. Very sad for Lorna. And what about Celeste? Had she not been aware of what was going on between her father and the housekeeper?

Not as far as I could tell. Apparently, she had not seen what she did not want to see. Even though I was certain that Annie and Philip were doing more than swimming together. I would have bet Celeste's thousand-dollar fee on that.

Marie looked over at the clock. "I need to go," she said. "We're opening for lunch soon and my dad's going to kill me if I don't go lend him a hand in the kitchen now."

I stood, too. "One more quick question," I said. "Steve and I would like to go see the Leeds family. Can you tell us where they live? Annie asked me to go see them, and tell them she said, "hi."

Marie scrunched up her nose, looking at me funny, like I'd lost my mind. "Really? She hates her folks. And her brothers. Her dad always beat her, and her mom never stopped him, and her brothers are all creepy. Annie always warned me to stay away from her four brothers. She would never say why, and I was afraid to ask."

They sounded like a fun bunch. Even more reason to pay them a visit. And anyway, I had a gun.

"I'd like to honor Annie's request and go see them," I said. "Do you have their address?"

Marie scoffed. "I don't remember their actual address, but they'll be easy enough to find. Take the main road out of town."

She pointed out the window, to the town's lone traffic light. "Head west about a mile or so. Look for a mailbox on the right. Big, rusted mailbox, kind of leaning to one side. Has the name Leeds painted on it in big red letters. You won't be able to see much of their shack from the road—but you can't miss it."

TWENTY-THREE

"What do you plan to talk to these people about?" Steve, back behind the wheel, shot me a glance out of the corner of his eye as we headed west toward the Leeds homestead.

Pressing my lips together, I sighed and admitted I wasn't sure. "Depends. On how they treat us. I'm just going to wing it. Just want to see what these people are like. Not even sure why. To satisfy my curiosity, I guess?"

"Good enough reason." Steve nodded. "All good private eyes are curious, or they wouldn't be in the business. We need to be more curious than cautious—and you're proving you have what it takes, gumshoe gal."

A compliment from Steve meant a lot. "Gee, thanks, Steve."

"You're welcome."

Then I realized what he was implying. "Wait. You think we're taking a risk by going to see the Leeds clan ... that they might really be dangerous."

He gave a wry grin. "Well, they're rumored to be related to the Jersey Devil—so there's a good chance."

"Guess we'll find out," I said. "Marie was a little vague about Annie's brothers. I want to see for myself what makes those boys so bad."

The place proved to be as easy to locate as Marie had claimed. Although someone had straightened up the mailbox and painted over the rust.

A narrow dirt drive, pitted with holes the size of craters, led to the cabin, partially visible through trees.

Steve pulled in a short distance and braked, keeping the engine running. He turned to me. "Well?"

"Well, what?"

"What do you want to do now? This is the place. Want to go up and knock?"

Was he serious? I couldn't tell if he was serious. I peered through a tangle of tree branches at the shack where Annie's family still lived, and a shiver skittered through me.

If the small wooden structure had ever worn a coat of paint, there was no sign of it now.

Broken steps led up to a small porch that tilted sideways. Grimy windows, covered with blackish looking curtains, were downright ghoulish. A chimney, missing a few bricks, jutted out of a rotted roof.

The pathetic house looked as if it had been slapped together haphazardly fifty years ago and was threatening to collapse into a pile of rotted wood at any minute.

I didn't even want to risk knocking on the door. Which, at closer glance, stood partially open. Maybe I should go to the porch and holler to see if anyone was home?

I glanced back at Steve. He was giving me an I-dare-you grin. Which faded when I gave him a just-watch-me-smile.

His hand shot out and grabbed my arm as I opened my car door. "No, Story, wait. I'll go."

I pulled away. "I can handle this." I picked up my purse and waved it at him. "My gun's in here, just in case."

Steve grabbed my arm again. "I'm going with you."

"Steve—"

BAM ...

A gunshot ... was that a gunshot?

Steve pulled me toward him and threw his body over mine.

"Is that somebody shooting at us?" I whispered.

"Sounds like it." Steve whispered back, his breath tickling my ear.

We waited. No more shots. Only silence. Eerie silence.

"I hope they didn't hit my car," I said.

"Don't think so. I think they were just trying to scare us off."

"What'll we do now?"

He reached over and opened my glove compartment.

"What are you doing?" I whispered.

"Getting my gun," he said grimly.

"I didn't know you brought it with you."

"Thought it might come in handy." Steve sat up, fired a shot in the air, and shouted, "We're armed, too. We don't want trouble. We just want to talk."

"About what?" A tall, skinny man with an unruly thatch of reddish-blonde hair that hadn't seen a haircut in many a moon ambled toward us with a rifle slung over his shoulder.

He had an odd, goofy grin on his face, made goofier by the fact that he was missing one of his top front teeth.

I sat up and gave him a friendly smile. "Hello." I wanted to say more, but the man's disheveled appearance temporarily rendered me speechless. He was wearing dirty denim overalls, much too big for his lanky frame, and was barefoot.

Goofy Grin looked at me, then at Steve, then lowered his rifle to his side. "What're you two city-slick-folk doing here? Pa said we had visitors and he sent me out to warn you we don't like visitors."

"Uhm ..." I was trying to figure out which one of Goofy Grin's eyes was looking at me. They seemed to work independently, when one looked up, the other looked down. "Uhm ... your sister, Annie sent us. She said to tell the family hello."

"Annie?" He gawked at me like I had completely lost my marbles. "Did you say Annie? We ain't seen that twit in years."

Steve, who was still holding his gun, put it down next to him on the seat. "We're friends of Annie's and my girlfriend here is right. Annie told us she used to live in Chatsworth and since we happened to be passing through town, we decided to come say hello. Give you the message that Annie misses all of you—hopes you're all well."

Knitting his mean-looking bushy eyebrows together in a baffled frown, Goofy Grin barked, "Who? Who the hell is Annie wishing well?"

"You and your brothers and your mom and dad," I said, as if we were talking about normal people and a normal family. People not related to a mythical devil.

A glint in one eye, then the other, conveyed suspicion. "What did Annie say my folks' names are?"

"Bert and Mattie. Bert and Mattie Leeds." I was proud of myself for remembering.

"Yeah, guess you really did come from Annie." He spat a stream of saliva on the ground. "She tell you my name?"

"No. She only said she had a bunch of brothers."

"It's Calvin." He squinted at me. "And I got a message for Annie. Go to hell."

"She's got a good job now," I said. "I wasn't sure if you knew—"

"Thinks she's a big deal, don't she? According to Marie, she's living in a big house with rich people. Why don't she ever come visit?"

"Maybe she will," I lied. I felt sorry for Calvin Leeds. Living in unwashed poverty, shunned, ridiculed by his neighbors, labeled dangerous and scary, when the scariest thing about him seemed to be his appearance.

Annie had escaped. But if Calvin was any indication, she had gotten all the looks and brains in the family.

"I'll tell Annie you miss her," I said.

"Tell her she broke Ma's heart," he said. "Tell her that. She broke Ma's heart by leaving and never coming back."

He almost had me in tears. Almost. "Sure." I nodded. "Sure. I'll give her the message."

"Now get out." Both eyes took on a mean look. "We don't like visitors. Pa especially. You don't want him coming out here."

Steve put the car in reverse. "Sure buddy. We're leaving. Just tell the folks we said, 'Hi,' for Annie. Bye now."

The T-Bird bounced into a crater.

Steve gunned the engine to get us out, throwing dirt, pebbles, and weedy stuff into the air.

I winced. Next time we'd be taking his car.

____

"Girlfriend?" I turned to face Steve as he drove us back to Chatsworth. "Did you call me your girlfriend back there?"

He laughed. "What of it?"

"I'm not your girlfriend."

"As you keep reminding me." He laughed again. "Relax. It was just a cover story. Tried to quick think of a good one since I had no idea what that strange man might do. He was armed." Steve reached over and gave my left hand a quick squeeze. "Couldn't exactly call you my wife because you're not wearing a ring."

I rubbed my bare ring finger, suddenly feeling silly. "Yeah. And we're not friends with Annie, either, but you claimed we were. Good job. Now I understand Annie better, for whatever that's worth."

He nodded. "And we know what Annie's family is like. Or, one of her brothers, anyway. Who, I'm willing to bet, is much like the rest of them."

"I can't believe that many people live in that dilapidated shack," I said. "I'm sorry we didn't meet the rest of the clan. Calvin was interesting."

"I agree." Steve gave me a sideways glance. "But what now? Where do you suggest we go from here?"

I sighed. "I'm so hungry right now, all I can think about is lunch."

With a teasing smile, Steve squeezed my hand again. "Okay, girlfriend. Let's go back to the Chatsworth Cafe. My treat."

____

Steve and I snagged the last available table at the café, where Marie—after a quick wink at Steve—treated us like all the other customers. She was too busy to do otherwise, and I was glad because I just wanted to eat.

We both ordered the meatloaf special, which was great. Then we climbed into my T-Bird and headed back to my office, where Steve picked up his Buick and I went in to type my daily report.

I was glad we had gone to Chatsworth. If nothing else came of it, I'd at least picked up some interesting tidbits about Annie from Marie. Most importantly that her alibi was far from solid because she had not left for the Shore as early as she'd implied.

I inserted a sheet of paper in my typewriter and began typing. Only the more I got down on paper, the more frustrated I became. After nine days, there were far too many questions and uncertainties in this case. And the man I'd been hired to prove innocent was now behind bars.

Who murdered Lorna Cranston?

Who murdered Francine Montague?

Were they murdered by the same person?

If so, why? And did that mean someone else might be next? Not if Philip was the killer, because he was locked up, behind bars. But deep down, I didn't believe he was the killer. Everything pointed to the fact that he was, but something was missing.

I'd left my office door partially open for air, and was staring into space, trying to think, when it opened all the way and Wendy walked in.

I greeted her with a smile. "Thanks for coming by. I needed a break."

"Fun day?" She plopped herself down in the chair next to my

desk. "You look a little windblown." Pressing her lips together in a pensive frown, she cocked her head. "Actually, I take that back. You look *a lot* windblown and kind of frazzled."

"Frazzled and frustrated." I ran my fingers through my hair, then winced. "My hair's a knotted mess. Steve and I took a road trip to the Pine Barrens today in my T-Bird, top down."

"Steve and you ... ooooh." Wendy gave me a knowing grin.

"Wipe that look off your face. It's not what you think."

She pursed her lips into an exaggerated pout. "Oh, darn."

"Don't get me wrong. The road trip was fun. But I'm frustrated because I don't feel like I'm getting anywhere with this latest case, even though Steve was recently hired to help me. There are so many puzzle pieces."

Wendy got up and shut the door, then came back and sat down. "Want to share with me what you can?" she asked in a loud whisper. "Maybe I can help."

I pressed my lips together and held her eager gaze. What would it hurt to talk things over with her? She was my part-time receptionist, as well as my new friend, and I trusted her.

"Okay," I said, then described my case and the people involved, and all the possible suspects, and then the second murder. I didn't name any names and Wendy didn't ask.

"Gadzooks," she said. "So, you're saying the maid, who sounds like one of your suspects, is from a crazy family in the woods."

"Well, poor. Strange and poor."

"And she's in love with her boss? A guy much older than she is?"

"She's acting like it."

"Hmmm. And you think they were probably carrying on behind his wife's back? His now-dead wife's back?"

"Probably."

"Come on, Story. This sounds like more than *probably*."

I sighed. "Right. But *so*? What does it *prove*?"

"As far as murder, nothing. But ..."

Wendy wiggled her eyebrows up and down. "It might mean something happened to that sweet young maid. You know, during all that fooling around with her boss. Maybe she planned it and maybe she didn't ... but even if she didn't ..."

I sucked in a breath. Oh, no. I stared at Wendy. "Oh my God," I whispered. "Sweet young maid ... she might be pregnant."

TWENTY-FOUR

The time had come. What I'd been putting off, dreading.

I needed to have a serious talk with Celeste about her father's philandering. Find out if she'd ever suspected anything, saw anything, heard anything that made her wonder.

At some point she must have had her moments. He'd been sneaking off to frolic with the next-door neighbor for years. Hadn't he ever returned home with hay in his hair?

And he'd been swimming with the pretty young housekeeper for who knows how long. Had Celeste ever come home and caught them together in the pool? Or just getting out of the pool? With wet hair, and sheepish smiles, when there was no reason for them to have wet hair or sheepish smiles?

I had to wonder the same thing about poor Lorna, but sadly, she wasn't around to ask.

Celeste was, and I had to confront her with the truth. Alone. I needed to speak to her alone, without Steve, because she acted different—distracted—around him.

With that plan in mind, I told Wendy goodbye, finished typing my report, went home, and got a good night's sleep.

Then the next morning, I called Steve's office and left a message with his secretary receptionist, Alice, for him to meet me at Grand Gables at noon.

Unlike me, Steve could afford full time help, and Alice was a jewel —an older woman, devoted to Steve, who treated him like her grandson. I'd met her once and liked her a lot.

"Steve tells me you two are working together again, dear," Alice said. "I think that's wonderful. You're good for him."

I was afraid to ask what she meant by that, so didn't, although it did give me a nice, warm feeling in the center of my chest. I didn't tell Alice why I wanted Steve to meet me at noon, only that there was something I needed to do first, and she sweetly agreed to give him the message.

No matter what Celeste ended up telling me, or didn't tell me, about her father's love life, Steve and I would need to pay a visit to the Cranston family doctor. It was a long shot, but we'd need to find out if Annie was his patient. And if—another long shot—he would reveal if she had visited him recently.

It was do that—or ask Annie to her face if she was pregnant. Which of course she would deny, so that wouldn't work.

No, I'd pay a morning visit to Celeste. And in the afternoon, call on the family physician, hopefully with Steve.

I got to Grand Gables at ten, hoping and praying that Celeste would be home and dressed and up and about.

She answered the door, not Annie.

"Story." She peered behind me. "Have you come alone? Where's Steve? Do you have news? Good news, I hope?"

"Steve will stop by later," I said. "We've been hard at work, and I want to bring you up to date, but I also need to talk to you privately about a delicate matter. Is there a place we can go?"

Celeste's face fell. "A delicate matter?" A look of alarm came into her eyes. "You're scaring me, Story." She waved me inside. "Let's go to the porch. We'll be alone there."

"Where's Annie?" I asked.

"Upstairs, vacuuming."

"And Rita?"

Celeste made a face. "Still in bed, I presume. She sleeps late."

No telling when Rita would get up, and I didn't want to be interrupted, so the porch made me nervous.

Celeste was wearing a flowered sundress, and I had on a skirt and sleeveless blouse. "It's a nice day," I said. "Why don't we go sit by the pool? We'll be sure to have privacy there."

Celeste shrugged. "Fine with me. Let's go."

The aquamarine water sparkled in the sun, so inviting I wished I'd brought my bathing suit to swim in the Olympic-size pool. Pushing that thought aside, I pointed to one of several patio tables shaded by yellow and white striped umbrellas.

We made our way around a line of lounge chairs facing the water. I took a patio chair facing the house to keep an eye out for potential interruptions.

Celeste sat across from me and waved a hand. "Okay, Story, what's this all about? Like I said, you have me worried."

Might as well just get to the point. I leaned toward her. "Was your father faithful to your mother? I mean, was there ever a time when you thought that maybe he wasn't?"

Her jaw dropped. She stared at me. "What are you talking about?"

Okay, so she wasn't going to make this easy. I leaned closer and held her gaze. "I'm wondering, Celeste, if your father might have had an affair. That you know about. Because as you've said, he's good-looking and charming, and women are attracted to him, even your Aunt Rita, and so ... I'm wondering ... if maybe he gave into the temptation to ... you know ..."

Celeste's gaze turned hostile. "No. I don't know. Why don't you tell me, Story. What should I know?"

I put my head back and sighed. Then I squinted at the long, softly padded lounge chairs, which were more than wide enough for two.

"Do you think your father, maybe, uhm, even once, succumbed to the charms of a beautiful woman who threw herself at him, and uh, took her to bed?"

"No!" Celeste narrowed her eyes at me. "How dare you even suggest such a thing? Why are you even suggesting such a thing?"

She paused, and the look she gave me shot daggers into my heart. "I know why you wanted to have this conversation in private. Just me and you. Without Steve being here. Which annoys me because I hired him to help you."

I shook my head, confused. "Why?"

"Because if he was here, I would fire you and hire him exclusively. Which I still might do."

"Please don't do that, Celeste." I willed myself to remain calm and professional. "You are misunderstanding me," I said. "I've been working hard to uncover the truth about your mother's murder, and it's taken me to some ugly places. I wish that were not so. I wish I could come up with a suspect and a scenario that has nothing to do with your father, but so far that's not the case. The truth is the truth, and my goal is to uncover it, which is Steve's goal, too."

"Steve ..." Celeste gave a humorless laugh. "Are you in love with him?"

Her question threw me. I was the one who was supposed to be asking questions. "This has nothing to do with me, or Steve," I said. "This has to do with your father and the women in his life."

"Is Steve in love with you?"

My heart jumped. "What are you talking about?"

"You're blushing, Story. You know exactly what I'm talking about."

She was changing the subject. And she was good at it. But was she doing it because she really believed her father had been the faithful, loving husband he'd pretended to be? Or because a part of her, which she didn't want to acknowledge, knew better?

"I want Steve back." She smiled. "And I'm going to get him back. I have never wanted any other man, and I never will."

"Again," I said firmly. "This is not about Steve. I came to ask you about your father and any possible affairs he might have had, and I came to ask you for a reason. I've uncovered evidence—and there are some things Steve and I have discovered together—that force me to ask these painful questions."

Then I blurted out the one thing I knew for sure would keep me from getting fired. "So, Celeste, if you really want Steve back, if you want him in your arms again, if you want him to fall in love with you, and I know you do ... then *do not* fire me. Because, as you know, from all the television and newspaper reports about our last case together,

Steve and I make a great team. And he would be furious with you if you let me go."

She blinked at me. "You're right." Her lips curved into a wry smile. "You're very clever, Story, I've got to hand you that. Fine, I won't fire you. But just know that if you have any designs on Steve romantically that I plan to win."

I matched her smile. "Believe me, I have no romantic designs on him, so he's ..." I stopped, caught off guard by a woman watching us from the porch. She started walking toward the pool.

It was Rita. And she had a strange look on her face.

She walked over to us. "I'm so glad to see you, Miss Detective," she told me. "I need to talk to you about that too-sexy housekeeper of ours, Annie."

Uh-oh. This couldn't be good. I braced myself. "Oh, what about her?" I asked.

Rita looked at Celeste, then back at me, then declared, "I think the little slut might be pregnant."

———

I gaped at Rita.

Had the truth about her brother-in-law finally penetrated her thick skull? She was always Philip's biggest defender. Had it finally occurred to her that maybe he wasn't the man she thought he was?

I was about to shout that out but held my tongue. I was learning. A savvy detective needed to know when to ask questions and when to shut up and listen.

Celeste jumped to her feet and put her hands on her hips, looking much less upset than I thought she would. Instead, she appeared rather intrigued by this juicy piece of gossip. "Pregnant?" she shouted. "Pregnant by *who*?"

"Shhh." I put a finger to my lips, then half-whispered in as casual a voice as I could muster, "This is shocking news, Rita. Tell us, who's the father?"

Gritting my teeth, I watched her face and waited for her to say what I had been too afraid to tell Celeste. This was too good to be true.

But Rita, flush-faced and smiling, was enjoying the attention Celeste and I were giving her, like she was an actress on a television soap opera about to reveal some dramatic tittle-tattle right before the commercial break.

Smiling? No, she shouldn't be smiling.

I couldn't stand it anymore. "Who could it be?" I asked in my most naïve and innocent voice. "Annie lives here, and she rarely goes anywhere on her days off, right? So ...?"

Rita looked at me like I was incredibly stupid, then at Celeste with a smirk. "Come on you two, isn't it obvious? It's got to be our stable guy, Clive. Or maybe Francine's stable guy, Gus."

I wanted to laugh. Not laughing was one of the hardest things I'd ever done.

A giggle welled up in my chest and threatened to break free from my lips. It was a good thing Steve wasn't there because I wouldn't have been able to keep it together. The thought of Annie and Clive or Annie and Gus making out was too, too funny.

No, those men were not Annie's type. She was much too ambitious for them.

I pressed my lips together, hard, and gave Rita a wow-you-might-be-right look, followed by "hmmm," which was the best I could do without losing it.

Celeste loved Rita's guesses about who might have knocked Annie up. "Oh my." She put a hand to her mouth and giggled into it. "Oh, my. I never liked that little hussy. Flitting around, showing off her cleavage in that low cut uniform, with that cute frilly apron tied tightly around her waist. I don't know why Mother put up with it."

My question, exactly.

"Have you noticed that she's tying that cute little apron a little looser around her waist lately?" Rita snickered. "Well, I have."

"Is that what makes you think she might be pregnant?" I asked, whispering the last word, like I was enjoying this girly gossip.

"That and the fact that she's been throwing up a lot." Rita sniffed. "I heard her doing it yesterday morning, and again today. In fact, she woke me up this morning with her loud gagging. I confronted her about it. But she just said she was sick. I doubt it."

I swallowed hard and looked over at the pool. Trying to think. How could I use this information to my best advantage, without making Celeste suspicious about what I really thought?

Then it came to me. "Things are bad enough here," I told Celeste. "You know, with your father in jail and all. I think I should find out if this is true. Because, what if Annie really is pregnant? Do you want her and her baby living here? Shouldn't she be fired?"

Celeste's eyes went big. "Oh horrors. Yes, Story. Yes, yes, please investigate this. See if you can find out if this is true. You're right, I do not need this on top of everything else I have to deal with."

"But how?" Rita asked me. "How can you find out if Annie is pregnant without her knowing?"

I shrugged. "I'll start with the family doctor." I turned to Celeste. "Could you give me his name and address?"

Celeste smiled. "I sure can. And I know for a fact that Annie has been to see him. I don't know if she has lately, but I do know that Mother took her to see him once and paid the bill."

She nodded. "Yes, indeed. Dr. Newport is the place to start."

Twenty-Five

Celeste seemed so entertained by the idea that Annie might be with child that she cheerfully invited me to stay for lunch. Any lingering resentment she might have had toward me for making insinuations about her father's character had vanished.

What a relief. She'd forgiven me, and I was hungry, and I had to wait for Steve anyway, so I gratefully accepted her offer.

I also wanted to take a fresh look at Annie, to see if she might have put on a little weight around the middle. Because I had not noticed and maybe Rita was just imagining it.

Celeste, Rita, and I sat down at the dining room table and watched Annie enter with a steaming hot quiche. Nobody said a word as she placed it in front of us because we were too busy sneaking looks at her waist, partially obscured by a frilly apron.

If Annie wondered why we were being so quiet, she didn't let on. Looking rather pale, she went back into the kitchen and came out with a salad, then went back into the kitchen and returned with a pitcher of iced tea.

"Thank you," I told her as she poured some into my glass.

Sneaking a closer look at her face, I noticed her complexion was downright pasty. I glanced back at her waist. Maybe a tiny bit plump? Hard to tell, her apron was so ruffled.

After she poured tea for the others and went back into the kitchen, she didn't come back.

I slid a piece of quiche onto my plate and dug in. Delicious, warm, cheesy. I took a bite of crunchy lettuce, then noticed Celeste wasn't eating.

"Annie!" Celeste shouted. "Could you please bring me the blue cheese salad dressing? It's in the refrigerator."

No answer.

"Annie," Celeste called again. "Did you hear me?"

No answer. Somewhere in the house, we heard a toilet flush.

"Annie!" Celeste pushed her chair back and stood up. "Annie?"

Annie hurried into the room. She looked green. Awful.

I almost felt sorry for her.

Almost.

"Where have you been?" Celeste sat back down.

Annie swallowed hard, then swallowed again. "I'm not feeling well, Miss Celeste," she said, her voice raspy and weak. "May I please go to my room?"

"What's wrong with you?" Rita took a sip of iced tea, then lowered her glass from her lips. "You woke me up this morning. You sounded really, really, really sick." She squinted at Annie. "Have you caught some kind of bug?"

I didn't like Annie, but I was growing uncomfortable for her. If the poor girl *was* pregnant, she was in for a world of trouble.

Maybe that was dawning on her. Since the man who was probably the father of her baby was sitting in jail, and would probably not be getting out anytime soon, if ever.

Then it hit me.

If Annie was pregnant, did Philip even know it?

If he did, had he murdered Lorna to keep her from finding out?

Or, had he and Annie worked as a team? Could they possibly have planned to take the million dollars from that life insurance policy and leave town? Leave the country?

No, Philip wouldn't do that to Celeste. Would he? His only child, who adored him?

My appetite gone, I put my fork down.

Annie clapped a hand over her mouth and ran out of the room.

We heard a knock on the door.

"I'll get it," I said.

I went and opened it.

Steve. Thank God. Steve.

Such a welcome sight for my quivering nerves. I felt as if I was living in some real-life television soap opera, with no way out.

He gave me a quizzical grin. "Story, you look like you've seen a ghost. What's going on?"

I pulled him inside, closed the door, and whispered in his ear. "A lot. But first, come have lunch."

———

Celeste was thrilled to see Steve and insisted he sit next to her at the table.

Annie was nowhere to be seen. Guessing that she was probably throwing up somewhere, I hurried to get Steve a plate, glass, and utensils.

I wished I'd had the opportunity to fill him in on Wendy's theory about Annie possibly being pregnant by Philip. But before I'd even had a chance to sit back down, Celeste was telling him about her and Rita's theories about Annie being knocked-up. By Clive or Gus.

"Really?" Steve matched Celeste's half-whispered tone, then shot me a raised-eyebrow-look that said, *what is she talking about*?

"Celeste wants you and me to investigate and she's given me the name of her family doctor," I said. Concerned that the subject of our dirty-linen-scuttlebutt might come back and overhear us, I half-whispered and half-mouthed, "I think it's a good idea. We can go after lunch."

"Be sure and let me know what the doctor tells you." Rita flicked me a sly grin. "This will be interesting."

Celeste put a hand on Steve's arm. "I need to go with you and Story. Doc Newport has known me all my life and he doesn't know you two at all."

"She's right," I said. "He might not be willing to tell us anything but at least Celeste can get us in the door."

A half hour later, after blueberry pie—which we served to ourselves because Annie never came back—Steve, Celeste and I headed for Dr. Newport's office in Steve's car.

Celeste jumped in the front passenger seat, and I climbed in the back. Then Celeste gave Steve directions to the physician's office, a small brick building in downtown Chad's Ford.

Inside the waiting room, an older woman behind a reception desk greeted us. "Miss Celeste," she said with an awkward, confused smile. "It's so nice to see you. Haven't seen you in an age. I'm terribly sorry about what happened to your dear mother." She cocked her head. "But are you ill? Because you don't have an appointment."

Celeste shook her head. "No, I'm fine, Miss Penn. I just need to speak to Doc about a private matter. It shouldn't take more than a few minutes." She gestured to Steve, then to me. "I've brought some friends along, who ... uhm ... are helping me with that, uh, private matter, so ... might you squeeze us in?"

Miss Penn blinked at Celeste from behind her round wireframe glasses. "I suppose that would be okay. You're in luck since no one else is waiting to see the doctor right now. He's in with a four-year old boy and his mother. Poor lad has a sore throat. Might need to get his tonsils out."

The door to the examination room opened and the worried mother and her son came out. The boy was happily sucking on a lollypop.

I flashed back to when I was a little girl. A lollypop from the doctor always made me feel better. Things sure get more complicated for grownups.

The white-coat-clad doctor waved us in. He had a pleasant face and a thick head of brown hair graying at the sides. He appeared to be around fifty.

Greeting Celeste, he closed the door to the examination room and turned to Steve and me. "Hello. I'm not sure we've met?"

"These are my friends, Story Smith," Celeste said, pointing to me, "and Steve Evans."

Nodding, he fingered the stethoscope around his neck. "Miss Penn said you've come about a private matter?"

"Yes." Celeste went over to the examination table and sat down on it, letting her legs dangle over the edge. "I believe my mother brought our housekeeper, Annie Leeds, to see you once." She took a deep breath. "I've come to ask you about her."

Doc Newport frowned. "Your housekeeper? You've come to ask about your housekeeper?"

Celeste nodded. "Is she a patient of yours?"

His frown deepened. "I don't understand. Why do you ask?"

Celeste met his gaze with sad eyes. "I'm afraid everyone in the Cranston household is having a difficult time right now." She sniffed. "We're still grieving the loss of my mother. So, please, doctor, could you please tell me if my maid is your patient?"

I noticed he was careful not to answer. Clever man. Instead, he countered with a question of his own. "Why? Are you worried about her? If you are, just have her come see me."

Celeste, flustered, looked over at Steve. "Steve, could you ..."

"I think what Celeste trying to say is that she is *extremely* worried about her maid," Steve said.

"I understand." The doc sighed. "Like I said, have her come see me. I'm sure your father would be happy to pay her bill, Celeste."

Had Philip already paid an earlier bill? I studied the doctor's face for any clues that he might know the real reason we were there. Did he even know Philip was in jail? If he did, he was giving nothing away.

He narrowed his eyes at Steve. "Evans ..." He studied Steve's face, a slow smile creasing his face. "Did Celeste say your last name is Evans?"

Steve nodded. "Yes."

"Are you the Evans boy?"

Steve looked confused. "I'm not sure what you mean. I was born a boy, and my last name is Evans."

Doc Newport looked as excited as if he'd just discovered gold. "I think my father might have delivered you as a baby," he mused, then beamed. "I'm certain he did."

Steve gave him a nervous smile. "What are you talking about?"

"My father, God rest his soul, was a doctor, too. And I remember when he came home one day and told my mother and me about the fine baby boy he'd just delivered to the Evans family."

Steve ran a hand over his chin. "It must have been a long time ago, doc. I'm thirty-three years old."

"A beautiful boy, with deep dimples, and a shock of dark brown hair, my father said."

"Might have been me." Steve shrugged. "But why are we talking about me?"

"The Evans family had several girls. And they were so happy to get a boy."

Steve shook his head, then frowned. "I am the only boy in my family. But I've never been made to feel special. My parents love my sisters, and I'm sure it was not that big a deal when I was born a boy. Maybe you're talking about someone else?"

"Perhaps ..."

"I bet Steve was that baby." Celeste giggled. "He's still beautiful, and he's still got those awesome dimples."

I pressed my lips together and forced back a sigh. This strange conversation about Steve as a baby was interesting, but we weren't getting any closer to finding out if Annie might be expecting a baby.

I decided to just ask. "Doctor," I said, waving my hand like a student who wanted a turn to speak. "I think Celeste is worried that her housekeeper, Annie, might be pregnant."

Silence.

Doc Newport stared at me.

Celeste nodded her head at me.

Steve gave me a way-to-go grin.

"I'm not sure why you are telling me this," Doc Newport told me, his voice tight. "I haven't even said that Annie is my patient."

But we could all see that Annie was his patient.

Because his face was growing red. People can often hide their feelings, but it's impossible for them to stop from blushing.

"*If* she was your patient, doctor, what would you tell her?" I pressed. "What advice do you offer women who come to you when they think they might be pregnant? I'm *not saying* that Annie Leeds did come to you—I'm just asking about women in general."

"I advise them to go see an obstetrician." He cleared his throat. "Things have changed since my father's time because doctors specialize now, and I'm not a baby doctor."

He turned to Celeste. "*If* Miss Leeds had come to see me. And *if* I had determined that she needed to see an obstetrician, then I would have sent her to one." He took a pad of paper and a pen from his coat pocket, then scribbled something, ripped the paper off, and handed it to Celeste. "This is the obstetrician I always recommend."

Then he went over and opened the door to the waiting room. "I hope I have been of some help to you folks," he said. "Good day."

———

"I believe the good doctor told us without telling us." Steve flashed me a grin in the rearview mirror as he drove us back to Grand Gables. "Good job, Story, I'm impressed."

"Thanks," I said, feeling pretty good about it myself.

Steve glanced at Celeste beside him. "What name did he write on that paper? Who's the obstetrician we need to go visit?"

Celeste fished the paper out of her purse. "Some doctor in Philadelphia who I don't know."

"Getting anything out of him will be more difficult," I said as Steve pulled into the Grand Gables drive.

Rita was waiting for us outside. And the look on her face told us we were about to face an even bigger problem.

She limped toward Steve's car, waving her arms, shouting, "Annie's gone! Annie's gone!"

We all got out and ran over to her.

"Calm down, Aunt Rita." Celeste grabbed her arms. "What are you saying? That Annie quit?"

Rita nodded. "She ran away."

"Ran away?" Steve looked at me, then back at Rita. "You mean she just ran off?"

Rita pressed a hand to her forehead. "She packed her suitcase, with all her stuff, then ran down the driveway. I couldn't stop her. Didn't know if I should even try."

Celeste grinned. "You did the right thing, Aunt Rita. She quit. She's gone. Hallelujah. Now I won't have to fire the little harlot."

Steve and I looked at each other. We weren't cheering.

"How do you know she quit?" I asked. "Maybe she's going to come back?"

Rita gave her head a solemn shake. "She's not coming back. She left a note."

"Let's go see it," Steve said, leading the way into the house. "Where is it?"

Rita called, "She left it on her bed."

We followed Steve to the third floor into Annie's tiny room.

As Rita had said, the maid had clearly taken everything she owned, which probably wasn't much if she'd fit it all into a suitcase. The bed was neatly made, and the closet was empty, as were the open drawers in the small bureau by the window.

A single piece of white paper lay in the middle of the bed.

"I left the note there, so you all could see it." Rita handed it to me.

Gripping the note, I read her message out loud: "To anyone who might care. I quit. It's not the same here without Mr. Philip. If he gets out of jail, tell him I went home. He'll know where to find me. Don't anybody else try—unless they want to die. Annie."

I looked at Steve. He looked at me. We knew. For Annie to go back to that hellish hovel she called home, her situation had to be dire. Which meant she must be pregnant ... with Philip's child.

Which meant she, and or Philip, had a motive other than money to murder Lorna.

And that Steve and I had to go find her.

Twenty-Six

This time we took Steve's car to the Pine Barrens.

"Do you think we should stop and see Philip first?" he asked as we set out for the Leeds's cabin the next morning.

"No, he won't admit to anything. We'd just be wasting our time."

"Do you think we should get the police involved?"

"No. Because it's not a crime to quit your job and leave a note about it," I said. "Which is all we can prove Annie has done at this point."

Frowning, Steve tightened his grip on the wheel. "She did threaten death to anyone who tries to find her."

"Right, but the cops aren't going to take that seriously. Besides, all Calvin said was that his family doesn't like visitors."

"He sure made that clear, didn't he?" Steve glanced over at me. "Personally, I found the guy more creepy than scary."

I patted my gun, which this time I was holding on my lap. "I think the Leeds like people to be afraid of them. I think they like the rumor about their connection to the Jersey Devil. I also think they are pathetic in a pitiable way and not very smart. I'm not afraid of them, but I do have my gun, just in case."

He slid me a sideways grin. "It's not in your purse—I call that progress."

"Gee, thanks. It's even loaded. But where's your weapon?"

"In a holster. Hidden under my shirt." He was wearing a loose-fitting black T-shirt over blue jeans and I was wearing blue pedal pushers and a short-sleeved black blouse. We hadn't planned it that way, but clothing wise, we sort of matched. We'd both dressed dark for a dark place.

"You scared, Steve?" I asked as we drove into the dense pine forest.

"Not really. I never allow myself to be scared. It's not good for business. Anyway, I have a plan."

"What is it?"

"This time, we're not going to just pull up to their cabin. We need the element of surprise because we don't want Pa coming out instead of Calvin. No telling what Pa will do, and the person we need to see is Annie. Which means we're going to park the car out of sight somewhere in the woods, then sneak up to the back of the house on foot to see what we can see."

"Hopefully Annie. Alone."

He grunted. "Right. Hopefully she'll be there. Don't know how she would have managed to get a ride home, but the family must have at least one vehicle, probably a truck."

"She hated them," I said, "but she went home anyway."

Steve gave a grim nod. "Yeah, family is family, and I'm betting that Annie's family's motto is *us against the world.*"

"I bet that's always been their creed. So how are we going to get Annie alone to talk to her?"

Steve reached over and put a hand on my shoulder. "That's where we'll have to get creative, partner. I don't see any other choice. We're just going to have to figure it out as we go along. If Annie is pregnant with Philip's child, and we can prove it, we'll have something to take to the police."

"As possible motive for killing Lorna?"

"Yes. It's a long shot, but it is a possible motive."

I didn't see how we were going to get Annie to admit to anything, but it was worth a try. Before setting eyes on her family's homestead, I couldn't have imagined the petite housekeeper shooting anyone. But after seeing for myself where she came from, it wasn't so hard to imagine.

Still ...

Rolling into Chatsworth, I was glad we had Steve's car this time because nobody gave us a second glance. We passed by the café, then kept going toward the Leeds's cabin, keeping our eye out for an opening in the woods.

About a half mile before the family's mailbox, we came to a narrow path on the same side of the road.

"Close enough, "Steve said, turning in. "Our destination can't be far."

The hard-packed dirt path led deep into the woods, then ended abruptly about a quarter mile in. Steve cut the engine and turned to me. "Ready?"

"As ever," I said, my heart thudding against my chest. Clutching my gun in my right hand, I scooped up my purse in my left. It was my summer handbag—big, beige, and roomy enough to hold extra ammunition, as well as my makeup, comb, and a thermos of water. No way was I going to leave it behind.

"That thing heavy?" Steve asked as he locked the car doors, then pocketed the key.

I shook my head.

"Okay." He shrugged and waved for me to follow. "Let's go."

We were both wearing sneakers, and the day hadn't heated up yet. We made our way through the pine-needle-carpeted-forest toward the Leeds's place.

Picking our way through thick brush and brambles, we came to a stream.

Steve whispered that it probably ran past the Leeds's home. We took the narrow path that ran along it.

After about fifteen minutes, Steve turned around, a finger to his lips, and let me catch up to him, then whispered, "I think we're getting close."

I nodded and we went on.

In my mind, I rehearsed what I might say to Annie if we did find her. I tried to put myself in her place. She had to be feeling awfully desperate to have come back to these woods. Maybe I could try to be her friend.

I thought about the threat in Annie's note—to not try to find her, or else—but pushed that out of my brain, concentrating instead on the soft sound of branches crunching under my feet, and the flickers of sunlight streaming through the tree canopy.

And being with Steve, on an adventure in the woods.

This was my life, and boy, it was exciting.

Until we spotted the Leeds's shack up ahead, through some trees.

And things got real. Real bad. Real fast.

A shot rang out. Then another. And another.

Bullets zipped past my head.

I threw myself on the ground and crawled over to Steve, who was crouched behind a bush.

"Pa must have spotted us," he whispered in my ear. "Stay close."

He had his gun drawn, and so did I, but I couldn't see who was shooting at us.

I eyed the cabin, the back of it was as ramshackle rundown as the front. The back door was half open. Dark curtains covered the windows. The wood porch was missing some slats. Beside the porch, a hand-operated water pump sat atop a clump of weeds.

How could people live like this? Where was Annie?

And what now?

"What do you want?" A voice shouted. A man, clutching a rifle, came out the back door. Not Pa, too young. Not Calvin, although he looked like Calvin. Same build, same wild hair.

"We just want to talk to Annie," Steve shouted. "We come as her friends. She knows us. Steve and Story. We want to help her."

"Damn you!" The man yelled. "Go away. Annie ain't going to talk to nobody. We hate visitors."

"Please," I cried. "I think she might be in trouble. She quit her job, but she didn't have to do that. I can help her. Just let me talk to her."

The man slapped his forehead, then turned toward the door and bellowed, "Annie, get yourself out here. Now. Tell these people to go away."

Annie walked out onto the porch. Followed by two other men who looked like Calvin. Then Calvin. All except Annie held rifles. They aimed them at us.

My mouth went dry. "Annie," I shouted. "It's me, Story. Can we talk? I'm here to help you."

"Bitch!" she screamed. "No! Leave me alone."

My heart was pounding against my ribs. "Please ... I know you're in trouble."

"No!" Her wail was the cry of a wounded animal.

"Get out of here, now." Calvin jerked his weapon at us. "*Now*."

"Annie," I yelled, desperate to get through to her, to shock her. "I know you're pregnant. And I can help you. Just let me—"

BAM.

A bullet zoomed past my head.

BAM, BAM, BAM, BAM.

Steve scrambled to his feet, grabbed my hand, pulled me up. "Time to go. Let's run."

We zig-zagged toward the stream up ahead.

Another shot rang out. Steve turned and fired.

I turned to look. They were following us.

Clutching my gun in one hand, I reached for Steve's hand with my other.

We ran into the stream. Splashed through shallow water to the other side. Raced through thick brush into deeper woods.

BAM, BAM, BAM. More bullets whizzed past.

Steve turned and fired another shot.

We crashed through the forest. Gunshots followed us.

They grew fainter and fainter. We seemed to be losing them.

Up ahead, a building loomed. It looked like it was made of concrete. Old. Abandoned. Dingy.

Covered with wild, twisting vines.

It had a door. Wooden. With a rusty latch.

Steve jerked it open. We hurried inside. He pushed the door closed. Slid an iron bolt into place.

It was dark and hot in there, with the only light coming from narrow open windows high above our heads. At least we had air.

"This must be some kind of fortress," Steve whispered. "I wonder what it was used for?"

"I don't know," I said, "but it feels safe." I was lying. I was terrified.

I looked down at the floor. Also concrete, it was covered with rotting, grimy straw. I didn't care. I sank to my knees. "Let's rest here," I said. "I'm exhausted."

"We'll stay here as long as we need to." Steve dropped down next to me and wrapped his arms around me, pulling me close. "I'm sure Annie's brothers know about this place," he whispered. "But they don't know for sure if we are in here. And if we keep quiet, maybe they'll leave.

I nodded. I was shaking all over, fear penetrating my body to the bones. I willed myself to relax in Steve's strong embrace.

Moments later, gunshots grew closer.

Angry hands pounded on the door. Furious voices shouted for us to come out.

Steve tightened his arms around me. I pressed my face to his chest to keep from whimpering.

"Shhh," he said in my ear. "Shhh, shhh, shhh. We'll be okay."

I nodded, but I didn't share his optimism.

Because the pounding went on and on and on.

"We know you're in there," a menacing voice shouted. "And we're not leaving till you come out with your hands up."

TWENTY-SEVEN

Steve and I froze.

With my face pressed against his chest, I felt his heart beating against mine, and took comfort from that. Forcing back tears, I told myself that if the Leeds brothers broke down the door, and shot us right there and then, huddled together like we were, there would be worse ways to die.

Only I didn't want to die.

Neither did Steve. Without moving a muscle, he whispered, "They'll have to leave eventually. We just need to stay quiet and wait them out."

"How long?"

"As long as it takes."

"Maybe days?"

"Hope not."

I hoped not, too, because we had no food and only a thermos of water.

Thank God I had brought my purse because at least we had water. It was probably around noon and the day was going to be a scorcher. It sure was growing hot and steamy inside our fortress. Although I couldn't blame all the heat on the weather.

Rivulets of sweat running down my back, I struggled to breathe as thoughts of impending doom raced through my terrified brain.

"How will we know when they've left?" I whispered after what felt like an eternity.

"Great question."

"Maybe they've left already." A girl could hope.

"It's only been about twenty minutes, so I doubt it."

"We know you're in there," the gruff voice shouted again. It was Calvin. "Might as well come out now."

"None of us is leaving," another gruff voice yelled. "Us Leeds boys stick together."

"We know how to track animals in the woods," Calvin shouted, "so we know you two are in there."

"We'll just wait them out." Steve's warm breath brushed my ear. "No matter how long it takes. We don't have a choice."

I nodded.

After that, we sat clutching each other in silence. Complete silence. For a very long time until Steve whispered that he needed to stand up to relieve the cramping in his legs.

I stood, too, stretching my arms to relieve the stiffness in my entire body.

Steve tiptoed over to the door and ran his hands over it. Then he walked slowly and quietly around our hideout, probing the concrete walls with his fingers, like he was searching for a secret passageway out.

But even from where I stood, I could see there was no way out.

Our fortress was roomy, about the size of a small barn, and it smelled horrible, musty, as if no one had been in it for a long time. The ceiling was made of the same concrete material as the walls and floor, and I wondered if the place had once housed animals. Or been used as a storehouse? Maybe for something valuable?

The high windows, four on each wall, were too small for a person to get in or get out. Not that we could have crawled out anyway, they were too high to reach.

"Whoever built this place meant business," Steve whispered as he came back over to me. "The door is about six inches thick, and the walls seem rock solid. No cracks."

"So, what now?"

He shrugged. "We wait."

"Until?"

He shook his head. "I have no idea."

I picked up my purse and removed the thermos of water. I sat down, patted the ground next to me, and waved the thermos at Steve. "Come on, I'll share."

He lowered himself down, facing me, and crossed his legs, smiling. "You brought water? Smart girl."

The thermos cap was in the shape of a small drinking cup. I unscrewed it and poured a couple of inches in it, then handed it to Steve.

"No. Ladies first."

I drank the water and poured more for Steve. He hesitated, then took the cup from me. "No telling how long we'll have to stay here." He drank the water and handed me back the cup. "We'll need to make this last."

I nodded.

Steve scooted closer, putting us back in whispering distance. "Bet you regret becoming a private eye now."

I shook my head. "Nope."

"It's not for the faint of heart." He grimaced. "My family worries about me all the time. I bet your parents do, too."

I shrugged. "My mother wishes I could be more like my friend, Brenda, from high school. Married with kids."

A slow grin spread across Steve's face. "That's funny. Somehow, I can't picture you like that. But maybe ... maybe you *should* consider the housewife life. The kind of life where you're not facing down death in an abandoned building in the middle of some woods."

"No, I'd be washing poopy diapers ..." I put a hand to my mouth to press back a giggle, then took a deep breath. "Or scrubbing a kitchen floor ..." I gulped down another giggle. "Or ..." I shook my head and tried to look serious. "Nope. The truth is that I'd much rather be doing this."

"With me." Steve grinned. "I'm flattered."

"Did I say with you?"

"Who else?" Steve winked. "Who else would you rather be with right now?"

I tore my gaze away from him. He was right. I couldn't deny it to myself. But I didn't have to admit it to him.

"How many women have you dated, Steve?" I looked back at him.

He stared at me, suddenly serious. "I'm not sure. I never counted."

"Were you ever in love with any of them long enough to consider marriage?"

"Not really." He looked uncomfortable. I'd hit a nerve. "No."

"My brother, Rob, says—"

"I know what your brother, Rob, says. You've told me what he says. That I break women's hearts. And you know, he's probably right. I probably have broken a few, including Celeste's, but I never meant to."

Somehow, that didn't make me feel any better. I suddenly had a need to get back up and stretch my legs. I walked around the perimeter of the building, running my hands along the walls, wishing there was a way out that didn't involve getting mowed down by a barrage of bullets.

With a sigh, I looked up—and my breath caught in my throat. Now that my eyes had adjusted to the dimness, I could see spiders in the spaces where the ceiling met the walls.

Big spiders. Little spiders. Lively spiders.

Aaaah. Terror shot through me. Goosebumps rippled up and down my arms. Every hair on my head stood straight up. I wanted to scream, but I couldn't, didn't dare—

Steve ran over and clamped a hand over my mouth. "Shhhh." He led me back to the center of the room, sat down, and pulled me down with him. When he saw that I wasn't going to scream, his lips twitched, like he was trying not to laugh. "I was hoping you wouldn't notice them," he whispered with a grin.

I swallowed hard. "I didn't scream. I wasn't going to scream."

He widened his grin and reached over and squeezed my hand. "I know but I wasn't going to take any chances."

"I'm hungry," I said to quickly change the subject.

"Me, too." Steve pointed to my purse. "Did you bring any food in there?"

"Sadly, no."

"We'll just have to be hungry, then."

"Okay." I wanted to lay down, stretch out my body, try to relax. But I didn't want to put my head on the filthy straw.

Steve seemed to notice. "Are you tired? I can give you my shirt for a pillow."

"What? No, you don't have to do that."

"I'm hot, anyway." He pulled his shirt off over his head and handed it to me.

Flustered, I took it from him, unable to take my eyes off his bare chest. Steve shirtless. Boy, did he look good shirtless. "Wow," I said. "Do you lift weights?"

He cocked his head. "Is that a compliment?"

"Answer the question."

"Of course I lift weights. Look at the profession I'm in. I better be in good shape."

I could only nod and resolve to take those karate lessons I'd been promising myself. As soon as I got out of this dirty, spider-infested prison. If I ever got out.

I bunched Steve's shirt up, put it down on the straw, and lay down on my makeshift pillow. It smelled like Steve. Strong, masculine, a bit piney, like the woods. I shut my eyes. Breathed in, breathed out. Tried to relax my muscles.

"Go to sleep, Story," Steve whispered, leaning over me. "Go ahead and take a nap. We're going to be here for a while. I'll keep guard."

I opened my eyes and looked up at him. "Thanks ..." But I knew I was not going to be able to sleep. Not with crazy men outside waiting to kill me. Not with creepy spiders on the ceiling waiting to bite me.

And not with Steve there, beside me, watching over me. I could try, though. I closed my eyes again and whispered, "Please don't let any spiders get me."

He gave a quiet chuckle. "Don't worry, I won't."

Twenty-Eight

Sleep was impossible, of course.

Though I was lying completely still, my heart pounded as if I were running a race.

The fortress was hot and muggy, but the blood in my veins felt arctic cold.

And my fear-wracked brain kept spinning with questions. How could we escape? Would we escape? And ... what made me think I could do this? What made me think I could make a living as a private eye?

I could have married my sweetheart, Dean, after college. Why had I called off our secret engagement? If we had gotten married, with that big, fancy wedding we'd talked about, he'd still be alive. He wouldn't have shot himself. He'd probably have a good job and we'd probably have a bunch of kids.

And Steve was right, I wouldn't be facing down death at the age of twenty-six.

Steve and I had faced danger together before. More than once.

My mind flashed back to us on that airplane ride, after our first case together. The plane hit violent turbulence and Steve calmed me down by singing me a song. A song he'd composed in his mind, at that moment, about us.

The lyrics and his amazing voice had made me smile.

He was a talented musician in his spare time, and I wished he could sing me a song now.

But he couldn't because we had to be quiet ...

BAM.

A muffled gunshot. Where?

I opened my eyes, my heart suddenly racing again. Steve was kneeling over me, a finger to his lips.

Had I fallen asleep after all? "What's going on?" I whispered.

"They just fired a shot to let us know they're still here," he whispered back. "Nice of them to keep us informed."

Strangely groggy, I struggled to sit up. "How long have I been laying here?"

"A few hours. I had to fend off a few spiders during that time, but don't worry, none got to you."

I widened my eyes in horror.

His gave me a got-you grin.

I swatted his arm. "Stop teasing me—it's not nice."

"But it's so much fun."

"I don't know how you can find any of this fun."

"Just the part about being with you, Story. The rest is no fun."

I handed him back his shirt. "We need to get out of here. Somehow. Someway."

He pulled his shirt on over his head. "I agree."

"Then we'll go to the police," I said. "We'll tell them that the Leeds family tried to kill us, tell them they need to bring Annie in for further questioning about Lorna's murder. Francine's, too. I'm starting to think she's the one. She's the murderer. Why else would her brothers be trying to silence us?"

"Good plan and I agree." Steve brushed straw off his shirt. "Only ... getting out of here is the tricky part. Exiting through the front door is not going to work. Even if we run with guns blasting, we won't get far without being mowed down."

I picked a piece of straw out of my hair. "Because the Leeds family is murderous and Annie's one of them, so she's clearly capable of murder."

Steve took a deep breath, let it out in a long sigh. "But where does that leave our client Philip?"

I shrugged. "I don't know."

"And what about Francine?"

I shook my head. "I don't know."

"None of our conjectures matter if we don't get out of here," Steve said.

I was horribly thirsty. I reached for my thermos, poured myself some water, gulped it down, then poured some for Steve.

"Do you think once it grows dark, we'll be able to slip out the door?" I asked, watching him drink. Based on the amount of water still left in the thermos, it was clear he had not touched a drop while I was lying there. What a brave, generous man.

He set the thermos aside. "Waiting for complete darkness might be our only hope. We'll just have to wait and see. It's growing darker in here." He yawned. "Which means we might not have to wait too long."

"Take a nap," I urged. "It's my turn to keep watch."

"Great idea. But what am I going to use for a pillow?" Staring at my blouse, he wagged his eyebrows.

Heat rose to my cheeks. "Uhm ..."

He chuckled. "Never mind. I'm teasing you again. I'll just put my head down on the vermin-infested straw."

"No." I scooted closer, arranging myself cross-legged across from him. "Lay your head on my lap."

Silence, then, "Really?"

"Yes, really." My cheeks were hot now.

"Alright, then." Steve lay down, with the back of his head in my lap, then stretched out the rest of his long body away from me. "This is nice," he murmured. "Thanks."

"You're welcome."

He didn't say anything for several minutes. Then, "I think I got the better pillow."

"Hush. Go to sleep."

"Not likely."

I didn't know what to say to that, so I sat still, and said nothing, and after a while Steve's breathing grew relaxed and regular.

It got darker and darker. Before long, we were in complete darkness. Off in the distance an owl hooted.

An hour went by, maybe two. My legs became increasingly cramped. Then, unbearably cramped. I didn't dare move because I didn't want to wake Steve.

Then, suddenly, he sat up, swiveled around, and reached for my hand. "Wow ... how long did I sleep?"

"Not long."

"It's completely dark."

"Yes."

He squeezed my hand, then let go. "Did you hear anything outside while I was asleep?"

"Only an owl."

"Maybe they left. Maybe we should try to make a run for it." He didn't sound so sure. I didn't like the hesitation in his voice.

"I'm scared, Steve. What if they're waiting right outside the door?"

He took my hand again. "I have an idea. I could try to make a run for it while you stay here."

"By myself?" My heart slammed against my chest.

"Yes. Bolt the door after I slip out. If I manage to get away, I'll send the police to help you. And if I don't—"

"No, Steve."

"If I don't ..." He squeezed my hand. "If I don't make it, at least you'll have enough water for a few more days. Hopefully by then Celeste will have sent a search party to look for us."

I could not believe what I was hearing. No way. "To look for *us*, Steve," I hissed. "To look for *us*. You and me. Meaning we need to stick together. Meaning we either both leave, or we both stay."

He didn't say anything. His hand was warm in mine. I was not going to be the one to let go. Then I knew. I couldn't go on living if Steve died trying to save me. I'd rather die with him.

"You're a strong woman, Story." He whispered. "You don't need me."

"Yes, I am strong, Steve. But I'm stronger with you."

"I can't believe you just admitted that."

"I know."

He scooted closer to me and put an arm around my shoulder. I snuggled against him.

"We'll wait another hour, then decide if we want to run for it or stay." His voice was husky. "Whatever we do, we'll do together."

I nodded.

"You realize we could die together."

I nodded again.

He sighed. "I might die with a woman I'm just getting to know."

I tensed up. "What do you mean?"

"There are so many things about you I don't know."

I smiled. "Like what?"

"Like, your car. You never did tell me how you got your awesome T-Bird."

"You mean because I'm clearly broke?"

"Well … yeah."

"It was a gift. From a grateful client of my brother, Rob."

"When?"

"Last Christmas. Rob and I drove my car at the time—a Hudson Hornet—to Maine to infiltrate a wedding undercover as man and wife. Rob's client, the wealthy father of the bride, suspected his daughter's fiancé was not the man he pretended to be, and he was right. Fortunately, we proved he was a scoundrel before vows were exchanged. Unfortunately, my Hornet got wrecked when Rob crashed it into a tree in the snow. The bride's father was so grateful we saved his daughter, he bought me a new car."

"Quite a tale." Steve sounded impressed.

"It inspired me to quit my job as a newspaper reporter and become a private eye. Rob has since joined the FBI."

"And this client of his bought you a brand new T-Bird?"

"Why not? He said I could have any car I wanted. Even better, Rob ended up marrying Piper, the bride we saved. A happy ending all around."

"Unbelievable ..." Steve hugged me closer. "You are amazing. You and I need a happy ending."

He wanted to kiss me. I could feel it. I could hear it in his voice.

And I wanted to kiss him. With every quivering cell in my body, I wanted to kiss him. We were probably going to die soon, anyway. Why not just surrender to my feelings?

Steve put a hand on my cheek.

Then someone pounded on the door.

"We're still here, fools," Calvin shouted. "So come on out. You might as well get it over with. Surrender, surrender."

That kind of surrender was out of the question.

Steve and I waited, frozen. Clutching each other, we braced for more. More loud knocks, more ominous threats. But that was it. Just that warning. In the middle of the night.

"I guess that's our answer," Steve whispered in my ear. "We're not leaving now. We'll just have to come up with a plan come dawn."

Twenty-Nine

I awoke at dawn to find myself cuddled against Steve, using his shoulder as a pillow.

Flat on his back on the hard straw-covered floor, he was asleep with his head on my purse.

Exhausted, we had surrendered to sleep that way. And now, confused, and disoriented, I wondered if we had died that way—and that this was some strange version of heaven.

Until I realized we were still in hell.

The cement floor made a poor mattress. Aching all over, I sat up slowly, trying not to wake Steve, then stood and stretched my arms toward the ceiling.

Wincing, I looked around. Nothing had changed. We were still imprisoned. And escape still looked hopeless.

I was hungry and my stomach hurt. I was thirsty and my mouth was so dry I could barely move my tongue.

My chest hurt because I was so filled with despair that it was hard to breathe.

I wanted to cry.

But I would not cry. Crying wouldn't help me find a way to escape.

Looking around at the walls, I tried to think. They were thick, solid, no cracks. I glanced up at the ceiling. It was as solidly constructed as the walls. No holes, no cracks, just spiders.

Then I looked down at the floor. Any cracks there? I got down on my hands and knees to inspect. Crawling around, I pushed dirty straw aside, examining every inch of floor as I made my way to the wall opposite the door.

What was I looking for? I wasn't sure, but I had nothing else to do, and maybe, just maybe, I could find a crack in the foundation. Then Steve and I could widen it and dig a tunnel to escape.

It was fantasy, pure fantasy.

Miraculously, I found something better. Pushing aside a thick clump of straw, my hand struck something sticking up from the floor. Ouch. A nail? I flinched and withdrew my hand. A drop of blood fell onto the hay. But I was too excited to care. I just may have found a way out of this dungeon. My heart did a happy flip.

A trap door crudely made of wide wooden boards, it was square, about two feet wide and two feet long. What could be under it? Somehow, if I could get it open ...

I ran my hand along the boards. Found a small iron handle. Grabbed it. Pulled. Nothing happened. I pulled harder. Nothing. I didn't want to break it ...

"Story?"

I turned around. Steve was awake. I eagerly waved him over.

"Wow." He squatted down to look, then grinned. "This could be interesting."

"I know, but I can't get it open."

"Let me try." He yanked on the handle. The wood creaked and moved. He yanked again. The trapdoor came up in his hands. He shoved it to one side.

Together we peered into a deep hole.

There was nothing in it. About four feet deep, it was empty. It must have been used for storage once, maybe as a secret hiding place. I smiled when I saw its walls were dirt. Not concrete. Hard packed dirt.

I glanced at Steve. "Do you know what this means?"

He nodded. "We might be able to dig our way out of here."

"Yep. Tunnel under the wall."

"It might take hours." He frowned. "We'll have to dig our way out by hand."

"It's either that or go out the front door."

"I'll get in the hole and start digging first." Steve put a hand on my shoulder. "I'll scoop out dirt, then hand it up to you. We'll take turns."

"I'm ready."

Steve dropped down, and with his hands, began carving a tunnel to the outside. He scooped out a handful of dark sandy soil, turned around, handed the dirt up to me, then went back for more.

We tunneled that way for an hour, then switched places, toiling our way toward freedom.

Dirt got in my eyes, my nose, my mouth.

We worked in silence as the day grew hotter and sweat turned the dirt on my body into mud.

Taking turns every hour or so in the hole, we ignored periodic poundings on the door, always followed by loud voices taunting us, shouting at us to surrender.

I took comfort from those threats because they were coming from the front of the building. And we'd be escaping out the back.

Finally, after making our way all the way under the wall, Steve, from down in the hole, called a halt to the digging. His face was so caked with dirt I could only see his eyes.

I went and got the thermos. We took turns drinking as much of the water as we dared.

"It's time to start digging our way up." He handed the thermos back up to me. "This will be the hardest part because we'll probably hit tree roots."

I shrugged. "We've gotten this far. I'm ready."

He nodded. "Good girl."

I didn't like the look in his eyes. "What's wrong, Steve?"

"When we reach daylight, you'll need to be the one to go."

"Me?" I hissed.

"Yes, you, by yourself. Our tunnel is too narrow for me to fit."

I shook my head. "No. I'm not leaving without you."

"You must. You're small enough to make it through, and when you do, you can sneak into the woods and run for help."

I swallowed hard. "But I can't leave you behind."

"You can and you must. Take your gun, nothing else, leave me the rest of the water."

I went numb. Numb with fear. Numb with grief. I shook my head.

"Story, listen to me." He took my hand. "If you're very, very quiet, you'll have a good chance of making it. And if you can get away, and send the cops, then my chances of surviving this hellhole go way up."

I still didn't like it. "Can't we widen the tunnel so you can come with me?"

"No. It will take too long. We're both exhausted. It's better this way."

I looked deep into his eyes, and what I saw in them now gave me courage. And conviction. There was courage in his eyes, and his courage gave me courage.

And even if the Leeds boys spotted me, and shot me down, they would not get Steve. Not if I could help it.

"Okay. I'll do it." I squeezed his hand. "But I'm going to cover the hole with brush before I sneak off. Even if they get me, they won't know how I got out, and they won't get you."

"Don't worry about me, Story. Just go."

"No."

Steve put his free hand on my cheek. Like he'd done the night before, in the dark. I couldn't see him at all then, and now all I could see under a thick mask of grime was his eyes.

And what I saw in them was desire.

And I knew ... that what he saw in my eyes ... was the same desire.

Then he moved his hand to the back of my neck, drew me to him, and kissed me.

And I kissed him back, mud-caked lips on mud-caked lips. And nothing had ever tasted or felt sweeter.

"I've been wanting to kiss you for a very long time," Steve whispered in my ear, then kissed me again. "And I know you've wanted this, too."

"Yes, but—"

"No buts." He kissed me again. Kissed my lips. Kissed my nose. Kissed my forehead. Then went back to my lips.

"No buts," I whispered, gazing into his eyes. I ran a mud-encrusted finger over his muddy lips and smiled. "*But* we still have a problem, you know."

"Oh, and what's that?" He gave me a dreamy smile back.

"We still need to get out of here. At least I do."

He sighed. "Oh, right. I'd almost forgotten."

"More digging," I said.

He stood and reached for my hand. "It's our last lap. Let's get to work."

THIRTY

It was probably mid-afternoon by the time I clawed my way out of our tunnel and into the woods, with the imprint of Steve's last kiss still on my lips.

I had my gun in my bra because there was no place else to put it. I was caked from head to toe in dirt and mud, and I could barely see because I had so much dirt in my eyes.

But I was free.

Hoisting myself up and onto the ground, I had to move fast.

I stood up and listened. Nothing but birds in the trees.

I was surrounded by trees, bushes, thick brush.

Quickly and quietly, I scooped up leaves and branches and arranged them over the hole. It disguised my exit point well enough. With any luck, the Leeds boys wouldn't even suspect I'd ever left, meaning Steve was safe.

I tiptoed away from the fortress, staying as light on my feet as I could, skirting sticks and branches on the ground the way I imagined the Indians had done long ago when they wanted to remain silent.

Ducking behind a tree, I looked back. No one was following me. My heart was racing, and I sucked in a deep breath of relief. So far, so good. *Keep going*, I told myself, *just keep going*.

I kept going. Whenever I needed to rest, I hid behind a tree. Peeking back at the fortress, I saw no one hanging around.

I heard no gun shots nor shouts of threat, just the silence of the woods on a hot, sunny day.

I was getting away, leaving the fortress behind. With no idea where I was going. I decided to keep moving until I found the stream that ran past the Leeds cabin and then head in the opposite direction.

Steve had given me the car keys, which were in my pants pocket. If I could make it to his car, all would be well.

But ... after making my way through a thick strand of trees and into a small clearing, I ran into Annie.

She was alone. Carrying a rifle. Which she pointed at me. "Stop. Put your hands up."

Frozen, I stared at her, hoping against hope she didn't recognize me with all the caked-on mud. But that was stupid. Of course she recognized me.

"Story Smith." She spit my name out. "Where the hell did you come from? Put your hands up."

I raised my hands, my heart slamming so hard against my ribs I couldn't breathe.

She stepped closer, keeping her rifle pointed at my chest. "You look a mess. Answer my question, where have you been?"

Keeping my hands high, I shrugged and forced out the words, "In the woods."

"Where's your partner?"

"Who?"

"Cut the crap—you know who."

"Steve?" I swallowed, sniffed, shook my head. "We lost each other. When your stupid brothers started shooting at us. Why did they do that? I just wanted to talk to you."

"We thought you were hiding in that old fort. My brothers swore you were in there." She narrowed her eyes at me. "How did you get out?"

I squinted at her. "What fort?"

She stared at me, obviously confused.

"I just want to talk to you," I pleaded. "Can you just please put your gun down?"

She kept it pointed at me. "No. Why did you have to track me down? I left a note that said do not try to find me, or else."

"I know why you left. You're pregnant. You need help. I can help you. Just turn yourself into the police."

Her eyes glittered coldly. "Why should I? I haven't committed any crime."

"You and your brothers tried to kill me and Steve." My gun was in my bra. Somehow, I needed to get my gun out of my bra.

Annie had not denied she was pregnant. "Is the baby Philip's?" I asked. "Because if the baby—"

"Shut up."

"Because if the baby is Philip's, then you've got a problem."

"I said, shut up."

I lowered my hands ... slowly ... hoping to grab my gun.

"Get your hands back up."

I raised them again. But not all the way. "What are you going to do, Annie? Your lover is in prison? Maybe I can help."

"Liar."

"Did you murder Lorna?"

"No."

"Did you murder Lorna so you could have Philip for yourself?"

"No."

"I think you killed Lorna and Francine."

She took another step closer. "Goodbye Miss Smith."

I dropped to the ground. BOOM. The shot whizzed over my head.

Before she could get off another, I whipped my gun out of my bra and fired at her—aiming for her leg. Even with my life at stake, I couldn't kill a pregnant woman.

She screamed but didn't go down. Though it was clear by the panicked look on her face that she'd been hit. She pressed a hand to her thigh, then pulled it away. Blood.

Confusion creased her brow. "You got me," she hissed.

Since she was still standing, it was probably only a flesh wound. But I wasn't going to hang around to find out.

I took off running, and when I looked back, she was gone.

———

What now?

I still needed to find Steve's car, but I'd lost all sense of direction.

Annie was probably heading home to get bandaged, and to alert her brothers that I was wandering the woods, armed. With their tracking skills, it wouldn't take them long to find me.

I walked and walked and walked until the sun started to go down. After a while I suspected I'd been walking in circles. Every weedy, overgrown path looked like every other weedy, overgrown path. Every towering pine tree looked like every other towering pine tree. Every dark, swampy bog looked like every other dark, swampy bog.

I was a city girl. I'd never spent much time in the woods. I'd never been lost in the woods. I was also weak from hunger and thirst and worried that Annie had the advantage because she'd grown up in these parts.

Suddenly, a branch snapped behind me. I didn't turn around to see if it was an animal a person, or my imagination.

I ran. And kept running.

Until the ground shifted under me, my feet got caught in branches, and I went flying.

My gun flew out of my hand. I came down hard on the ground. Pain shot through my ankle.

Then Annie limped over to me, pointing her rifle, this time at my face.

Panic and despair shot through me as I stared up at her. I'd run into a booby trap she'd set for me. The clever backwoods woman had dug a shallow hole and covered it with branches, then used fear to steer me into it.

I was staring death in the face and there was nothing I could do.

She pulled the trigger.

Click.

Nothing happened. I was still alive ... oh, my God, I was still alive.

Her gun had jammed.

She tried again. Again, nothing.

She stared at me. I stared back at her.

I didn't have my gun. She saw that. She looked around for it, clutching her useless rifle in one hand, pressing her other hand against her wounded leg.

I held my breath, in too much agony to stand. My ankle felt like it was broken.

Annie stopped searching for my gun. She, too, was clearly in pain. Her face was ghastly pale, and a dark red blob was blooming on her light brown dress, right where I'd grazed her.

She turned back to me, breathing hard, a savage gleam in her eyes.

"Bitch," she hissed, then half-running, half-limping, took off into the trees.

Thirty-One

I had to move, and fast. Broken ankle or no broken ankle, I didn't have much time. Annie was going to sic her brothers on me, and if they found me, I'd be a dead woman.

Stumbling to my feet, I put pressure on my ankle and took a step. Pain shot up my leg, but I didn't fall. Looking down, I saw swelling but no broken bones sticking through the skin. Thank God for small mercies.

Gingerly I attempted another step, then another. If I had to, I'd crawl, but I didn't want to crawl. I kept limping, heading in the opposite direction from Annie, enduring the pain with clenched teeth, telling myself to keep going, keep going.

The forest was dense, nothing but pine trees in every direction, and it was growing darker by the minute.

With no idea where I was, and no idea how to get to Steve's car, I just limped on, pushing through thick, buggy, scratchy brush, enduring the agony that grew worse with every step.

I came to a small stream and hobbled across it. I came to a fallen tree and crawled over it. Adrenaline surging through my veins, I kept moving. If Steve and I were going to survive this, I had to find his car or find someone who could call the police.

After what seemed like an hour, I heard a car. Somewhere up ahead. I was coming to a road.

Bleeding from scratches on my face, arms, and legs, I crashed through more underbrush. Looked around. Spotted it. Through some trees.

In too much pain to go any further, I crawled the rest of the way to the narrow two-lane road, leaned against a tree, and waited for another vehicle to come along.

Fifteen long minutes later, the headlights of an old truck burned through the gloom.

The driver didn't seem to be in any hurry. Taking my chances that their last name wasn't Leeds, I waved my hands in the air, begging for them to stop.

The truck pulled over and an older man wearing overalls and a baseball cap came out and hurried over to me. "You look like you need help, missy."

"Yes, please, thank you, thank you." I struggled to stand up. "Someone is trying to kill me."

"Kill you?" Frowning, he looked me up and down. "Who? How?"

"A woman. Back in the woods. She tried to shoot me. I hurt my ankle trying to get away. Please, I need to get to a phone to call police."

Taking in the distressed look on my face, and my pitiful, muddy, bloody appearance, I could tell he believed me. He took hold of my arm and helped me hobble to the passenger side of his truck, then yanked the door open and helped me in.

"Looks like you need to see a doctor, missy," he said as he got back behind the wheel.

"Probably, but I need the police more right now. I escaped from some bad people, but my friend is still back there, and I need to get him help. Fast."

My Good Samaritan blinked pale blue eyes at me in confusion. "You left a friend back there? Where?"

"We've been hiding out in some old building that looks like a fort. Deep in the woods. Concrete, covered with vines. Abandoned."

His eyes widened. "Oh, you mean the old Stoneman Depot? Used to be on the outskirts of a town that's long ago gone. Only thing left of the place is that building the Stoneman family used to store food, weapons, animals ... hogs, I think. I think they kept hogs there for a while."

I nodded. "That sounds like it. The only windows are up near the roof."

"Yep. Place must be more than a hundred years old. Rumor has it that it was once part of the Underground Railroad. Might have even been used by Pineys, years before that, after the Revolutionary War. Many Pineys were British-loving Tories, and their Patriot neighbors considered them traitors and hunted them down."

"Makes sense," I said, trying to be patient with my rescuer's deep historical knowledge. "It was a good place to hide. Could you please drive me to Chatsworth so I can call police? My friend is still back there. I escaped out a tunnel that we dug in the rear but he's still being held hostage."

"Sounds like you've had quite a day." My savior pulled back onto the road, made a U-turn, and headed back in the direction from which he'd come. "But I don't understand. Who's trying to kill you, missy?"

I didn't answer right away. I didn't know this man's name. What if he was a friend of the Leeds, or one of them? I decided not to take any chances. "Some nasty men ... and their sister."

He snickered. "Oh, you must mean the Leeds gang."

I tensed up. "Do you know them?"

"Everybody in these parts knows them. And fears them." He glanced over at me. "Only you must be mistaken about their sister. She left town couple a years ago. Smart girl."

"She's back."

"Really? You don't say."

"When she fired at me and missed, I shot her in the leg. I think she was headed back to her family's cabin. They sure are evil. I can see why people think they're related to the Jersey Devil."

Good Samaritan chuckled. "People don't think it, honey, they know it." He glanced over at me again. "My name's Gil. What's yours?"

"Story Smith, I'm a private eye from Philadelphia and I'm investigating the murder of two women."

"A private eye, you say?" Gil tightened his grip on the wheel and shook his head. "I wouldn't put it past any of the Leeds to commit murder if that's why you're here. But you sure don't look like a private eye."

"I was at the Chatsworth Café the other day. They know me, and they'll let me use their phone."

He grunted. "Alrighty then, we'll head there."

"Thank you," I said. "I can't thank you enough. You've literally saved my life."

Minutes later, when we pulled into town, Gil parked in front of the café, and I limped in.

Sam Hale was behind the cash register. His daughter Marie was waiting on dinner customers. The Hales and everyone in the eatery stared at me when I asked if I could use the phone to call police.

"It's upstairs, I'll take you," Sam said, then hustled me through the kitchen to a set of stairs that led to the family's apartment.

He didn't ask why I needed to call the police. But I'm sure he wanted to get me out of his café since my dirty, bloody, frightful appearance would have ruined anyone's meal.

It took every ounce of strength I had just to climb the stairs and follow him over to a phone on a table in the living room.

"There's a state police headquarters not far from here." He dialed the number, then handed me the phone.

A female dispatcher came on the line. I told her that someone had tried to kill me, that my partner was still in jeopardy, and begged her to send an officer to the café.

Ten minutes later, a police car pulled up. A young baby-faced officer got out. I met him out on the porch and gave him a quick version of what had happened to me and Steve.

"The old Stoneman Depot? You say you've been hiding out *there*?" Looking me up and down, with an incredulous, concerned look on his face, he ordered me to get in his car.

"Do you know how to get to there?" I asked as he pulled away. "Calvin Leeds and his brothers are holding my friend hostage there."

He gave a grim nod. "Sure, I know where it is, but it won't be easy to get to. There's no road."

"I know, and the Leeds boys are all armed. Are there any more officers you could send?"

He got on the radio and requested back-up assistance, then cut his eyes to me. "Nothing surprises me when it comes to the Leeds. You're lucky to be alive."

I rubbed my ankle, which was swelling so bad that I had to loosen the laces on my sneakers. "Believe me, I know."

"You also look like you need a doctor."

"I do, but my pain isn't what's important right now. I'll be okay."

"You sure?"

"Positive. First, we need to rescue my friend. And Annie Leeds needs to be arrested."

"For ...?"

"For trying to kill me, and for possibly murdering two women in Pennsylvania—Lorna Cranston and Francine Montague."

———

The young officer refused to let me go with him to the depot. Which was just as well, since I could barely walk, and the only way there, once we parked at the edge of the woods, was on foot.

Instructing me to wait in his patrol car, he disappeared down a faint path, gun drawn.

Minutes later, two more patrol vehicles pulled up and four more armed officers got out and followed him.

The only thing I could do was wait and hope they could rescue Steve without a gun battle.

That's all I cared about. Was Steve making it out alive. And after that? I couldn't think beyond that. Steve and I had kissed. I'd spent the night in his arms. Together, we'd dug my way to freedom. Things between us would never be the same. But I didn't care about that now. All that mattered now was for him to make it out alive.

I heard gunshots and then more shots and shouting. My heart jumped into my throat. *No.* I opened the car door. *No, no, no.*

I tumbled out onto the ground. Tears filled my eyes. I started to crawl toward the depot, my ankle throbbing with pain, my legs too shaky to stand.

Then I heard someone running toward me.

It was Steve. *Steve ...*

Joy flooded through me.

He ran up to me, carrying my purse.

I couldn't believe it. The man was running for his life—and he remembered to bring my purse.

Behind him, police officers marched Calvin Leeds and his brothers out of the woods with their hands up.

I struggled to stand. My knees wobbled. Steve caught me in his arms and hugged me tight. "Way to go, Story," he said, his voice breaking with emotion. "I knew you could do it. You saved us both."

I put my head back and gazed into his eyes, only vaguely aware of the drama unfolding around us as the officers handcuffed the Leeds boys and ordered them into the patrol cars.

"I lost my gun," I blurted. "Annie shot at me, and I shot at her, and then I lost my gun."

Steve pulled me closer. He kissed my forehead. "Don't worry about it," he said with a smile that I could hear in his voice. "We'll get you another one."

THIRTY-TWO

he New Jersey State Police building was a few miles outside Chatsworth.

A middle-aged, dark-haired woman with a long face—most likely the one I'd talked to on the phone—took Steve and me into a small meeting room overlooking a waiting area just beyond the entrance.

She gestured for us to sit at the table, left, then returned a few minutes later with a pitcher of water, two glasses, and peanut butter cookies.

"I'm afraid cookies are all we have right now," she said with an apologetic smile. "I'm Miss Marble, by the way. I'm the dispatcher here, also receptionist, secretary, and chief bottle washer. I'll see if I can get one of the officers to go out and get you guys some sandwiches or something. I understand you're hungry."

"Starving," I said, reaching for a cookie. "Thank you."

Steve nodded. "The cookies are great. Thanks so much."

"You're welcome." She turned to leave, then hesitated and looked back at me. "I also sent for Doc Henry. He makes house calls and he'll examine your ankle, miss, see if it's broken. You'll need to go to the hospital if it is, but if it's just sprained, he can probably wrap it. He'll take care of those scratches, too, honey. They look nasty."

The scratches on my face, arms, and legs did sting, but they, along with my ankle, could wait. "I appreciate your help," I told her. "But I don't want to leave here before they bring in Annie Leeds. I need to be here when they question her because I have questions of my own."

Miss Marble shrugged. "That will be up to the detectives. I'll leave your door open. If you need anything else, holler. I'll be right outside."

Steve poured me a glass of water. I gulped it down. He poured himself one, gulped it down.

We were gobbling down cookies when we heard a commotion outside the room.

Calvin and his brothers were filing into the station with their hands cuffed behind their backs.

"This way," the officer leading them shouted as they shuffled past us single file. "Jail's this way. We need to talk to you guys one at a time."

"Annie's the important one," I whispered to Steve.

He pointed. "And there she is."

She was being led into the station by another officer, and she too was handcuffed. Relief washed over me.

Still limping, she had changed her clothes. Someone had also bandaged her leg because she no longer appeared to be bleeding.

Catching my gaze, she came to a sudden halt.

My breath caught in my throat. The look in her eyes was not what

I'd expected. I'd expected pure hate. What I saw instead was pure panic.

"Wait," she told the officer. "Where are we going?"

"Keep moving," he ordered.

"No. I want to know where you're taking me."

"Into the interrogation room. We need to talk to you."

"Help," she shouted to me. "Help me, Miss Smith ... please." Her panic didn't appear to be an act. She was truly afraid. Her eyes were welling with tears and her voice had a desperate high-pitched squeal.

I stared at her, shocked. This woman had just tried to kill me. The last time I saw her she was pointing a rifle at my head. It was only through the grace of God that her weapon jammed.

Now, her transformation was stunning. And it occurred to me that it boded well.

"Get a move on," the officer demanded.

"Wait," I limped to the door. "What do you want from me, Annie?"

"You said you would help me. With my baby."

I widened my eyes. "So, you're admitting that you are pregnant?"

She gave a sorrowful nod. "And I need help, I need help real, real bad."

Her plea was pitiful. And, in different circumstances, I might have been moved to tears. But I had no tears for this woman. Only a plan.

"I did say I could help you," I admitted, "but only if you tell us the truth."

Steve came over and stood next to me by the door.

She looked at me, then at Steve, then back at me. "The truth about what?"

"You know," Steve snapped.

"We want you to tell us the truth about how Miss Lorna died," I said. "And Miss Francine, too, because we're sure you had something to do with it."

"We also need to know the real story about you and Mr. Philip," Steve said. "Give permission for us to go with you in the interrogation room because only the truth is going to help you now."

Annie sniffed and looked at the officer. "I give permission."

Shrugging, he waved for Steve and me to follow.

We went down a hall and into a larger room, one with a long wooden table and six chairs.

He ordered Annie to sit at the end of the table furthest from the door, then removed her handcuffs. Steve sat on one side of her, and I sat on the other.

Two men came in and dismissed the officer. Unlike him, they wore plain clothes.

One nearly bald, introduced himself as Detective Larson, and his younger rusty-haired partner as Detective Pettway.

Larson sat next to Steve and Pettway took a seat next to me.

"We understand you want these two folks in the room with you," Larson told Annie. "Is that correct?"

She nodded meekly. "Yessir."

"Why? They're not your lawyers, are they?"

"No sir."

"We're private eyes," I said. "I'm Story Smith and this is Steve Evans. We met Annie while investigating the murder of a woman in Pennsylvania. Earlier today, she tried to kill me—but now it seems she's had a change of mind about me, because she believes I can help her."

"You promised me you would," Annie hissed. "You promised."

Larson looked at me, his gaze relaxed and confident. "Let's start at the beginning, shall we, Miss Smith? I have a feeling this is complicated."

"Very," Steve muttered..

I appreciated having the floor. I told them about Annie's job as the Cranston housekeeper. About her being one of many suspects in Lorna's murder. That after Lorna's best friend, Francine, was killed, Steve and I suspected Annie could be involved in that, too. And that we then began to suspect Annie was having an affair with Philip Cranston, and that she might be pregnant with his baby.

"Is that true?" I leaned toward Annie. "Is Philip the father of your baby?"

She stared straight ahead, stone-faced. No answer.

"You killed Miss Lorna because you wanted to become the next Mrs. Cranston, didn't you?"

She didn't move. No answer.

"You and Philip had been having an affair for a long time," I pressed. "Then, when you found out you were pregnant, you got desperate. Didn't you?"

She said nothing, didn't even blink.

"You shot Miss Lorna, knowing that Mr. Philip would collect a million dollars from her insurance policy, didn't you?"

She blinked. A tear slid down her cheek.

"Then you found out that Philip was also having an affair with Miss Francine, didn't you?"

She swiped the tear away.

"You killed her, too, didn't you?"

Annie shot me a hostile glare. "You said you would help me."

"And I will," I said softly. "But first you need to tell us the truth. About everything."

"Why should I?"

"Because you're going to go to prison for trying to kill me regardless. Which means even if you don't admit to killing Miss Lorna or Miss Francine, you won't be able to keep your baby. Your brothers will also be going to prison—and from what I've heard about your parents, I don't think you want them raising your child. You will need help finding your baby a good home. And I promise, I will help you find him or her a good, loving home."

No one said a word. We watched Annie absorb what I had just said.

I couldn't believe I was promising to help arrange the adoption of her baby. I had no experience with such a thing, but it was the right thing to do.

Unless Philip wanted to raise the child, which I doubted. He would probably deny being the father to his dying day.

Annie crumpled. She folded her arms on the table, buried her face in them, and started to sob. Pitiful piercing wails filled the room. She cried and cried and cried. When it seemed that she had no more tears left, we all continued to sit silently and wait for her to lift her head.

Finally, she did. Her eyes were tiny slits in her puffy cheeks, but there was something in her eyes I hadn't seen before.

Surrender.

She blinked at me. "Mr. Philip knew," she said. "He knew I shot Miss Lorna. And he kept my secret."

Boom.

There it was. Like a bomb going off. Fragments of the ugly truth flew across the room and rained down on my head.

Numb, I glanced at Steve, who was staring at Annie in disbelief. "What are you saying? That Mr. Philip—"

"Mr. Philip didn't care that I killed Miss Lorna," she said, her voice monotone, devoid of expression, as if she was reporting the weather, or what she was going to have for dinner.

"I didn't tell him I was going to do it, but when I told him I did, he wasn't upset. He said he wouldn't tell anyone. That he loved me and not her and that we could get married soon as he got his insurance money."

I choked back a gasp. Hearing her say it made the evil horribly real.

"Did you know about the insurance policy before you killed her?" Steve asked.

She turned to him. "I found it in a drawer in his desk. Mr. Philip kept telling me he wanted to marry me—said he would if he could. Then when I found out I was going to have his baby, I needed to speed things up. A million dollars made it even better. Meant we'd be rich."

Annie narrowed her eyes at Steve. "But he never got the money, thanks to you. Then the cops kept thinking he did it and then I found out he was loving Miss Francine, too. Doing with her what he was doing with me."

I nodded. "You found them together in the barn ..."

"Sneaked up on them. Saw them naked in the hay. Rolling around like two pigs. I had my gun with me. I was so mad I shot Miss Francine in the head, just like I did Miss Lorna. Pig deserved it."

Steve leaned toward her. "And Mr. Philip? What did he do?"

Annie sniffed. "He grabbed his clothes and ran off. I wanted to shoot him, and I could have shot him, too, because us Leeds are good shots. But I couldn't. I loved him. We were going to get married. Till the cops arrested him for Miss Lorna's murder and hauled him off to jail. Even then, he still didn't tell no one I did it. Which means he does love me, right? Don't that mean he loves me?"

It meant he didn't want anyone to find out about his affair with her. And by keeping her secret, he was an accessory to murder. The only person Philip truly loved was himself.

I felt nauseous, like someone had punched me in the stomach.

Annie had murdered Lorna and Francine and she had just confessed. But Philip was guilty, too. Which meant he would be spending many years in prison.

Celeste had hired me to prove her father's innocence, but he was guilty as hell. Not only had she lost her mother, now Steve and I would have to deliver the bad news that she had also lost her father. That he had never been the man she believed he was. That his life had been a lie.

Larson and Pettway stood and went over to Annie. Larson told her to stand up and put her hands back behind her back.

"You're under arrest for the murder of Lorna Cranston and Francine Montague," he said, "and the attempted murder of Story Smith."

———

My ankle was only sprained. Severely sprained, but thank God, not broken.

After the police locked Annie away in a jail cell, Doc Henry arrived, wrapped my ankle in bandages, gave me crutches, cleaned, and bandaged my scratches, and instructed me to take it easy for a few days.

But how?

Steve and I still needed to wrap things up. We still needed to go see Celeste and Rita at Grand Gables—and visit Philip in jail. I was not looking forward to telling Celeste the bad news about her father, but I was looking forward to seeing his reaction to Annie's confession.

After the doc left, Mrs. Marble brought sandwiches to Steve and me. The two detectives interviewed us at length. Then they drove us back to Steve's car in the woods.

By then, it was nearing midnight. I sensed that Steve might be even more exhausted than I was because he was uncharacteristically quiet and looked emotionally drained.

I couldn't blame him. It had been a wild, rollercoaster day.

"It's much too late to go see Celeste and Rita now," I said, fishing his car key out of my pocket. "I need to go home and get a good night's sleep so let's go see them in the morning."

He unlocked my door and helped me in. "Good idea."

He slid behind the wheel. Then just sat there with the key in his hand.

It was too dark to see his face, but something was bothering him.

"Steve? What's wrong?"

He reached for my hand and squeezed it.

My chest went tight. A lot had happened to us. We'd survived a close call with death. We'd solved the murders of two women. And ... we'd spent a night in each other's arms. And then, there were those kisses ...

Oh, no. He didn't want to talk about *that* now, did he?

"It's about Annie's baby," he said.

What? That was the last thing I'd expected him to say. "Annie's baby?"

"Yes."

"What about Annie's baby? Are you worried that I promised to help get her baby adopted? Maybe I shouldn't have blurted that out—but I thought it was the right thing to do."

He squeezed my hand again. "It's not that."

"Then what is it? Are you worried that Celeste or Rita will want to raise the baby?"

"Lord, no. I'm not worried about that."

"Then what are you worried—"

"I'm adopted," he whispered.

What? "What?"

"I'm adopted, Story. And Annie's baby hit a nerve with me."

I blinked at him, confused. What was he was talking about?

"My birth mother was in jail when I was born," he said. "So was my birth father. They were bank robbers. They robbed banks for a living."

I was too shocked to say anything. Then, "Oh, Steve ... I had no idea."

"During their last heist, a bank teller was killed. Maybe they didn't intend for anyone to die, but they were charged with murder on top of robbery."

Disbelief disabled my brain. I couldn't believe what Steve was saying. "Oh ... oh, I'm so sorry, Steve."

"Turned out my mother was pregnant with me when they robbed that bank. Two months pregnant. It was never reported in the news, and when it came time for me to be born, a secret adoption was arranged with the Evans family. They had money and had always wanted a boy. No one knew, and no one knows now, and they've never even told me. I found out on my own ... and I never told them that I know."

Steve's hand felt cold in mine.

I squeezed it in sympathy.

"When Annie's doctor started talking about me as a baby, it made me nervous," he said. "Because when he mentioned that his father had delivered a baby boy to the Evans family, what really happened was that his father delivered me to them as a newborn, wrapped in a blanket, direct from the prison where my mother was locked up for life."

There was a sadness in Steve's voice that I'd never heard. Low and deep and broken, and in it a hushed shame. Shame he didn't deserve. I was touched that he'd told me, but I didn't see him as any different than before. He was still Steve.

"I think you ended up being one lucky baby," I said, with tears in my eyes. "From what you've told me about your family, you were placed in the arms of wonderful parents. A mother and father who loved you as much as if you had been born to them."

"My parents managed to forge my birth certificate. Thomas and Martha Evans are listed as my birth parents."

"That just proves how much they love you. In my opinion, they are the lucky ones to have you as their son."

"That's nice of you to say."

"It's true."

"The problem ..." He hesitated, two heartbeats, three. "The problem is that erasing my birth parents' names from the record doesn't change the fact that I come from criminals."

That's what he believed? I was horrified. "No, Steve," I said, "they have nothing to do with you. You are your own person. And you are a good person."

He went very still. "It's the real reason I've never let myself fall in love, get married, have children. Because I come from bad stock. I'm afraid of passing on bad genes. I'm not who the world believes I am."

"Steve ..." I didn't know what to say. But everything suddenly made sense. Outwardly, Steve showed the world a charming, dashingly handsome, confident, successful man. Someone who had it all.

Inwardly, he was hiding a secret, a shame that he'd locked away in a part of himself that no one could ever see.

Now he was showing it to me. I leaned toward him. "Steve, you are *you*. You're smart, you're kind, you're brave. You would make a wonderful husband and a wonderful father. You are not those bank robbers. Since your birth, they have had nothing to do with you, and they never will. You must believe that."

"People would be shocked if they knew."

"It's no one's business, and as you said, their names are not even on your birth certificate, so you are officially an Evans. I'm curious, though. How did *you* find out?"

"When I was thirteen, I overheard my parents having a conversation about me being adopted. They were in the living room, and they assumed I was upstairs asleep in bed. Only I'd snuck down into the kitchen for some milk, so I crept closer because I could tell they were taking about something important. They had no idea I heard them, and I was confused at the time, and didn't want to believe it. For a long time, I told myself it wasn't true. And then ..."

"And then what?"

"That's what got me into the P.I. business." I heard him smile. "My father had always wanted me to be a lawyer, like him. So ... being the dutiful son I was ... I went to law school. The summer after my first year, I went to work for my father's firm to gain experience, and there I met his private investigator, Al Dunlap. Al and I hit it off immediately. One day, I confided to him that I might be secretly adopted and asked if he could find out if it was true. He did, and after that I decided I didn't want to be a lawyer. I wanted to be a private eye, like Al."

"And you dropped out of law school ..."

"To my father's disappointment."

"And Al ...?"

"Became my mentor. And when he died three years ago, he left me his business—his clients, his office, and his secretary receptionist, Alice."

"Wow. Even Alice. She's awesome." We were still holding hands. Steve's felt warm now and I could tell he was feeling better. "Thank you for telling me this," I whispered. "I think I understand you better."

"I hope in a good way."

"In a very good way."

"Good." He leaned over and kissed me. Once, on the lips, then started the car, backed it out of the woods, and drove me home.

THIRTY-THREE

The next morning, Steve and I agreed to go see Philip first. He came to my office so we could go together in my T-Bird, with him driving, since I was on crutches.

Steve was clearly feeling much better. His heart-clutching grin was back, along with his air of carefree confidence, and he'd cleaned up nicely, looking dapper in a pale blue shirt and khakis.

A good night's sleep had also revived me. The pain in my ankle had subsided to a dull ache, and I felt refreshed and cheery in my new red-white-and-blue-striped sundress, cinched at the waist with a sparkly red sequined belt.

"You look mighty pretty today, crutches and all." Steve glanced over at me as we headed, top down, toward the jail. "I see you remembered what day it is."

"Sure did. It's Monday. And the Fourth of July. And the day we get to wrap up our case. For most people, today will mean parades and picnics and fireworks, but not for us." I sighed. "I doubt the people we need to see will be in a festive mood."

Philip was anything but festive. When a guard took us back to his cell, we found him sitting on his cot, slumped over, holding his head in his hands.

Had he been told that Annie had confessed? I hoped not. I wanted us to be the ones to give him the news.

He jumped up when he saw us and came over. "Where have you two been?" Grabbing the bars, he pressed his face against them and scowled at us with frustrated fury. With his unkept hair, unshaved face, and sunken, dark-circled eyes, he reminded me of a caged gorilla I'd once seen at the Philadelphia Zoo.

Except the gorilla had not done anything to deserve a life behind bars. Philip deserved his fate. Wrapped up in his own self-pity, he didn't even seem to notice I was leaning on crutches.

"We've been busy, old fellow." Steve cocked his head. "Or we would have been here sooner, I assure you."

A wary flicker of hope entered Philip's eyes. "Oh, yeah? I hope that means you have good news for me. Just get me out of this place —now."

Okay, so clearly no one had told him. Steve and I would get to do the honors.

Goody.

"I'm afraid we have bad news for you, Philip," I said.

"What?" He narrowed his eyes at me, then noticed my appearance for the first time. "What the hell happened to you?"

So, I told him. Everything.

Every damning thing.

The showdown in the Pine Barrens. That Annie had confessed to murdering Lorna. That she'd confessed to murdering Francine. That she'd confessed to having an affair with him.

And that she was now sitting in a jail cell, pregnant with his child.

"But the worst thing for you, Philip, is that Annie claims you knew she'd killed Lorna," I said, "and that you covered for her. Making you an accessory to murder."

I paused to let that sink in. "She also claims that you witnessed her shooting Francine and kept quiet about that, too. Another accessory to murder."

"The irony being," Steve quickly added, "that if you had turned Annie in for murdering your wife, your mistress would still be alive, and you wouldn't be charged with anything."

Philip looked like he was about to throw up. His face turned a ghastly shade of gray. He let go of the bars and stumbled backward to his cot. "None of that is true," he hissed. "Lies, lies, it's all lies."

"Is that how you're going to play it?" Steve asked. "You're calling your girlfriend a liar?"

"She's not my girlfriend."

"You tried to collect that million dollars so you two could run off together," I said. "But what about Celeste? What were you going to tell Celeste? Or were you going to tell Celeste anything? Did you plan to just disappear? Scurry off into the sunset with your twenty-year-old maid? Start another family with her somewhere far, far away?"

"No." Philip shook his head. "No, no, of course not. I didn't plan anything. I didn't have a plan."

He tore at his hair. His mouth twisted into a sneer. "Damn-fool women in my life," he howled, his eyes bugging out as he glared at me.

"Annie shoots Lorna, then tells me later that she did it because she loves me. Celeste hires you, then tells me later that she did it because she loves me. Francine threw herself at me—and what was I supposed to do? She said she loved me. I can't help it if women love me."

Wow. I stared at him in shock. Philip painting himself as the victim was beyond nauseating. "Annie is prepared to testify against you in court," I said.

Philip groaned. "No. No she won't. Annie loves me."

"She's pregnant and she's scared. I promised her that when her baby is born, I will make sure her child gets adopted into a wonderful, loving home. She grew up in a house of horrors. She knows what it's like to go without love. She loves that baby, and she'll do the right thing."

"But Annie loves me." He was whining now.

It made me cringe. "She loves her baby more. You've lost the game to a baby."

"I can't believe she's doing this to me. I covered for her. I went to jail rather than tell anyone what she did ..." Philip's eyes went unfocused as he stared into space. Slack jawed. Wide eyed. In disbelief.

Then he turned back to me, and I saw something new his eyes.

Defeat. Total, complete defeat.

"We're going to go see Celeste now," I said softly. "What do you want me to tell her?"

He looked at me and blinked. "Tell her I'm sorry," he said. "Tell her I'm sorry."

———

Celeste took the news pretty much as I'd expected. Raging denial, followed by angry acceptance, followed by buckets of tears. For her mother, for her father, for herself.

Steve had called her from the police station to let her know we were on our way with news and suggested that she might want to have her Aunt Rita and grandfather, Arthur McKay, there as well.

When we arrived, Steve did most of the talking since we agreed the truth would be easier for Celeste to accept if it came from him.

I felt sorry for Celeste as I watched her cry. Witnessing her grief was as painful as I'd feared. She didn't deserve what had happened to her. The brutal slaying of her mother, the awful betrayal of her father, the tragic truth that her beloved father would spend the rest of his life in prison.

Which I felt guilty about, even though I knew I shouldn't. She had hired me to clear his name, and I'd tried. Trying had almost cost me my life.

But Philip had sealed his own fate with the choices he'd made. And in the end, justice won.

Only, it wasn't quite the end.

Rita, sobbing, excused herself to go up to her room.

But not Celeste. Deepening her cries, she threw herself into Steve's arms, dramatically seeking solace in her despair.

Of course. Of course she did.

"Umm ... If it makes you feel any better, your father said to tell you he's sorry." Steve awkwardly patted Celeste's back as he shot me an embarrassed, I-can't-help-it-if-she-loves-me look.

I sighed. I'd been feeling sorry for Celeste but now ...

Steve couldn't help it if women threw themselves at him. Any better than Philip could. Not that Steve was the monster Philip was. But Steve seemed to be enjoying it. He wasn't letting Celeste go.

A hole formed in my chest and expanded and expanded, becoming a deeper and deeper place of emptiness the longer Steve let Celeste remain in his arms. Emptiness? No, jealousy.

I turned away and caught Arthur McKay's sympathetic eye. "My granddaughter will be fine," he told me. "It will take time for her to heal. But she has me and she has Rita and together we will see to it that she has whatever she needs to go on with her life."

"Thank you," I said. The rational part of me knew that wouldn't be Steve. Celeste wasn't his type, he'd said. The emotional part of me went cold with fear that maybe it would be Steve. Maybe he'd change his mind about her. What did I know?

All I knew was that I shouldn't be thinking these things about Steve. We'd kissed. Passionately. He'd told me his secret. I loved him. Couldn't deny that I wanted him. But that didn't change anything. Because nothing had really changed. He hadn't changed.

I had to focus on my job. And it occurred to me that I still had a loose end to attend to.

"Mr. McKay," I said, "has a man named Victor Bravo been in touch with you about Lorna's will?"

He smiled. "Oh, yes, I meant to speak with you about that. He called the other day and talked to Celeste. Lorna wanted him to have her horses if anything happened to her—and Celeste urged him to go ahead and take them. She doesn't want them, and I concur with her decision."

"Interesting." I glanced over at Steve. He whispered something in Celeste's ear. With a tearful pout, she pulled away.

Steve, his face flushed, came over to me. "I think I've calmed Celeste down. Are you ready to go, Story?"

"Yes." I swallowed hard, knowing that my cheeks were as red as his, while pretending he didn't notice. "We have one more place we need to go today. We need to go see Lorna's psychic medium, Victor Bravo."

Thirty-Four

Victor Bravo was dressed for the holiday. Blue turban atop his bald head. Loose fitting, tent-like red and white striped shirt that reached his knees. Billowy snow-white pants. Nothing on his feet but three toe rings. Red, white, and blue toe rings.

He seemed genuinely thrilled to see me standing at his door, holding onto Steve's arm because I'd left my crutches in the car.

"Story Smith …" He smiled at me, then at Steve, then cut his eyes back to me and beamed. "This is an easy one," he said, swirling his hands in the air, fluttering his fingers. "You two are made for each other—so I say yes, yes, a thousand times, yes."

"What?" I blinked, confused. "Yes … to what?"

"To your relationship. Isn't that why you've come? To ask me if I see a future for the two of you. And yes, I do, I certainly do."

I felt my face go hot.

Steve laughed. "That's cool. So cool. Seeing as how you claim to be psychic, right?"

"Right." Victor scrunched his nose. "Oh, wait, you haven't come to seek my advice about your relationship, have you? No, no, I'm sorry. I got carried away. You're here about Lorna's will."

We nodded.

"Well, in that case, come on in. I'm expecting some friends to stop by later to help me celebrate the Fourth, but I have time to see you guys. Especially if it pertains to Lorna's horses, because it seems I will be inheriting them, and I've no idea what that will mean."

The inside of the flamboyant man's house was as decorated as he was. Red, white, and blue streamers hung from the ceiling. Red, white, and blue balloons bobbed about. He even had red, white, and blue plastic palm trees in his living room—one of each color—where he waved for us to take a seat on his sofa.

Plastic palm trees? Really? What did plastic palm trees have to do with the events of 1776? I grinned. Nothing. That's what made them so much fun. Victor was fun. A free spirit, a breath of fresh air after the horrors I'd just been through.

Victor took a seat across from us. I introduced him to Steve, then brought him up to date on Lorna's murder. "You'll be relieved to know that you are no longer a suspect," I said, "which allows you to move forward with the will free and clear."

He chuckled. "I never was a suspect, my dear. The police came to see me, but I think they found me more amusing than anything else."

"I'm glad you've agreed to take Lorna's horses because I've been worrying about them in the back of my mind," I said. "Especially Thunderbolt, her favorite. Thunderbolt and I hit it off."

Victor leaned forward, suddenly serious. "I could never abandon those animals even though I have no idea how I am going to care for them."

"Story said that you were worried because you don't have the land," Steve said. "You obviously don't have a place for them here."

Victor studied Steve's face. For several long minutes. Like he was reading him. "I see horses around you," he said in a deep, low-pitched croon. "Why am I seeing horses?"

Steve frowned. "I'm afraid I don't know what you're talking about."

He squinted at something invisible behind Steve. "Do you own any horses?"

Steve shook his head. "No ..."

"Have you ever owned horses?"

Steve shrugged. "I grew up with them. My parents have an estate near here, and they have horses."

"Ah." Victor beamed. "That explains it."

"Explains what?"

"Why I see horses all around you. I like you, Evans. And I would like to give Lorna's horses to your parents."

The look on Steve's face was a mix of shock and cautious respect for the psychic's abilities. Then he shook his head. "Wait. Those horses are worth a fortune. Are you saying you want to sell them?"

"No. I want to give them to your parents. Where I'm sure they will have a good home. And where Story will be able to visit Thunderbolt whenever she likes." He spread his hands wide. "I'm sensing incredibly good energy between you and Miss Smith. Which does indeed indicate a promising future."

Wait ... what? I stared at the psychic. "What are you—"

"I'm sure my parents would be happy to accept your gift." Steve flashed me a this-is-fun grin. "I'll discuss it with them and get back to you soon."

Victor clapped his hands. "Excellent. I'm glad that's settled." He stood up. "Now, if you'll please excuse me, I need to go put icing on two dozen cupcakes I baked for my party. Which you are welcome to stay for—don't feel you need to rush off."

My brain was still trying to process what Victor had predicted. And I was having trouble breathing because my chest was so tight. Breathe in, breathe out, I told myself, and don't worry about what Victor said. His powers could be real. Or he could be a complete phony— incredibly good at getting people to believe he could see things others couldn't.

Especially if he told them what they wanted to hear.

Did I want to believe Steve and I could have a future together? Of course, I wasn't an idiot. The problem was that I was one of a long line of women who'd believed that fairytale. And they had all been burned.

"We need to go," I said. "I appreciate the kind invitation, but I have a lot of work to do."

Steve gave me a funny look. "Like what?"

"I need to type up a report for Celeste. Get everything that happened down on paper while it's still fresh in my mind."

Steve gave me an even funnier look. "I don't think you're going to forget any of it any time soon, if ever. But if you want to go, let's go."

"You'll miss seeing Madame Z." Victor slid me a sly smile. "I'll tell her you said hello."

My jaw dropped. "Madame Z? But—"

"She's changed, my dear. I know I warned you to beware of her, but she and I had a good long talk and now we're friends. She's now billing herself as a tarot card reader who can summon the power of angels. Turns out that all that bragging about fending off the forces of evil was scaring people away. Bad for business."

"It sure scared me." I gave Steve a let's-get-out-of-here-look. "Please tell her I said hello."

"Certainly. But her sister, Madame B, is coming to the party, too. She's a hoot. Are you sure you don't want to stay?"

"Doubly sure. I met Madame B when I was looking for Madame Z, so no thank you."

Victor shrugged. "Alrighty, then. Happy Fourth of July. And you will be happy to know that I'm waving my fee today."

I frowned. "Your fee?"

"For my services."

"Services?"

"For my fortune telling services." Victor patted his turban. "I see a bright future for you two pretty people. All I ask is that you invite me to your wedding."

———

"So ... let's talk about our wedding." Steve was in a jovial mood as we headed back to my office. Humming "Here Comes the Bride," he turned to me with a grin as wide as the Grand Canyon. "Shall we set a date?"

"Very funny," I said.

He chuckled. "Seriously, you and I do need to talk."

"Oh ... about what?"

"You know, stop pretending."

I glanced at him out of the corner of my eye. That smile. Damn his cute smile. "You mean the way you kissed me when we thought we were going to die?"

"Yes, and the way you kissed me."

"We thought we were going to die."

"Oh, come on. Those kisses meant something to me, and I know they meant something to you. That Bravo fellow is right. There *is* an undeniable energy between us."

That undeniable energy was zinging through my body right now. But I didn't want to think about it or talk about it. "We make a great team," I said, wincing at how lame that sounded.

"A great team in more ways than one."

I couldn't look at him. We had the top down, of course, and I turned and stared out at the people merrily celebrating the holiday as we passed by. Kids riding bikes decorated with parade streamers. Yards filled with small American flags flapping in the breeze. Dads firing up the family grill—the mouth-watering smell of roasting hamburgers and hotdogs filling the air.

"I wrote you another song," Steve said softly.

Another song ...he'd written me another song. My heart melted. I turned back to him and gave him a trembling smile. "Wow, thank you."

"Do you want to hear it?"

I combed shaky fingers through my hair. "Yes, yes, of course I want to hear it."

"Great." He pulled over to the side of the road and parked under a big oak tree. He cut the engine and turned to face me.

My breath caught in my throat.

Cars whizzed by, and somewhere off in the distance—*boom, boom, boom*—kids were shooting off fireworks.

But that was nothing compared to what was going off in me. My heart was beating faster and louder than any drum. Every nerve in my body was exploding.

Steve wiggled his eyebrows. "Before I start singing, I'd like to ask you a question."

Oh boy. I took a deep breath. "Okay ...."

"Are you really planning to spend the rest of the day in your office, typing up a report that could easily wait until tomorrow?"

Geez Louise. That was not the question I'd expected—to my relief. I relaxed and smiled. "I was planning to, but now that I think about it, it would be rather lonely in that building. I'm sure no one is working today, not even Wendy."

"Then don't do it." Steve reached for my hand. "My parents are back from Europe. They always host a big Fourth of July barbeque. Come with me."

My nerves went back to twanging. "Your parents?" I bit down on my lower lip. "You want me to meet your parents?"

"Sure. Why not?"

"But how would you introduce me? Not as your girlfriend, right?"

He grinned. "Sure. Not as my girlfriend. I'll just say, 'Hi, Mom and Dad, meet Story Smith. She's not my girlfriend.'"

I pulled my hand away. "That's not what I meant."

"Okay, how about I introduce you as my friend and colleague, Story Smith, super sleuth?"

"I like that."

"Okay, it's a date, then. Let's go." He put the key in the ignition.

"Wait," I said. "I want to hear your song."

"Oh, right." He gazed into my eyes and swallowed hard, like he was suddenly feeling shy.

Then he started singing, in that wonderful tenor voice of his that torched my soul.

"Some enchanted day, we will be together ... For now, it's but my dream ... But no matter how it may seem ... For me, it's always been you ... It's always, always been you."

Oh wow, oh wow. I took a deep, shuddering breath and smiled.

He reached for my hand. "Do you like it?"

I loved it. How could I not? Tears filled my eyes. Tears filled my throat. A tear slid down my cheek. "I love it," I whispered. "But I still can't let myself fall in love with you, Steve."

He didn't say anything. Then he gave me that heart-grabbing grin. "Ah, but Story ..." He pressed a finger to his lips, then reached over and touched my tear. "I think you already have."

Acknowledgments

I am blessed to have many people in my life who support my writing. Thank you, thank you, thank you to all my family, friends, fans, and fellow writers—including members of First Coast Romance Writers— who have traveled with me on my journey as a novelist.

I also feel extremely lucky to have a fantastic editor, Caren Burmeister, who is also a wonderful friend and a great writing coach. She has edited all my books and helped me grow my career as an author in many ways. I'm also grateful for my superb cover designer, Robin Johnson of Florida Girl Design, Inc., who has created the covers for all my books and continually amazes me with her talent.

Thank you as well to all my readers. I write to bring you joy, and it would mean the world to me if you would take a few minutes to post a review for this book. Thank you! And happy reading!

About the Author

Maggie FitzRoy lives with her husband, dog, and two cats in Ponte Vedra Beach, Florida.

She is the author of historical romance, romantic suspense, and romantic mystery thriller novels. She fell in love with reading fiction when she discovered Nancy Drew in third grade and always wanted to create her own female detective. Weaving together mystery and romance, *Tuesday Means Trouble* is the second book in the Story Smith Mystery series, following *Never on Monday*. For information about all of Maggie's novels, and to receive updates on her future books, including the next Story Smith and Steve Evans adventure, *Woe is Wednesday*, visit her website www.maggiefitzroy.com.

www.ingramcontent.com/pod-product-compliance
Lightning Source LLC
Chambersburg PA
CBHW061639190726
48289CB00006B/1662